BAPTISTE

BLOOD
OF
MIDGARD

BOOK ONE OF THE ARMY OF ONE TRILOGY

Blood of Midgard

The Army of One (Book 1)

Copyright © 2024 by Baptiste Pinson Wu

All rights reserved.

No part of this book may be reproduced in any form or by any electronic or mechanical means, including information storage and retrieval systems, without written permission from the author, except for the use of brief quotations in a book review.

Cover art by Miblart

❀ Created with Vellum

To Johanna,

Who would go through Ragnarök like it's another Tuesday.

Brothers shall fight and slaughter each other;

And sisters' sons shall sin together.

Ill days on earth, many a whoredom.

An axe-age, a sword-age, shields shall be cloven;

A wind-age, a wolf-age, till the world totters.

And never shall a man spare another.

Völuspá

PROLOGUE

Now...

The plop of a drop stirred me from a violent, painful dream, and what the sound failed to wake, the sudden, pungent smell of sulfur achieved. The acid landed an inch from my cheek, yet it burned nonetheless. By instinct, I tried to wriggle from the heat, but the chain binding me to the stone was solid and infused with some gods' *seidr* magic. According to legends, those chains had been made of entrails, but they felt like metal to me as they dug into my skin.

However, the snake above my head was as real as the legend suggested.

I heard it before I saw it, my eyes still growing accustomed to the darkness of the cave. It rasped with anger, heinous from having missed its target. Its venom was said to bring the worst pain known to gods and men. While I would rather not have tested this theory, the dark light shining in its little dead eyes, an arm's length from my face, led me to believe it was true.

I have awakened to scary things over the many years of my existence: blades, angry women, angry husbands, a bear once, but never a snake. This was a first, and when you've lived more than three centuries, firsts are rare. I could have done without this one, though. Skadi claimed she had chosen the meanest snake of the nine realms. It would not age, Skadi made sure of it, and it didn't need to eat, but its appetite remained.

This was an ugly, vicious beast if I ever saw one. Its scales were a sickly mix of black and ocher; its fangs, the size of a middle finger, gleamed in the dim light. Its jaw stretched open at such an angle that my head could fit in with ease. No, not my head—

"Don't worry," said a familiar, husky voice, "it misses more than it hits."

I followed the voice, and fury surged through my veins. The man standing between me and the cave's exit, leisurely unbuttoning his shirt, was not just my enemy but the enemy of all life. A being the gods, the *skalds,* and pretty much anything with a mouth had warned me against, but like an idiot, I had not listened.

Another drop fell, closer this time. The snake hissed again, stretching its body as much as it could from the stalactite of granite it was trapped inside. It shook with years of rage from being denied the bite. Skadi had not wanted the snake to kill its prey, just hurt him until the end of time, which, judging by the situation, was upon us.

Loki was loose, which meant one thing, Ragnarök would soon follow. Such was the prophecy. And no one would recognize him.

His hair was short and dark, and his plaited black beard shone with silver beads reflecting what little light made it into the cave. Small scars marred his hard face here and there, none of them new, and eyes like those of an old wolf shone with an unnatural look of delight. The grin splitting his face was even less natural. This, all of this, wasn't the Loki I or anyone else knew.

This face and body belonged to the leader of Odin's warriors, the Einherjar, a man they called Drake, the Dragon. A man known to everyone on Asgard. One who could open doors without raising suspicion and the only human warrior with direct access to the All-Father.

As Drake, Loki could return to Asgard, surrounded by the Wolves of Odin, elite warriors famed among all the Einherjar. He would salute Tyr, Heimdallr, and even Thor, maybe, if Loki's wounded pride allowed it. He would need to wait for an audience in the silver antechamber of Odin's hall, where few of the Æsir dared go since the death of his favored son. But Drake would be welcome. Decades upon decades of good service earned him this right.

I knew all this because until a few minutes ago, I was Drake, and Drake was me.

Loki would approach Odin, and Odin wouldn't notice the change. His mind had been absent for a long time. He would fail to recognize Loki, and... well, Loki would kill him somehow. The trickster probably had a plan for that as well.

"I won't kill Odin," Loki said, wincing as he peeled the blood-stained shirt from his wound. "He needs to be alive for Ragnarök, remember?"

"Get the fuck away from my head," I shouted in an unrecognizable voice, higher pitched than my own. Seemingly younger, too.

"*Your* head?" Loki asked with a smirk. "Be careful," he said, nodding toward the snake. I rolled my head just in time to avoid the venom and had to keep it at an odd angle while it fizzled out.

"Wait, how do you know about Ragnarök?"

Ragnarök had been part of the gods' lives for as long as they existed, but the details of its unfolding were revealed after Loki's imprisonment. No one had been allowed here besides his wife, Sigyn, and she had not returned to Asgard since.

"What do you think?" he asked as footsteps approached from the exit, soon revealing a vision I had yearned for years.

Muninn stopped in her tracks when she noticed my eyes on her. For a second, I forgot and loved her again. Then I remembered how she had tricked me here. *She* had told Loki about Ragnarök, of course. He always had a way with women. She refused to look at me, and I read guilt in her eyes. She could keep it for herself.

"I couldn't find white mistletoe around here," she said, offering Loki a small wooden bowl. "I replaced it with ivy leaves; it should do it." She helped him out of the blood-heavy shirt, which fell with a wet splash.

It was the first time I could see my own body so clearly. It was the body of a warrior. Strong and supple. Round shoulders that rolled with the arms, biceps bulked by decades wielding swords, and an abdomen where muscles and fat mixed to give the best of both. The blood dripping from the left side was worrisome, but I had known worse, and at least this time, it did not hurt *me*. She applied the green and white mixture to the wound, careful not to hurt him with her touch. Loki still hissed, just like the snake.

"Sorry," she said without looking at him.

"Don't be," he replied. "I have longed for another kind of pain." His eyes stared at the snake, and I felt his hatred and fear for the beast.

I pulled on the chains, but there was no budging them. If a Jötunn like Loki couldn't move them, how could I, even in his body? Muninn expertly tore a piece of my old shirt and bound Loki with it. How many times had I dreamed she would be as close to me as she was to him right now? From the eyes I watched her with at this moment, she seemed even more beautiful.

"Love can do that," Loki said, hearing my thoughts as they came.

Of course, she was in love with him. What a fool I had been, thinking that maybe the dark and beautiful Muninn could ever love a man such as me, or any man really. It wasn't enough for Loki to steal my body and my title; he also had to take her. May the both of them freeze in Hel.

"What do you want?" I foolishly asked.

"You know," he answered as he wriggled inside my old mail shirt. "Ragnarök, the end of the world, death to the Æsir, all of that."

"Why?" I even more foolishly demanded.

His head popped from the collar of small iron rings. "You know why. You know how they treated me."

I did know. During my first couple of centuries within the ranks, I witnessed the cruelty of the gods toward Loki. I even felt pity for him at times. But on top of all his mischief, Loki had killed Baldur, Odin's favorite son. There was no pity to be had after that.

If he heard my thoughts then, he said nothing.

My beloved knife found his grasp, and he stabbed it a couple of times in the air with obvious satisfaction before sheathing it. He left my shield behind and took a last look at the snake, a smile full of victory on *my* lips. He meant to turn away, but Muninn put her hand on his arm.

"Remember—" she said.

"I know," he replied, "you can trust me."

"Trust," I spat. "Trusting the god of lies. You are indeed not the woman I thought you were."

"I *am* a liar," Loki replied before she could say anything, "but when I give my word, I mean it."

"So do I," I said, "and I give you my word today that I will find you and end your miserable life." My threat lost its power on his satisfied face. I was a worm threatening a rooster.

"I welcome your attempt," he said as he lowered himself to my level and caressed a strand of long black hair off my right ear. "I do wish to see how Odin's Drake will find his way out of this."

He winked as he stood up, and I hated my face more than ever before.

"My wife will be back soon," Loki said as he and Muninn made for the cave entrance. "She'll keep you company. Until then, enjoy that of our little friend." And as if it heard, the snake opened its mouth again, and another drop slid along its fangs. I heard my heart beating hard against my chest; the snake was right on top of me.

"And Drake," Loki called from under the arch of stones separating him from the gray sky, "enjoy the end of the world, my friend."

Muninn embraced him in her pale arms. Two wings of dark feathers sprouted from her back and enfolded them both before they flew away from my sight.

I turned my attention just in time to see the drop detach from the fang. I tried to dodge, but the snake had aimed well. It plopped on my left cheek. Its heat crept under my skin, then inside my flesh. Every nerve from my teeth to my eyeballs trembled as I shrieked. My mind blacked out fast, but not fast enough.

The stories were right; nothing had ever hurt so badly.

Fuck the stories.

1

Somewhere on Midgard. One week before.

A fresh pinkish sun loomed above the hills to spectate the macabre show the night had left for her. The breeze was getting warmer already, transporting a fragrance of pine trees and salty spray from the sea. The smell of iron was mixing into it, proof of our offering to the All-Father. It was one of those dawns the *skalds* sang about at great length to impress young women. Yet this moment was odd. It disturbed me. It bothered me.

I always favored fighting at dawn. Men fight better then. Maybe because they had yet to fully emerge from their dreams and fought as if they would wake up soon. A fool's kind of bravery, but bravery nonetheless, and Odin wasn't too picky about bravery anymore. He cared more about its quantity than its quality. But it wasn't just that. Fighting at the edge of night and day felt right, almost poetic. A beautiful metaphor for what was war, the passing from one state to another. From peace to chaos, man to beast, from life to death, or from life to... well, to something else.

But among my many battles at dawn, this one had a different taste. It was different because it wasn't unique, and it bothered me.

If there was one thing you could count on with a bloodbath, it was its uniqueness. You could strike the same blow to two men, and they would react differently. One would sink to his knees, calling for his mother, while another would take it and use whatever was left of him to avenge himself. War is always the same, but battles are unique. They may appear similar, like the trees of a forest from afar, but from up close, one could notice the specific pattern along the bark of each specimen. I'd fought in hundreds of battles and had yet to fall upon two similar patterns—until that moment.

I'd lived it before. I had already been wiping blood from my sword with a piece of cloth torn from my last victim while squinting at this exact sun on this exact patch of land facing a quiet sea. And, for some reason, it bothered me.

"What is it, Drake?" Bjorn asked as he passed a comb of bones through the mess of his gory beard. Still sweating, my friend stared toward the horizon as well, as if the answer to his question lay there. The shadow of his massive body broke the touch of the sun and took me back to the present.

"Nothing. I just have a feeling we've fought here before," I replied, tucking the blade back in my belt. It wasn't entirely clean, but it soon wouldn't matter.

"We may have," he said. "I don't think there are many places where we haven't fought on Midgard." Bjorn fought like an animal in the melee but regained his calm in a matter of seconds once the last opponent dropped his blade. I envied him for it. He behaved as most men do after having lain with a woman, as if the ball of anger we carried with us at all times had vanished. Me—I fumed for long minutes and could shake for much longer, though I'd learned to keep it down over the years.

"Hey," he called to the men behind us. One was on his ass, having a cut on his scalp checked by another. "Was there ever a fight here?"

The man with the cut was the leader of a small trading town, a jarl in his own right, and he didn't care for Bjorn's tone. He spat a red gob in our direction, which made Bjorn chuckle. We'd won him his fight, but I felt no gratitude. His name was Sigurd, son of Sigurd, I think.

"Not since my grandfather's time," the jarl replied after a wince of pain. I could see part of his skull and thought he would die within a week.

"There you go," Bjorn said, turning back to face me. "We probably fought here some fifty years ago or something."

"I guess we did."

Bjorn was right, of course. Wherever Norsemen lived, we'd fought. But I knew I would be picking this bone for a while.

"If you ladies are done smelling flowers and admiring the scenery, we should get going." Karl was in a mood. Then again, when wasn't Karl grumpy? This time, it came from a crudely bound cut on his right thigh that made him limp, but someone rattling mucus down their throat in his presence would birth the same mood in old Karl. Despite his impatience, he still took a deep breath of fresh air when he reached us and sighed with something resembling pleasure. For someone used to Asgard, Midgard smelled like shit, but it felt amazing.

"Who died this time?" I asked, pretending once more to

ignore his tone. The old man had earned this right, many times over.

"Snekke died first," Karl answered while massaging his wounded leg.

"I could have guessed as much," Bjorn replied with a chuckle. "I saw Cross-Eyes fall with an arrow in his throat."

"And I saw Einar and Eigil fall in the shield wall," I said, remembering their screams more than their actual fall.

"Both father and son at the same time?" Bjorn asked. He sounded amused. "Oh, they'll hear about it."

Four out of ten, I thought, not too bad. This time, we'd won. Both sides suffered many casualties, and I'd personally witnessed several acts of courage. The last man I'd killed—barely a man at all—had died with honor and nearly took my eye. I expected to see him again on the other side.

"Rune and Titus are almost done piling them up on a cart," Karl said. "Let's go once it's done."

"Are you giving the orders now?" I put a hint of steel in my tone. Karl needed to be reminded of his place once in a while.

"All I'm saying is that if we wait too long, you'll have another body to drag," he replied, opening his bloody palm toward me.

"We have to wait for her," I said, and both my men puffed. I understood their annoyance but let it slide. "I think Einar's arm was cut off. Make sure to pick it up before we go."

Karl didn't dignify me with an answer, so I followed him with my eyes as he dragged his useless leg to the cart and bent to pick up our comrade's arm. He tossed it in the cart where four of us lay dead. Titus stood by it in his usual straight-like-an-oak posture while Rune, the youngest of my men, got ready to pull the cart. Ulf would be looting some dead man. An old habit that hadn't died with him.

We did our part; the Valkyries would do theirs next. And between us, *she* would show herself to me. We didn't need to wait for her. Muninn was just a witness, but I would not leave before I saw her. Sometimes, I came down to Midgard for that opportunity alone.

"Fuck the gods," Bjorn said, playing with the bit of bowel dangling from under his shirt he hadn't noticed before. "I didn't even feel it," he went on, looking at me with his typical stupid smug.

"Last night's mead might have gotten you a bit too numbed." I slapped his back as a signal for us to join our brothers. He pushed it back inside as best he could but knew it would soon hurt.

With the grace of a falling tree, he climbed on the cart and lay himself by the bodies of our dead.

"Now I have to pull you as well?" Rune asked in his young, pristine voice. He tried to sound tough and complaining, as warriors do, but he was too pretty to be taken seriously. "I start to wish I had fallen too."

"I'm surprised you haven't," I said as I added the weight of my helmet to the cart. "Those men we faced were good fighters. You did well, Rune," I said while removing one of my arm rings.

"Thank you, sir," he said as he accepted the offering, pride gleaming in his pristine eyes.

He deserved it for surviving, if nothing else. Rune had joined the Wolves only two years ago and, in that time, had gained our respect, even Karl's, though the old man would never admit it. Even among the Einherjar, Rune was a young recruit, probably less than twenty years on Asgard. I appreciated his youthful optimism; it was refreshing. He'd be truly formidable if he could stop himself from shoving his foot in his mouth.

"They may have been good fighters, but they were poor as dead sheep," Ulf said with a tone showing the result of his looting. "Might as well go back home now."

Home.

Asgard was home, but purely because I couldn't even remember what *home* used to be.

"Still waiting for the little bird," Bjorn said, playing with dead Eigil's mouth to make it look like he'd been the one speaking. Ulf knew better than to complain on this point, but the absence of complaining from this particular friend was heavy with meaning. He threw his bow and quiver in the cart and stood next to Titus behind the vehicle. As the bow landed by the body of Sven Cross-Eyes, I saw her through the gaps in the cart's sideboards, dark and beautiful like a moonless night, standing at the tree line.

Muninn.

"There's a small cave down the beach, maybe ten minutes north. I'll see you there," I said without taking my eyes off her. She looked back at me and gave me the most discreet nod.

"I guess it means we're pushing this thing on the sand," Ulf complained as the cart departed, leaving nothing but space between me and Muninn.

She wouldn't come any closer, so I did.

The patch of land separating us was littered with bodies. Fifty men or so had perished. I'd claimed three lives this time, I think. Not a bad day of work. Mass killing wasn't my purpose; I left it to the likes of Bjorn or Eigil. Three was good enough for me. I walked by my last victim and knelt. He was even younger than I had thought, probably fourteen.

Two lines of clean skin went from the corner of his eyes

down to his ears, splitting his face full of dirt and sweat. A clean stab through the ribs had taken his life, but he had still tried to return the favor before falling. I traced the three triangles of the Valknut on his chest, hoping the Valkyries would notice him among the dead. A superstition I kept since my first kill as a Wolf, two hundred and sixty-seven years ago.

"See you soon, brother," I said as I stood and crossed the battlefield to join Muninn.

"He died well," she said when I greeted her with a nod. Her voice was icy but not unkind, like a winter breeze on the morning of a rainy night.

"He did. Many did."

"Many didn't," she said, "but *you* fought bravely, Drake, as usual."

To Hel with bravery, I thought. I did not want her appraisal of my skills. I was still angry from the fight and found her presence soothing and exciting at the same time. She must have known how I felt about her. How could she not? I was not a discreet man, to say the least, especially with my emotions.

She must have known all I wanted was to push her against the closest pine tree, lift her black dress, and consume the last of my rage in her embrace. I wanted to tell her that, among our world of golden gods and exuberant warriors, she was the only thing that made sense. I wanted to lose myself in the black of her eyes, the paleness of her skin, and the silk of her darker-than-night hair.

I would have done nothing about it, though. Muninn scared me as much as she fascinated me. For more years than I could remember, I only enjoyed those moments between the killing and the reviving. Had I been smart, I would have left it at that, and the world would have been safer. I was in love with Muninn but my feelings were tainted with fear. And this fear that kept my hands on my hips came from her true nature. I knew what she was and hated what it meant. Odin was fond of playing with people's minds, and I often thought Muninn was his very own trick for me.

She was his little pet, a creation of his mind to observe the world for him. She was his *memory;* she was part of him. The All-Father had sired many children through his innumerable affairs and even some through his marriage, but he had only created two from himself: Muninn and her brother.

Thus, I only allowed myself to enjoy her presence, her lack of smell, and her clever eyes as they scanned the battlefield, committing to memory every detail for her report to Odin. The ghost Valkyries would choose the brave among the dead and bring them to Asgard. Muninn would tell the story to Odin and Bragi so that the god of poetry could spring one of his interminable tales in honor of our new brothers. They seldom spoke of the Wolves anymore, those verses. They used to, but the Einherjar grew tired of it through the centuries.

The living would also not mention us in their tales, for Muninn's role wasn't only to fill her memory but also to erase and modify that of the men who fought with us. In a few minutes, those warriors would forget how Bjorn broke a shield wall with one swing of his axe. They would think one of theirs did that. It didn't matter. Fame had been sweet as a living man and sweeter still among Odin's warriors. But no longer. The feeling of futility was growing on me.

Muninn must have felt my unease, for she dropped her cold hand on mine.

"What is it, Drake?" Her eyes shone with compassion. It

was enough to make the air freeze in my chest. Here it was again, this terrible hope that she felt as I did.

"Nothing," I told her gently, masking my state of mind.

"You should go," she said, nodding toward the beach where my comrades had vanished.

"Will I see you this evening?" I felt stupid as soon as the words came out.

"If Odin wants me to," she replied, the exact answer I should have expected.

"Let's hope the All-Father is in a good mood today then."

That was it, the few minutes of life that got me through the years of killing. They seldom left a good taste in my mouth, but I thirsted after those rare moments, nonetheless.

"Send the ravens if the fire isn't enough," I told her with a last look over my shoulder. She nodded, already focused on her task. To those who do not possess the gift, *seidr* doesn't look like much. I had developed a sense of it after many years in Asgard, a feeling of heat compressing my heart like a hot rain in autumn. Bjorn said he heard a ringing in his left ear when someone used the magic. Some had weirder claims.

Those with a sharper affinity for the forbidden art told stories of ghosts and pain, of horrors worse than war. I saw nothing of it at this moment. Muninn was as beautiful as ever, tracing runes in the air with a middle finger stained in black ink. The men and women on the battlefield would forget us and go home, some with new and undeserved fame.

It had been a simple mission, this time. Sigurd's men and their enemies were already at each other's throats, blades sharp and shields freshly painted. All it took was a small push to make sure war claimed enough lives and packed Valhöll's benches a little more. When our missions needed more interference, Muninn would spend more time on Midgard, cleaning the memories of anyone who interacted with the Wolves.

Sometimes, though, Muninn could not find all those we had met. A man might have fled before the battle, or a woman might have taken her children deep into a wide forest—those cases were not uncommon. Which is why we also kept our identities hidden. She could stay for weeks in search of the missing ones, but as Odin said, "*It wouldn't help if folks knew I picked sides. Especially if they knew I always pick the losing one.*"

How many thousands of Einherjar had the Wolves made? How many more until Ragnarök and our last death? There seemed to be no end and no way to prevail over the prophecy.

Or so most Asgardians believed.

My thoughts led me through the carnage to the beach, making me oblivious to the cries and laughter of the survivors. The waves crashing on the pebbles took me back. We Einherjar feared the sea. It could undo what Odin had done and take us away from the eternal glory of fighting for the All-Father.

It might just have been stories, but many among us believed Ran, goddess of the sea, had sworn to swallow even her Æsir brethren to the depth of her kingdom if she could. Since she'd been found guilty of helping Loki, no one dared approach her. I veered to the left when my feet got wet in the white surf and followed the trail of blood leading toward the cave where my men were getting ready to head back *home*.

If I had known then where my road would lead, I would have avoided caves, but it was better to deal with our return in a discreet place. When Odin created the Bifröst, the bridge connecting Asgard to Midgard, he hadn't thought it through. I guessed Bjorn's next words before they passed his lips just as the shadow of the cave's roof chilled the back of my neck.

"Fuck Bifröst."

"As you say, brother."

Ulf and Titus prepared a fire under the cart while Rune helped Karl in it. They were efficient, my Wolves.

"You want me to go last?" Bjorn asked.

"I'm the leader of this sorry bunch," I told him with a gesture inviting him to lie down. "I'll go last."

"Thank the gods," he said with a sigh of relief. He was pale as bones. "I don't think I could have lasted that long."

Bjorn was our best fighter. A bear of a man who could pass for the son of Thor. No one had won the *brawl* as many times as he did. But even the best fall in battle. I dropped my hand on his shoulder to thank him for offering to take my responsibility despite being so close to death. He was shivering.

"Technically, I didn't die in battle," he said through bluing lips.

"You did if you die from this wound," cranky old Karl said as he dropped himself on top of Cross-Eyes' cold body. "Just as I will if this fire doesn't start soon enough."

"Come help if you're not happy, old man," Titus replied from the nest of twigs he was setting on fire.

"If I get down, it will be to kick your ass, *framling*," Karl snapped back at Titus, who was a foreigner indeed and proud to be. Odin had granted a handful of non-Norsemen a seat in his great hall, and among them, Titus alone joined the Wolves.

When not on a mission, Titus was often in charge of training the Einherjar. It had to be said that this former general came from a people who knew discipline and how to fight wars. He looked my age, somewhere in his late thirties, and had a similar build gained from a life, and afterlife, on the battlefield. His skin was darker, and his eyes darker still.

He was also responsible for many of us, myself included, keeping our hair short. A choice the Æsir had not liked but allowed, for it meant better hygiene. Lice, sadly, also thrived on Asgard. But even if we could respect and adopt this habit, we would never go as far as washing as often as he did, nor would we clip our beards to the skin like children. A man needed to preserve his pride.

Titus did not reply. He was a man with more restraint than us. It pissed off Karl even more, which I suspected Titus knew. The old man grumbled as he lay down.

"I'm ready when anyone feels like—" He never finished this sentence. Ulf had crept up on the other side of the cart and taken the old man by surprise.

"He prefers not to know when it happens," Ulf said to no one in particular as he pulled his long knife from Karl's ear with the sound of metal scraping bone.

"I thought I got to kill Karl this time," Rune whined.

"You'll kill him when you're a man," Ulf replied. Titus and I chuckled, but Rune did not.

"You know very well I never will be." I almost felt sorry for him; he was right.

Einherjar don't age, at least in Asgard. We remain as we were at the time of our first death. We could grow stronger or weaker, improve our skills, and learn new tricks, but we did not age, not even mentally. Especially not mentally. Karl would remain a grumpy old bastard and Rune a young, daring, beardless pup.

The cumulation of our missions on Midgard meant he

might have aged a bit at some point, but it would be a slow process. By my estimations, I had spent nearly five years on Midgard since my first death.

Rune had been the third son of a Geat's jarl and died in his first battle at the age of sixteen. Not one of the battles we'd taken part in. I envied him for remembering his life, which had ended only twenty years before. Mine had gone from blurry to forgotten. Even my real name I could not remember. Drake was my title. Drake, the Dragon who leads the Wolves. I had known two other Drakes before me.

"Do you want me to help you too?" Ulf asked Rune as the young man sat somewhere between Karl and Bjorn, who, I just noticed, had already crossed the rainbow bridge.

"No need, I'll use those," he said, fishing a pair of brown and white mushrooms from his pocket.

"Suit yourself," Ulf said before crouching to help Titus with the fire under the cart.

It was considered a cowardly thing to use poison over metal, but I had let the practice take root among my men. They faced enough as it was. Let the other "heroes" judge them after coming down to Midgard over and over again.

"Did you eat your nail first?" I asked. His eyes grew with shock. I was right, he hadn't.

"By Frigg's ass," he said before tapping on the small leather bag hanging from his neck, "almost forgot."

"That's why you should take it *before* the fight," I reminded him. "No nail—"

"—No Valhöll," the three of them echoed.

"I know," Rune said.

Odin's nails were our way back home. Swallowing one before we died ensured we would be sent up the Bifröst, not down to Hel. Of course, if we ate them and spent too long on Midgard, they came out the natural way, and eating them again was not an appealing idea, so we usually swallowed the nails at the last moment before a fight.

They had to be pulled from the All-Father's hands before we left Asgard. It pained him greatly, but it was his price to pay for having fucked up Bifröst so badly. The gods could use it down and up as they pleased, and the Valkyries had this power, too, though only in their ghost forms. *Our* return path was more... lethal. It was also the reason only ten people could join the Wolves. I don't know if it didn't work with Odin's toenails or if he didn't want them removed, but ten was our maximum.

The mushrooms followed the nail, and Rune started breathing frantically. He would need a couple of minutes before death truly took him. Mushrooms were painless, but it didn't make things much easier. Smoke enveloped the cart, and my last two men rose. Titus put on his helmet and took his sword. He knelt by the entrance of the small cave, just passed the line of shade to die under the sun, and planted the tip of the blade in the sand while inclining his forehead toward the pommel.

"*Mars pater, ego pro vestra sapientia*—" he mumbled. A prayer to his old god of war that he had tried to teach me.

"How many centuries with our gods for him to stop this nonsense?" Ulf asked mockingly. I replied in kind, for I knew Ulf meant no disrespect.

"Your gods are real," Titus said without moving. "Mine are somewhere, too. Once I have proven that your prophecy about the end of the world is worth horse manure, I will find them."

"I pray you're right," I told him without believing it. Prophecies always had a way of happening. Ragnarök would be no different.

Titus stretched his collar, his signal. I stood behind him

and stabbed between his neck and shoulder, as he always asked. It wasn't the gentlest method, but Titus insisted on it.

After hundreds of times, we had developed our preferences. Sometimes, one of us tried something new. But it usually ended in a colossal failure of pain for him and laughter for the others. Like the time Eigil and Cross-Eyes tried to drink themselves to death. It didn't work, and they had to eat the nails again after throwing them up. Ulf had planted the idea in their minds, and it became a favored story among us.

Titus made no sound as he fell face-first. The heat from the fire and the thickness of the smoke made carrying him to the cart difficult. Hair and leather were already burning, starting with the men at the bottom.

"Is he getting heavier?" Ulf asked as we dropped Titus on the heap of bodies.

"I don't think he would allow it," I replied.

"Maybe I'm just getting older," my friend said as a joke told too many times. He was nervous, as usual. Ulf had been my first recruit as the Wolves' Drake, and it had made many people doubt me. He was, by his own words, afraid of death. How he had managed to be chosen by a Valkyrie in the first place was a mystery to me, and to him as well. But his fear was precious to us more daring and fame-hungry warriors.

I have lost count of occasions where he sensed the trap, the weakness in our plan, or when he was the last one standing and sent us home. His fear was a valued asset and made him the best damn archer I ever met. But the last moment was always tough on him.

"How?" I asked, my eyes squinted against the smoke as he pulled himself onto the cart.

"Don't snap my neck," he said, "it hurts for hours after."

He didn't like the easy ways out because they took too

long and frightened him even more than the pain of a quick death. I chose the heart this time, just as he closed his eyes in expectation. He sighed with something like relief when I accompanied him down.

By then, the cave was mostly black with smoke, and I had to ready myself.

Fire sent everything back to Asgard: body, metal, fabric, everything. When it so happened that we failed in our missions and all got killed, we had to count on crows, Muninn's pets, to eat the flesh from our bones. This was her third and last role. But even a murder of them needed days to devour us and send us whole to Asgard, and we arrived there buck naked and ashamed. A professional hazard. Yes, fire was better.

The slain—the new ones, that is—would go straight to Asgard, carried by the mystical hands of the Valkyries. At least the ones who had fought and died bravely enough. In Asgard, they would become our brothers and feast and fight until Ragnarök.

I waited until the flames roared strong enough, then fished the small leather bag containing the nail of the All-Father from my mail shirt. The nail looked exactly like a human one and even had dirt on it. Odin had bitten it nervously.

This was my way home, and for a second, I wondered if I should take it. I had not forgotten to eat it before the battle; I just hadn't. Even now, I'm not sure why; probably just a way to tempt fate. We could still go to Asgard without the nail if we fought bravely, but it was a great risk. One wrong move, a spear in the back, a moment of terror, and I would have joined the cursed in Hel, waiting for the end of time, when the army of the dead would rise to fight Asgard and end the nine realms.

Not a great option, but many chose it, more than we liked to think. My first Drake had chosen this option. He sent me up the Bifröst at the end of a mission and never followed us. If I lived until Ragnarök, I would meet him again, and we would fight once more. I swallowed the nail for him. Usually, it was for Muninn, or the Wolves, or a number of other reasons. There was always a reason to keep on fighting.

But I was tired.

It wasn't the first time I felt the exhaustion from this existence creeping into me. We all did from time to time. This was usually when the Wolves switched a member. Not an option for the Drake.

I ate mushrooms like Rune had. Not out of fear; I was just exhausted and didn't want to suffer. Flames engulfed the cart now, sending a smell of burning meat up my nose. The mushrooms numbed my senses quickly but not fast enough that I didn't feel my skin heating up to the point of pain. Thankfully, my mind retreated on itself, and the colors of the Bifröst opened up toward Valhöll.

Home.

᛭

"Crossing the bridge is like sex. The first time goes too fast to remember anything. Then it gets more interesting, then boring, then interesting again."

Karl, member of the Wolves.

2

Asgard.

Rays of color met at the center of my vision and mixed into a white flashing light. There was no sound, no worries, and no air until the world returned in a splash of icy water. I gasped as soon as my head jutted from the surface. A hand grabbed me by the shoulder, dragged me away from the source of Bifröst, and dropped me on the muddy earth surrounding it.

"By the gods, you took your sweet time," Bjorn said after pulling me far enough so that I could lie on the grass.

"Everybody made it?" I asked. The same question I always asked. No one had failed the crossing in decades, but the last occasion still haunted me.

"Aye, we did, but you got us four waiting," Cross-Eyes said in a rich Saxon accent that we never managed to cure.

"Not our fault you made a point of dying so fast," Karl mocked him before pressing on a nostril and expertly expelling some snot. "Now, which of you bastards killed me?" he asked, pointing an accusing finger at Rune, who lifted his hands innocently.

"That was me," Ulf answered, still lying, hands shielding his face as he exerted his mind to forget. Someday, I told myself, Ulf would refuse to join us.

A brother once told me passing through the Bifröst was probably like birth. It made sense when he explained his theory, though he had added that at least on the other side you didn't connect with a freshly made shit. Most of the time, though, we connected with our thoughts, which was worse.

Many stories about the gods are exaggerated. I could say as much after three hundred years by their sides, but the beauty of Asgard could not be explained in words, for none exist to describe its beauty. It was an island lost in a sea of ice patches and pristine water reflecting a sky of blue and green. A single mountain stood east of the island. A tall, thin, dark brown peak, its tip forever lost inside a hanging cloud from which a lively stream ran down to the valley, just enough water to nourish the lush nature surrounding the mountain and to fill Mimir's well.

I never went higher than the cloud, nor did any of my brothers, for the cold and the lack of air made any effort too painful. But from where I had stood, in what I would call my youth as an Einheri, I saw the island in its entirety. Everything was held in a green that approached silver.

Trees patched with the colors of their many fruits, seas of grass and wheat dancing with a gentle breeze, and hills on which played wild game, the likes of which did not exist on Midgard. The day I climbed the mountain, I thought the whole of Asgard could be crossed in a day or two, but when I attempted it, I gave up after ten. Space worked in a funny way here, and it was one of the things you gave up trying to understand after some time.

Heimdallr, who, along with Tyr, was the only god I considered a friend, once told me the mountain was a root from Yggdrasil, the tree of life, sprouting at an odd angle. But Heimdallr was prone to making fun of us mortals, and I never discovered if he was honest in that matter.

Sharp alabaster cliffs surrounded the island and made it impregnable. Its lowest point was a small pond of non-salted water connected to every lake or river in Midgard, with few exceptions. This pond, wide as the length of a longship, was the source of the Bifröst.

We came out of the pond to face a side cliff that could only be climbed from a narrow path dug in the rock. It snaked up to the plateau island in a leg-breaking, lung-testing fifteen-minute climb that left us panting. Of course, intruders who managed to use the Bifröst without the approval of its guardian, Heimdallr the Golden, would enjoy the hike as much as we did.

"I was wondering when I'd see your sorry face," Heimdallr said, offering his hand for me to stand up. My godly friend was always down by the pond when someone crossed the Bifröst. It was his duty and, in our case, his pleasure, or so he said.

"We barely left a couple of days ago," I told him after he lifted me as easily as if I were a child.

"Well, Asgard is dull without its mad dogs," the Æsir replied, offering me a smile of golden teeth to warm my heart.

I often thought Odin had chosen Heimdallr as the gatekeeper of Asgard not only because his sight and hearing were the sharpest among the gods, though not as amazing as he claimed, but also because of his appearance. None looked more like the image we have of the Æsir than Heimdallr.

He was of Bjorn's height and had a chest to rival Thor's. His beard and hair, which he kept well-oiled at all times, was a pale blond that shone like gold under the sun, as did his teeth. The best of his features, however, was his personality. Gentle by nature, Heimdallr was easy to laugh with and, despite his role, was welcoming and respectful of those less powerful than him, a unique trait among the Æsir.

Maybe this was why he had been happy to accept this role so far from the other gods and their halls. That and the one thing he had negotiated with the All-Father in exchange for his compliance, an infinite quantity of the best mead to be found on Asgard. Said mead was the reason for his paunch and for my men's presence in Heimdallr's hall as often as time allowed.

"What is it, my friend?" he asked as we made our way toward the Snake Path.

"What do you mean?"

"You are even more sullen than usual. It's like I'm talking to Tyr." I realized then that he had been talking while I was lost in my thoughts. Most of my men were already halfway up. Einar was scolding his son, Eigil, for the way he had fought down there, while Cross-Eyes, Snekke, Titus, and Karl passed a skin of mead among themselves.

Rune jogged a few steps behind and would have a hard time getting any of the drink. Behind us, Bjorn was helping Ulf to his feet and would wait for him to feel better before ascending the path. No one would hear us. Some things you just did not share with your subordinates, especially doubts.

"I fought there before," I told Heimdallr.

"So?" he asked as he handed me his skin of mead. I gulped some and felt warmer already. It was amazing, this mead. Sweet and strong, the best of what nature had to offer.

"So, what's the point of all of this?" I asked, doing my best not to sound like a spoiled child. "The benches of Valhöll fill up regularly, but the more they do, the stronger our enemy gets. They always collect at least half the slain."

"The weaker half," Heimdallr quickly replied as he tucked the skin back in his belt.

"It doesn't mean they're weak either." Heimdallr had led some of our missions in the past and witnessed the value of the folks on Midgard. He knew men could swing an axe even when their guts failed them.

"Odin has bet on bravery. He has placed his hope in human courage; there's nothing new here. Nothing has changed except you, apparently."

I was doing my best to follow his steps, and he did not seem to notice my struggles.

"The prophecy changed things," I said, which made him hum from the back of his throat. The prophecy made everyone feel uneasy. For twenty-three years, it had hung over our heads like a bad dream from which no one seemed able to wake up. A dark cloud of bad news everyone, gods and Einherjar alike, freely interpreted. "The prophecy says we will all die. Odin will die, so will Thor; even you will die."

"Ah," Heimdallr scoffed, booming like the thunder. "I'm to die killing Loki; that's worth it." The prophecy mentioned that Heimdallr and Loki would kill each other, and like most of the Æsir, Heimdallr had reasons to want to end Loki's life. I did not share his eagerness, though.

There was no mention of Muninn, nor any of my brothers in particular. We were to stand by Odin's side when the battle began; that's all we knew. "Not all of us will die,"

Heimdallr went on seriously. "A few gods will make it, as will two humans, and life will start anew, bright and beautiful."

"A heavy price for a handful of Æsir and a couple of humans," I said, immediately realizing how my words could be interpreted. "I meant no offense."

"None taken. I'm sure some of the worst pieces of shit on Asgard will be among the survivors." I chuckled at that, barely surprised by his blunt honesty. "But it's not like we have a choice."

"What if we did? What if there was a way to change the outcome?" I regretted asking right away. This was dangerous talk. Not forbidden, but this conversation falling on the wrong ears could see me stripped of my title. The gods had played with enough prophecies through their eons to take them seriously. "A way to save you," *and Muninn,* I thought. Heimdallr sighed and stopped in his tracks. His heavy hand dropped on my shoulder, making me wince with pain. The gods were effortlessly strong.

"Don't play with prophecies," he said, his golden hawk eyes fixed on mine. "You may think you know things, being the Drake and all, but believe me, my friend, you don't want to play with prophecies." He weighed each word down with gravitas. I also detected a hint of threat.

We were almost up the path, and I could hear the tumult of voices; some I knew, others I didn't, but Heimdallr had a point to make and spoke before I could. "You think Ragnarök a disaster, and many of my people agree with you. But to me, it is a promise that life will continue. If someone somehow altered the prophecy, there is no guarantee that anyone will survive Ragnarök. If I see you trying anything, Drake, I will have to stop you; you hear me?"

I nodded but had heard more stubbornness than

wisdom in Heimdallr's words. I should have listened harder. "One last thing," he said as the path ended, turning to a lush plain of grass, fresh with dew. "Don't mention any of it to Odin."

"No chance of that happening," I replied.

Odin had changed. More than any of them. Ragnarök had always been a reality for the All-Father, something he had knowledge of since he had sacrificed himself to himself ages ago. But the revelation of the prophecy by Mimir's head, twenty-three years ago, had achieved what Loki started with the murder of Baldur only seven years before that.

Odin had aged like no other Æsir ever had and seemed ready to break like a twig at the slightest provocation. Anytime I met with him since the revelation of the prophecy, I expected him to either burn with rage or weep like a crazy old man. Sometimes, though, Odin mustered a bit of his old self and became the witty Æsir I had known and loved for centuries. He would delight us with stories of past debaucheries, tales lurid enough to make a berserker blush or recount his most glorious battles. I loved this Odin, but he made himself rare.

No, I would not tell the All-Father.

"Is that you?" an unknown voice called with enough vehemence that my hand went by itself to my sword's handle. "You're the son of a whore who killed me, aren't you?"

Every time there was one.

The man stomping toward me was short and burly, the kind who never cooled down. I didn't remember him, but I had not seen my second victim clearly, and he might have been the one. The group he emerged from comprised sixteen or seventeen slain, less than the twenty-five Odin had expected. The Valkyries had been picky. Those men had naturally split into the two sides of the battle, something that would quickly change here.

"You should thank him," Heimdallr said before I could reply to the insult. I don't remember my mother very well, but she was no whore, of that I'm certain.

The short, angry man had paid no attention to the god, but just then, the cloud masking the sun vanished, and the light made Heimdallr shine in bright gold. My new brother gasped and remained dumbfounded.

"Because of Drake here," Heimdallr continued with a theatrical gesture toward me, "you have become a soldier of Odin, an Einheri, one of the heroes who will accompany us in the final battle."

The slain were being taken to Asgard by the ghost Valkyries, who would lovingly drop our new brothers at the top of the Snake Path with no explanation. Sometimes, if none of the Wolves had been killed, the new Einherjar could wait a long time before someone guided them toward Valhöll and the citadel. Usually, one of us, Snekke, more often than not, would join them and clarify the situation.

Snekke was skilled with words, a rare trait among warriors, though his most extraordinary talent was his understanding of people. He could fire up a crowd like no one else, speaking in such a way that everyone felt his words on a personal level. But he was just as capable of soothing them, bringing survivors to tears, or seducing a widow in mere seconds. I often thought he must have been a *skald* in his life, but he never agreed or denied it, and I never learned the truth.

There were two problems with Snekke. First, he wasn't the best of fighters. Of average height and less than average build, he did not impress in the shield wall. He had long, straight hair the color of hay, a thin beard framing a thin face, and two remarkable blue eyes. While he was a passable spearman, his fighting ability rarely let him survive long in battle. But by then, his part was done, anyway.

Second, he was fake. Such was the case with a lot of those master manipulators; they always sought a way to gain something. And once you understood this about Snekke, there was no trusting him completely.

This was why it had taken me a long time to appreciate him. But as a Wolf, I dare say he had filled the benches of Valhöll more than any other, myself included. Folks will always look for a way out of battle. In those occurrences, Snekke was the one reminding them why they needed to fight, how their pride had been stung, what the enemy would do to their wives, or the loot they would bring back to their huts.

He would sometimes mention the glory of dying in battle and being chosen by Odin, and at least he was honest in that. But calming pride-wounded slain and revengeful warriors wasn't his priority. He just didn't care much at that point. Snekke, like most of the Wolves, had his reasons for being part of the crew—Midgard's women, mostly. Once back home, his motivation melted fast.

"I told him you would explain," Snekke said, emerging from the group of slain, thumbs tucked into his belt.

"My apologies for the pain," I told the angry man, extending an arm. He took it without realizing, his eyes still lost on the Æsir.

"It did hurt," he replied more mildly. He blinked and came back to me. "Is this really Asgard?" he whispered as if the question would offend Heimdallr, somehow forgetting the stories of his extraordinary hearing.

"You didn't even mention that?" I asked Snekke, who

shrugged. I sighed and tried hard to remember how it felt to land on Asgard for the first time. "This is indeed Asgard," I told the man before moving my attention to the others. This was when I noticed with pleasure the presence of my last kill, the young man on whom I had traced the Valknut. "You will remain here, feasting with the gods, training with your brothers, until Ragnarök and the end of the world."

I did not bother to explain what Ragnarök was. At this point, the prophecy was known far and wide on Midgard. Stories traveled faster than the plague, even between realms. If I had to bet, I'd say Thor had blabbered it out during his several journeys among men. He was never satisfied, our god of thunder, neither with his wife nor our mead.

"Should you prove yourselves among the best," I said as grins showed many decayed teeth among them, "you may join the Wolves of Asgard and return to Midgard to gather more brave men, just as we have gathered you."

I've never been a man for speeches, but I had practiced this one, and my men knew it so well that they gathered around me on cue, even Karl, who liked to be noticed by the newcomers. Ulf had regained his pride, and more than a few heads turned to Bjorn, probably wondering if he was a god himself.

Even Einar stopped scolding Eigil to let the solemnity of the moment absorb our new brothers. It did the trick, and curiosity changed to admiration. In front of them stood Valhöll's best, something to be respected. Some of my men were not actually the greatest fighters, but each excelled at something and deserved their spot. I was proud of my Wolves, not like a father, but more like a big brother.

Many Einherjar came to Asgard with no help from the Wolves. There were too many battles, especially in summer. We tipped the scales and raised the stakes, but were not always needed. And the Wolves had not always existed for the sole purpose of recruiting more warriors. Our responsibilities had shrunk over the centuries, and with any sign of the approaching end, we focused more heavily on gathering brave men.

This was when the questions usually started pouring, the first almost always being whether they would lie with Valkyries. They'd soon realize that Valkyries aren't more extraordinary than regular women. Some were beautiful, some were not, and they were not as willing as the stories made them, and being Odin or Freyja's creations, most were stronger than us.

A few Valkyries had started what could be described as relationships with some of my brothers, but the cases were rare. Only Titus had such luck among the Wolves. She looked a lot like his wife, he said. And he, being a rare and exotic sight, had no problem seducing her. We envied him greatly, but at least it gave me hope about my foolish and secret desire.

Then would come the questions on the gods themselves, especially Thor, favored by warriors, or the quality of the mead, the daily battles we were supposed to practice, or any detail they had heard rumors of. We just replied that they would have their answers soon.

But one of them asked a question we were hearing more often.

"When is Ragnarök happening?"

A wave of murmurs spread throughout the group, and a few approved of the question. In my days, Ragnarök was but a fable. You always found some lunatic who claimed the end was near, but they lived in the woods and survived on dead squirrels. Folks used to turn Einherjar with the prospect of a never-ending second life on Asgard. But now, it's like they expected to be shoved into the shield wall upon their arrival. Even on Midgard, they felt the looming tension of the end of the world.

"No one knows," Snekke replied, marching toward the man who had spoken, a tall and not-so-bright-looking fellow who barely flinched when my man grabbed him by the shoulder. "But it will be a moment of glory, I can tell you that. Wave after wave of scum from Jötunheimr, fiery beasts from Múspellsheimr, and dead men from Hel, crashing against our shields, and..." The whole group followed him like a herd of peaceful goats as he spoke. The young slain nodded at me before joining his comrades. He was even younger than Rune.

"Will you be joining us this evening?" I asked Heimdallr, an echo of the question I had asked Muninn.

"Not sure," he gravely replied, making me understand he preferred to remain close to the Bifröst. Heimdallr spent more time by Asgard's passage since Loki's imprisonment, and even more so since the prophecy. Some beings could force it open, and he would be the first to signal and repel any threats. I left him there to return to his small hall dug in the cliff, with his exceptional mead, telling myself that if Muninn did not attend the feast, I would join him.

Bjorn and Ulf were waiting for me. Together, we caught up with the group, who now stood silent, eyes wide-open in wonder at the sight of the *wall*.

The city of Asgard was much, much more impressive than anything I have ever seen. In the past, before the wall was erected, long before me, the new Einherjar saw it from the moment they arrived, which is why they were dropped at the top of the hill rather than by Bifröst like us.

Now, the only thing they could see of the citadel was a huge, white wall masking the bottom third of the mountain.

It went around it in a near-perfect circle of high stones the color of chalk but smooth, the same stone the entire island was made of.

The ground was still flat where the wall stood and remained so for another five-minute walk before the slope of the mountain started. The wall shined with silvery veins that seemed to pulse, giving it a lifelike feeling.

"The stories are true," one of my new brothers said in astonishment.

"The stories are almost always true," I replied grimly, "though they are often exaggerated."

The wall surrounding Asgard was already famous in Midgard when I was a boy. I never learned how accurate the story of its construction was, but let's say Loki had played a part in it that some gods would never forgive, Freyja among them. Though, as often as not, when it came to the god of lies, his punishment had been excessive. I used to pity him, before Baldur, and before... Well, before he stole my body.

To me, he acted like those boys who thirsted for attention and only knew one way to get it: mischief. Doesn't mean they shouldn't receive a beating, but it's never the only reason for their misdeeds. And, as with most stories involving Loki, by the end of it, the gods had been blessed with much, while he only received a lesson he would never learn.

The palisade looked like a range of teeth standing next to each other in perfect order, not blocks of stones as we sometimes see on Midgard but huge chunks of rock taken whole from the cliff. How the Jötunn, who had built the wall, arranged them with such efficiency was a wonder, and I slept better for its presence.

One of the new men pressed his hand to the wall with

apprehension before letting out a breath when the touch felt familiar. He seemed disappointed.

"How do we get in?" the young one asked. I did not think he was the kind to speak out, but I was glad he did.

"Like this," I said, grabbing his wrist while unsheathing the long knife from my belt. He meant to retrieve his hand from my grasp, but I was much stronger. I waited for him to give up. "Open your hand."

I told myself I would keep an eye on him, a thought I often had about new brothers but always managed to forget. More careful than usual, I drew the blade across his palm. Immediately, a thin red line bloomed. If it pained him, he didn't show it, and I felt sorry for him for a second. Had I not killed him, he would have become a great warrior on Midgard.

"The blood of the heroes is the key to Asgard," I told them while I pulled his hand to the wall. *It's always a question of blood*, I thought, but did not say. This was the greatest day of their existence; no need to spoil it with my grumpiness.

"The blood of *dead* heroes," Karl said with scorn, as if he had not been slain once himself.

There was a rumble coming from the stone, and the ground shook. Then, just as the new men checked their feet, the rock shrunk before them. It disappeared slowly at its base as if the earth were eating it in one slow, big gulp. Those rocks were as wide as four men standing side by side with their arms stretched and as high as fifteen standing on each other's shoulders. Their descent was deafening and veiled our sight with thick clouds of dust.

"Let's go," I said, dropping the young man's hand before stepping into the cloud on the other side of which stood the citadel.

I took a deep breath as I took in the sight of the place. No matter my mood, this was a view with no match. The mountain was covered at its base with hundreds of halls and houses. They formed a disorganized pattern of white, brown, and gold structures linked by paths of white pebbles. Some halls were dug into the mountain itself, while others had been built with materials that didn't belong here.

Valhöll, the first hall in front of us, was the least remarkable in the citadel by its appearance, though its size, from the outside, put it in the top three or four. Huge shields hung under the roof's crossed beams, and a gigantic golden tree stooped over the hall's main entrance. That's all there was to say on the topic of Valhöll. Beauty wasn't its purpose.

Most of the other gods' halls were more conspicuous, and there were more than just halls in the city. Scented trees, quiet ponds, waterfalls, and, more importantly, life painted the citadel.

On Midgard, the stories we heard of Asgard back in my days revolved around the same gods, as if Asgard belonged to a very elite group. Nothing was further from the truth.

Asgard was beaming with life, so to speak. A beehive buzzing with countless people traveling the paths, most of them Einherjar, but not only. Valkyries in their human forms wandered peacefully, wearing robes of linen or silk, their hair floating freely in the gentle breeze.

Æsir, dozens and dozens of them, lived among the rest, some high and mighty from their obvious divinity while others looked no more formidable than a Midgard's farmer. Of course, even the least impressive Æsir could crush my skull with two fingers if he wanted to.

In fact, in all my time as an Einheri, I have only witnessed two men defeating a god in combat. Bjorn was one of them and had been given a house as a prize. Not as comfortable as the one granted to me on behalf of my title, but a great possession nonetheless, which he sadly lost in a game of *tafl*. Everyone knew Bjorn sucked at *tafl*.

The Æsir were not the only clan of gods on Asgard. The Vanir were fewer in this realm but easier to spot. I had no love for this clan. No matter what we did, they looked at us as if we were made from the same stuff they had dumped in the morning. The gods, just like any other creature of the Nine Realms, had to empty their bowels. They barfed when drunk and suffered hangovers and bad days, just like the rest of us. But the Vanir did not accept the similarities and stuck to their snooty behavior and not-so-mysterious ways. Freyja, for example, the goddess of love and war, was a real cunt at the best of times. And she was the nicest of them, which says a lot.

Of course, the Einherjar were the most numerous beings you could see in Asgard. Thousands upon thousands of my brothers roamed the city at any given time. We had built a center of life, the likes of which existed nowhere else in the nine realms, despite Titus's ridiculous claim regarding his mother city.

Einherjar had built smitheries, bakeries, and gambling houses. We worked our wooden and stone crafts for each other and for the gods, at a price. Some men even accepted the degrading tasks of sewing and fashioning clothes. We mocked them, but they grew silver-rich faster than anyone else.

The less talented or ambitious among us tended the farms belonging to the gods, but Asgard's soil was so rich that it barely needed working hands. We were loud and unruly, the perfect opposite of the Vanir, yet Asgard was more ours than anyone else's.

We trained, then fought, then feasted every day, per

Odin's order, which was good enough for most of us. At least for some time. But even the great citadel could not accommodate us all. At any given time, half of the Einherjar remained inside Valhöll, which, as explained for the rest of the island, worked with an unexplainable concept of space. The others could wander the mountain, the city, or the rest of the island as they wanted while there was no training or *brawl*. When I say they could wander, this was not without consequence. Asgard remained a wild, dangerous realm.

"Listen to me," I barked, turning to a group of wide-open mouths. "As long as you stay within the citadel, you cannot die," I said the last while pointing at the wall. I nodded at Eigil to get ready for the next part, the most enjoyable moment of the tour. "Or rather, I should say *you cannot remain dead*."

Eigil acted before any of them could ask the meaning of my words. His hammer swooshed in a wide arc above his head, then landed with a monstrous crunching sound on top of someone's head. I was pleased he'd chosen the short man who had been so vocal earlier. His brain and blood splashed the others, and he fell like a tree, leaving only a scrap of scalp glued to Eigil's hammer. My new brothers jumped away with curses, hands going to the hilts of their weapons, but Eigil remained unimpressed, his big, deer eyes oblivious to the change in atmosphere.

Bjorn and Ulf chuckled, and I can't lie; I enjoyed this part every time, too.

The man who had fallen, Erik, according to his comrade's screams, suddenly gave a few spasms, which got the small crowd quiet. Erik got to his knees, his head still nothing but a puddle of broken bones and torn muscles. Already, the gruesome resurrection was taking place. I had become numb to it over the years, but it was disgusting. One of the new men vomited when he saw his friend's face reconstructing itself piece by piece. It did not take long, and by the time his mouth was whole again, his scream was deafening.

"I should also mention that depending on how you die, coming back hurts like a bitch," I said loud enough to cover Erik's shrieks.

They were in a trance as he fell on his ass, sweating and panting like a woman who had just given birth. I could have explained all of it, or I could have told them to check the young man's hand which had healed soon after we passed the wall, but where was the fun in that? Now they got the message. We couldn't die in the citadel, but we sure as Hel did not want to let ourselves get killed either.

"Does that mean we can die outside?" a man asked, his thumb pointing toward the wall before it slowly went up again.

"Not only can you die, but you will die," Einar said to the man who towered over him by a good head, which was the case for most men. "Anything out there will try to kill you and will probably succeed." The island of Asgard was beautiful beyond words, but it was far from safe.

"Don't worry," Karl said, "most of you won't leave the city before Ragnarök, anyway."

"Well, I still don't want that to happen to me," one of them said as Erik stood up, hatred and exhaustion creeping on his face.

"Oh, that will happen a lot," Eigil said as he picked the rest of Erik from his hammer. The Wolves laughed, for Eigil had not meant to mock the new men. His face flushed when he realized the effect of his words, but by then, the sounds of hundreds of men approaching drowned the rest.

They had taken their time, but the Einherjar were

coming to welcome their brothers, old and new. Grim warriors carrying shields, swords, spears, axes, and the aura of deadly fighters formed a wide arc twenty paces from us. One of them beat his fist on his bare chest, then another followed with a sword on a shield, and suddenly, they all picked up the rhythm. They barked, howled, and cheered, and a chill ran up my spine.

Fuck Ragnarök, I thought, nothing could beat us.

The weariness of this existence momentarily gave way to the pride of being a leader among this savage lot.

Our new brothers watched in awe, stuck between fear and pride. I walked into the crowd as if nothing stood in front of me. They parted on both sides, creating a corridor of men leading to the Hall of the Slain. My Wolves followed me, for such was their role, and behind them, seventeen new warriors to fill the benches of Valhöll.

ᛦ

"My father used to say I was good for nothing and would get killed on my first raid."
"Did you?"
"Raided for twelve years before some bugger stabbed me between the balls."
"And your father?"
"Never saw him again. The bastard probably died a straw death in the same shit hole he's known all his life. Can't wait to face him during Ragnarök."

Sieg Astridson and Oleg White Eye
Square twenty-one

3

The stories of Valhöll claimed that the Einherjar fought all day, slaying each other before coming back to life for a grand feast. It's close to the truth, but as usual, not accurate either. We trained during the day, most days, not just to fight, but for every step of what will be the final battle of our time.

We practiced gearing up, forming up, leaving the hall in good order after just one note of the horn, how to stand in the shield wall, look as fearsome as possible, and yes, we fought. And within the fighting part of our training was the heart of the stories, a great melee, Valhöll's Brawl.

At some point, it had some silly name like "the contest of champions," an idea coming straight from some Vanir's ass and just as quickly forgotten. It happened randomly. Anywhere from once a month to three times a week, but always in the evening. We gathered in Valhöll, the only place where all of us could fit. There, we welcomed our new brothers before the madness shook the walls under the blows of thousands upon thousands of men fighting to the death.

Valhöll was a strange place, to say the least. On the outside, it was a massive building of wood and thatch fit for four or five hundred people. But once inside, you quickly realized it was, in fact, much bigger. From the dais on which stood Odin's chair, a massive seat carved in a single piece of oak covered with the fur of a white bear, you could not see the end of the hall. I think there was no real end.

Valhöll grew according to the number of people in it; it was as simple as that, though how it worked was far from my understanding. It always remained as wide as a longship, with sturdy, beautifully dragon-carved poles lined every twenty paces, and the ceiling's highest point was the height of a mast.

Men who ventured into the woods would return with the pelts of hunted beasts and display them on the beams crossing under the roof, the greatest of which hung right before the gods' dais. The practice had claimed too many lives among my people, so Odin had forbidden us to hunt, and the pelts, antlers, or giant shield-shaped scales adorning the front of the hall had remained unchanged for a century.

On the evening of the brawls, we pushed the tables and benches to the sides of the hall and traced squares in the ground with branches of ash trees infused with *seidr* magic. We made them big enough for twenty men to fight. The best fighters battled inside the closest squares to Odin and whichever gods attended the brawl, eager to show the All-Father their worth. As you moved from square to square, the quality of the fights decreased until it was more an act than a proper battle. No one checked past the thirtieth square, so what was the point of maiming each other to death?

It was an honor to fight in the front squares, and all the arrangements were purely voluntary. Men fought where they thought they could distinguish themselves. If they did not feel like they could that day, they just withdrew to a lower square and faked defeat before taking a seat at a bench of the many tables lining both sides of the hall.

Not an option for the Drake, though. My spot was in the first square, where some of my men would stand as well, though they were not on anyone's side at this moment. Some of the new recruits would usually join us, invited by snarling men before being dispatched in a matter of heartbeats under the laughter of spectators. You could have been a prow man on Midgard, have songs to your name, and a byname inspiring fear in men's hearts; in Valhöll you were nothing until you proved yourself in the square.

I never thought the brawl was a great place to judge the quality of a fighter, a point on which Titus agreed. The strength of the Einherjar was in their number, not in their individual skills. Still, it was good entertainment and an even better source of healthy competition. On that evening, though, I cared very little about any of it; my thoughts were focused on Muninn's absence.

A large swing of Eigil's hammer grazed my nose, bringing me out of my daydreaming.

The square was still packed; I'd only missed the beginning of the brawl, but I had to pull myself up if I wanted to avoid being shamed by one of my men. Why Eigil had chosen me as an opponent was a mystery. In terms of pure strength, he was the best of my men, even stronger than Bjorn. But what he had in muscle, he lacked in brain. Choosing me as a first opponent was a mistake, but at least he had tried something new by doing so.

He stared at me with his big, blue eyes, trying hard to avoid giving a clue about his next attack. I knew where it would come from anyway and just waited for it. The head of his long hammer waited on the ground. Just as he meant to lift it again, I kicked it down with the sole of my right foot before slapping him with my left hand. It wouldn't have hurt his spirit as much if it had been a fist.

"Don't leave it on the ground," I told him, having to shout the words to be heard above the tumult of the brawl. "It's useless there." His face flushed with the shame of having been slapped. I thought he would charge like a crazed goat, something he often did, but he surprised me. He tossed his hammer at me.

The throw was not dangerous, so I naturally grabbed it in the air and realized my mistake when Eigil's shoulder drove the air from my lungs. He was a monster of strength. I could not find the ceiling from the ground for a second, just long enough for him to take his hammer back and attempt a new swing. I rolled to the side, and the chunk of metal landed right by my cheek. Had he aimed for my chest, I could not have avoided it.

"Don't stay on the ground," he said as he lifted the hammer again. "You're useless there." Someone cheered at his jest, and I wondered if he had ever said anything as clever before. That's when his mistake in choosing me showed.

He was about to bring his deadly weapon down when someone bumped into him, another brawler lost in his fight. It caught Eigil's attention just long enough for me to sit up and drive my blade up his groin, a good hand's length of it.

He shrieked like a child and dropped his hammer to clutch his inner leg when I removed my blade.

"You're too big for the square; wait for it to get less crowded before you attack a nimbler opponent," I told him as I placed my hand under his armpit. He nodded while biting his lower lip, and I shoved him outside the square, where he immediately started feeling better.

Many things influence a fight, skills and brute force among them, but patience and brains help too, especially when the opponent is as big as an ox and fights in a tight space with a hammer as long as his leg.

Bringing my attention back to the fight, I noticed that nearly half the men had been pushed out or chosen to exit. At the center, Bjorn was toying with one of the new men, whirling his axe for the crowd's pleasure, especially for Freyja, who happened to be there that night.

Magnus Stone-Fists, the second-best fighter among the Einherjar and probably the most hated of our kind, was finishing his opponent slowly, pulling him back at the center of the square even as the man struggled to flee.

I spat toward Magnus before a cheer took my attention to Cross-Eyes, who raised his arms victoriously after he managed to stab his spear through his opponent's skull. The poor man had to be dragged outside the square as I took his place to face my warrior. Cross-Eyes did not look anxious and had no reason to be; this was his element.

He was a lean man, on the short side, with more strength than his scrawny arms let you believe, and he was dangerous. The tail of his long red hair swooped behind him as he took his stance, pointing the tip of his spear toward my throat. If Cross-Eyes didn't feel nervous, I did.

Odin had once sent us on a mission for a single man whose reputation as an incredible fighter had spread all the way to Asgard. It was highly unusual, and I had doubted the nature of the mission until I met said man. His fame claimed he had won over fifty *holmgang* without a single scratch.

I had scoffed at the sight of him, had challenged him,

and been killed in less time than it takes to say *Mjölnir*. Three more comrades joined me back to Asgard before Bjorn finally took care of him. I remember telling myself before he struck me on that day that dueling with a spear was the dumbest idea ever. Yet the most unnerving part of fighting this expert of one-on-ones wasn't his choice of weapon; it was his eyes.

His real name was Sven, but no one called him that. We called him Cross-Eyes because his eyes could not both look in the same direction, which made fighting him a pain in the ass. You never knew where he was looking and, thus, where he would strike.

As usual, his first jab took me by surprise. I only managed to avoid it because I knew he favored the thigh as his first target, an advantage another opponent wouldn't have. I pulled my leg back just in time and parried the spear away with my sword. But Cross-Eyes brought it back before I could step in, and I had to block the next lunge with less grace.

He smiled as if victorious already, which pissed me off a great deal. I thought I had bested him enough times to gain a bit of fear, but apparently not. I rushed, not following the advice I had just given Eigil, but Sven expected it. He reversed his grip and slammed the butt of his spear toward my face. But I knew this trick as well and simply stopped the staff with my left palm.

It hurt, but not as much as if I had taken it straight on the side of the head. I could see the surprise on Cross-Eyes' face, but I had one more for him. Before he could step back and regroup, I stomped his left foot, grabbed his wrist, and rocked my head back. He cursed as I rammed my forehead against his nose.

I heard the bone break, then a gasp of agony. Few things

hurt more acutely than a broken nose. He shook his head to regain his senses. I could take my time with him now. Blood ran from his twisted nose down to his beardless chin, and his knees were shaking. Cross-Eyes was our *holmgang* fighter, but if you took his mobility out, he wasn't *as* dangerous.

From the corner of my eye, I saw two fighters in the next square engaged in the last bout of their group. I proudly noticed one of them was Rune, giving Titus a hard time, or so he thought. Rune was a unique case among the Einherjar. He started very far from the main square and had not moved for five or six years. And suddenly, he escalated the squares. Half a year was all it took to see him in the second one.

When I asked Rune how he had improved so fast, he shrugged and claimed he had done nothing differently. Ever the instructor, Titus had kept his eye on him since he reached the upper fights but couldn't explain it either. Rune's talent had just bloomed.

I discarded both of them from my mind as Sven picked up his spear.

"You yield?" I asked him.

"In your dreams," he replied, defiance back in his eyes.

"Suit yourself." I brought my sword hand back to my hip, regretting that I had not taken a shield this time. They are cumbersome in such a tight space and quickly prove useless against the likes of Eigil, Bjorn, or Magnus. But against Cross-Eyes, shields helped.

Thinking to end this quickly, I stepped forward just as a great shadow loomed over me from the side. The impact of Magnus's back threw me out of the square and into a thick column. I stood up, cursing his mother.

My fight was done, made short by the violence of our

legendary duel, Magnus against Bjorn. Most brawls ended with the two champions fighting like rutting bears, not using any weapons other than their fists. Bjorn was a couple inches taller and altogether better built, but Magnus had trunk-like thighs and calves as thick as my biceps. Being a berserker, he also displayed a more savage nature than our jolly Bjorn.

My champion had won this fight more often, but if he let it continue, Stone-Fists would summon the beast trapped within him, and Bjorn would be in trouble. The fight was still under his control for now, and they seemed happy enough to wrestle for the upper hand in a contest of strength.

"There isn't much you can do when they're like this," Cross-Eyes said as he came to my side, his nose returning to its normal shape in front of my eyes.

"They could have let us finish," I replied. Cross-Eyes nodded absently, already enthralled by the madness of the duel. I took this chance to check the dais where the gods sat or stood, but Muninn remained absent. At least she had not witnessed my failure.

Odin sat on his throne, patting the shaggy head of Freki, one of his two hounds. His face bore no expression, which was the best we could hope for since Baldur's death. Both master and dog looked bored, though the latter swung its head from the square to its master, tongue lolling in anticipation of some treat.

The All-Father had not physically aged since I became one of his warriors, but his weariness weighed on his posture, and his eyes drooped as if about to fall asleep. He, who used to stand like the mountain and roar like the thunder, was now but the shell of an old man. I loved Odin and missed him dearly.

From where I came from, we often claimed that shit came in threes. For Odin, the first was Baldur's death thirty years ago. The second, seven years later, when he prophesied the details of Ragnarök. And last, Huginn's disappearance.

Odin had conjured two ravens. Muninn was Odin's memory and traveled the world as a witness, while Huginn was his thoughts and acted more as a messenger. I remembered Huginn as a good-looking young man, the twin of my beloved Muninn.

One day, maybe twenty years ago, Huginn left for Midgard and never returned. The All-Father had raged like never before, certain that one more of his children had been killed. Some claimed that since Odin had lost his *thoughts*, he surely had lost his mind as well. I don't know how Muninn took it, for I never dared approach the topic with her. Some rumors claimed she spent her free days flying over Midgard in search of her brother.

Freyja was here too, surrounded by her handsome, richly oiled male guards, wearing the bare minimum amount of clothing. Our goddess of love and war was never one for sleeves and collar, but that night, one could guess the temperature just by looking at her. Maybe Bjorn would get his wish this time.

Next to her sat Bragi, who snored with his lyre on his lap. Further down the dais, Sif patiently waited for all of this to stop while her husband, Thor, bellowed like the drunk he was, shouting for the two men to rip each other apart, his wide horn cup splashing mead all over himself. He almost got what he wished, for the two champions were caught in the heat of the moment.

Bjorn lay under Magnus as the berserker pushed his thumbs into my friend's eyes. But while shouting with pain,

Bjorn grabbed Stone-Fists by the balls and forced him to relent. I winced for both of them. It doesn't matter how strong you are; eyes and balls remain sensitive attributes.

"He's enjoying it too much," Titus said as he and Rune came by our side. The bruise around Rune's eye was vanishing, and Titus grinned as he offered me a horn of mead. His was filled with water, the prize for squares' victors.

Einherjar only drank the mead flowing from the udders of Heidrun, Odin's smelly goat. And while it tastes better than most mead we could find on Midgard, we got bored with it to the point that men sulked after clear water, which sadly was reserved for the gods. For many among us, this cup of water was the only reason to fight those brawls. That and the Valkyries serving them.

"It's just because the goddess of tits is here," Einar said from behind, standing on a table. His head weaved left and right so he could keep the fight in sight. Eigil would not look at me. He needed some time to digest the shame of our fight.

"You're right," I said. And just as if he had heard us, Bjorn managed to get rid of Magnus long enough to send a kiss toward Freyja, who scoffed as if insulted.

"You fought well," I told Eigil. Those words would go a long way to mend his pride, especially when spoken in front of his father. Einar slapped his son's back, and I smiled at this odd duo.

No two people could look more different. Einar was as short and energetic as Eigil was tall and placid. The father never stopped speaking in his squeaky voice, while the son never uttered a sentence with more than five words. Einar scolded his son for anything, but I never met a father with more love for his son than Einar.

I had chosen him because Eigil fared much better when

his father was around. And even though Einar wasn't an exceptional warrior, he had enough bravery for ten men and knew his way around a boat. The saddest part for him was not being able to sail the open sea, something he missed as much as his wife, a woman who, by the look of Eigil, must have been a giantess.

"Who do you bet on?" Titus asked, going back to the only vice I knew him to have, gambling. A vice shared by all his people, he assured me.

"Einar is right," I replied, "Freyja is here; Bjorn won't lose."

"My cup of water for a night in your house he loses then," Titus said, offering me one of his rare grins. I nodded. It never did to bet against Bjorn.

I immediately focused on the fight. This had gotten personal.

Magnus was losing his mind, and I could see foam at the corners of his mouth. He was going berserker. I wondered for a second if Titus had seen it before offering the bet. His discreet smile told me he had.

Shredding his tunic to bits, Magnus howled like a bear and charged Bjorn, arms wide-open. Bjorn took it and locked his left arm around Magnus's neck before catching his own wrist with the other hand. For a few seconds, Magnus's momentum drove Bjorn backward, dangerously close to the square's edge, but when my friend managed to stop the charge, it became a still battle.

Bjorn, veins popping on his forehead, intended to choke his opponent, while Magnus punched blindly at whatever piece of Bjorn he could hit. Magnus's face turned from red to purple; his punches lost their spirit, and soon, he just dropped his arms as if asleep.

"Shit," Titus spat.

The fight was over, but Bjorn kept the pressure on Magnus's neck. Then came a sound like when one breaks a chicken's carcass at the end of the meal, except it came from Magnus.

Bjorn dropped his opponent's body and threw his hands to the ceiling under a chorus of cheers. He turned toward the gods, all panting and sweating, and bowed to them, though we all knew it was for Freyja's benefit. Titus shoved his cup into my hand with a curse in his language. He and his woman would have to consume their passion somewhere else than my house.

Odin stood and raised his hand, quieting the room in a second, except for Thor, whose guffaw took a moment to die down. That's when I noticed Muninn by Odin's side. I had not seen her entering the hall, and my heart skipped a beat. Our last encounter was a few hours old, but felt like years. She found me in the crowd and gratified me with a corner smile. The merciless hope that she had feelings for me struck again, if she had feelings at all.

"You fought bravely, Bjorn Bjarnisson," the All-Father said. "You know the drill. As our champion, I grant you a wish. What do you want?"

Still searching for his breath, Bjorn stood arms akimbo, five or six steps from the All-Father, and though he had his back on me, I could guess his stupid grin.

"Same as usual, All-Father, I want to bed Freyja," Bjorn replied loud enough for us to hear. The named goddess rolled her eyes and puffed with her arms crossed under her perfect bosom. I was close enough to notice the corner of her mouth slightly rising.

Everyone wanted to bed Freyja, but since her story with the three Dwarves, she played hard to get. I often thought she enjoyed us lusting after her. Even Odin's desire for his fellow goddess was famous. His wife had made it clear she would never forgive him if something happened between them. So, as far as we knew, Freyja remained off-limits to him as well.

"Freyja, what do you say?" Odin asked.

"As usual," Freyja replied, her smooth, silky voice the perfect embodiment of her sensuality. The crowd cheered, and I lost myself upon the sight of the goddess as she threw her head back with laughter, wondering how smooth her skin must be to shine as such.

My bowel twisted when I noticed Muninn looking at me and shaking her head disapprovingly. Suddenly, I wished she hadn't been there to witness this brief moment of weakness.

Thor smacked his lips, passed his horn to his wife, then rolled his shoulders as he climbed down the deck. The men all around raised their fists again and again as our favored god took his place in the square, cracking the knuckles of both hands in a sign of intimidation.

How many times had it happened, I wondered? Since his first victory in the brawl, Bjorn had only asked for one thing: Freyja. She had scoffed the first time, declaring that she would give herself to him if he could defeat a god in battle. It took him decades, but he did defeat one, a brother of Thor named Meili.

But Freyja insisted that she meant Thor, and though we all knew it to be a lie, Bjorn played along, as did Thor. No need to say that Bjorn rarely managed to lay a finger on the strongest of the gods, and the said finger would usually snap in a matter of heartbeats.

"Eigil," Bjorn called, a hand open toward us. Eigil understood what Bjorn wanted and tossed his hammer to our friend.

"Ready to get your ass kicked again, Bjorn?" Thor asked as he closed his fists. That he used his name showed the hint of respect Thor held for Bjorn. I was the Drake, but more often than not, he would call me short-ass or something of the sort. Thor was the Æsir I disliked the most, though I liked him a great deal more than any Vanir.

"Not this time," Bjorn replied defiantly.

Still too far to strike, Bjorn swirled the hammer left and right. It gained speed and whooshed as it grazed the floor. Thor seemed bemused at this new strategy. He chose to ignore it and stepped closer, just close enough to throw the first punch, but Bjorn stepped back fast enough while keeping his hammer moving.

"Now you watch Bjorn, my boy; that's how you use a hammer," Einar told Eigil without taking his eyes away from the fight.

"Yes, Pa," Eigil replied without enthusiasm.

Not for the first time, I was amazed at the resemblance between the two fighters. Thor's hair and beard were bright red, while Bjorn's was dark brown, but so much of the rest was the same. Some claimed the gods had spread their seed on Midgard. That would explain Bjorn.

Thor leaped forward, higher than a man could, high enough to step on his opponent's face. But Bjorn stepped on the side at the last second and brought the hammer down at Thor's skull. The god rolled away in time, but many a man clenched his teeth at how close it had come.

As they faced each other again, Bjorn showed signs of fatigue. His breathing got heavier, and his shoulder shook from the strain of swinging the hammer. Thor noticed and paused. Unwilling to let his chance pass, my friend moved first and changed his grip on his weapon to give more length to his attack. Using the last of his strength, he whirled the hammer faster, and when he could not have given more momentum to it, he made a longer step and aimed at Thor's skull once more. Thor saw it coming and simply grabbed the hammer shaft as if a child wielded it.

He snatched it from Bjorn's grasp, and his next move was so fast that I missed it. In the blink of an eye, he grabbed Bjorn by the throat. My friend rose a few feet from the ground, fighting for air as the crowd quieted. This fight was as good as done.

To be fair to Bjorn, he still fought and even managed to bash his knee into Thor's stomach. That would have dazed any man, but Thor was something else and barely flinched. It pissed him off, though, and Thor shook Bjorn like a hound with a hare until we heard something snap. Bjorn became still.

Thor kept his victim in one hand and opened the other arm to a cheering, adoring crowd. With little care, he tossed our champion at the feet of the god's stage, out of the square, where his chest heaved again. Freyja gave Bjorn a disgusted look as he regained consciousness, then left the hall when he leaned on his elbow, her immaculate guards on her trail.

I saw a small chuckle on Odin's lips as he witnessed the scene, though it may have been my imagination. I was more concerned about Muninn, who I could no longer spot. She had already left, as would Odin soon. He used to spend the night with us unless some bed called him, usually not his. Since Baldur, though, Odin entertained us only as long as needed to reward the champion, then retreated to one of his halls.

"Going to check on the others," I said to recover from an involuntary sigh.

I would find the rest of my men farther down the hall,

some thirty tables on the left. The official Wolves' table stood just in front of the Æsir's dais, but some of us preferred the intimacy of the crowd, especially since several of the gods heard better than owls, and our conversations contained a lot of swearing in their names.

We might have been a pack when our duty took us to Midgard, but things were different here. Some of us liked to keep a respectful distance from the others after a mission. Karl was probably somewhere farther down the hall, enjoying the attention of the latest addition to our army and no doubt making them believe he had a say in who would join the Wolves in the future. He often claimed to be my right-hand man when none of us were around. I found it amusing and let him perpetrate his lie as long as it didn't disturb the peace of Valhöll.

At least the young man who had joined us today—whose name was Thrasir, as I would later learn—would not be listening to my old comrade's fables, for he was sitting at our second table. Ulf had his arm around the young man's shoulder while Snekke regaled them with some story that ended with a burst of laughter. It died naturally as I sat across from Thrasir.

"Who won?" Ulf asked.

"Thor," I replied as the boy filled my cup.

Ulf cursed in his beard and went for the inside of his tunic, from which he fished a piece of hacked silver. He did not even look at Snekke when he tossed the silver to its new owner. Snekke kissed it and winked at Ulf, who cursed in his cup.

"You bet on Bjorn?" For a man with such a profound love for silver, this was a stupid bet.

"I bet on you," he replied, surprising me even more.

"Why on Midgard would you do that? I haven't won the damn thing in ages."

"He always bets on you," the man beside me said. His name was Arn. A Wolf through and through. We had joined the crew at the same time, and for decades, the competition had been fierce and brotherly between us. He looked barely over twenty, but as with many of us, it was deceiving. He still joined us occasionally when one of us could not or would not, and I always felt better for his presence in our shield wall.

"Well, that explains why he always needs to loot the dead," I replied, which got a few chuckles, even from Ulf.

"Did you loot me?" Thrasir asked in his young, breaking voice, his tone more curious than angry. It silenced the table in a heartbeat, but Ulf replied before it got awkward.

"I didn't." He sounded honest, so I didn't believe it.

"Too bad," Thrasir said. He checked his own cup and found it empty. "I had a ring given to me by my lover before we left for the war. I died wearing it, but it's not on me anymore."

"You fought well, but your side lost," I said. "One of the victors might have taken it before you crossed."

I checked Ulf while Thrasir lost himself in his memory, probably thinking of the young woman who would never see him again. We exchanged a look only old friends could, and I knew the ring was somewhere nearby.

"Was she important to you?" Snekke asked.

"We were supposed to get married. I was going to ask her father after the fight. She'll marry someone else now." I heard the knot in his throat and pretended not to notice the tears pearling in the corners of his eyes.

"Thor's hairy balls," Ulf cursed as his hand went once more inside his tunic. One second later, he thumped the ring on the table. Thrasir jerked and stared at it as if it were made of pure gold. "Really not my evening."

Thrasir bore no resentment. He had every right to be angry, and things could have turned ugly, but the boy was apparently more gentle than most Norsemen. He was a good kid, and if a part of me felt guilty for parting this young man from his lover, I was also glad to find him among us. He reminded me a lot of Rune when I first saw him, straight as an arrow. Rune had turned more... enigmatic with time, though.

I enjoyed a few minutes with those men until a hand dropped on my shoulder, light as a feather, cold as silver. I shivered at the touch and spilled some of my mead. I've always been proud of my instinct, but this time, I was caught by surprise. I turned around, hand going to the handle of my long knife.

"Muninn," I called, making a fool of myself as I clumsily sprang while trying to wipe the mead foam from my beard. "Anything wrong?"

"Do I need to have an issue to see you?" she asked, a perfect, witty smile on her lips. My heart skipped a beat.

"Of course not," I replied a bit too fast. The others chuckled, and I closed my eyes in shame. I was the Drake of Odin's Wolves, leader of our most elite crew, but here I stood, stuttering like a beardless teenager.

"Sit with us," Arn offered, sliding from his spot to let her sit between him and me on the bench.

"I can't," she replied, "but thank you, Arn. Drake," she called softly. My title sounded both sharp and light on her tongue. I would have loved to hear my real name spoken by her and would need to ask one of my men if they remembered it. "Odin wants to see you."

4

Loki's cave, now.

I watched Loki leave with everything that was mine. My blade, my body, the woman I loved, who, in fact, wasn't mine at all, and my title. In exchange, he had given me his curse, a raging snake, a humid cave, unbreakable chains, and a wife, who joined me and the reptile after it managed to spill its venom over my face for the third time. It did not hurt less.

"Oh, you poor boy," Sigyn said, rushing to my aid when she saw the liquid fuming from my eyebrow.

I had trouble recognizing her, for she had changed more than I thought the gods could. Loki's wife had never been an amazing beauty, but she used to have a childlike, fresh energy and the traits to match this description.

Now, she was mostly bald besides some widely spread strands of hair, sick yellow eyes, and spotted skin blemished by fatigue. Her clothes had been white and silver but now went from piss color to brown. There was nothing of the

Æsir, only a wretch of the poorest sort. She carried a large, empty bowl of crystal. It, too, had seen better days.

"Sigyn, thank the Æsir," I said, surprising myself with my new voice.

"That's how you should greet me every time, husband," she replied. A wide grin covered her broken face as she raised the bowl between the snake and me.

"No, Sigyn, I am not Loki. I am Drake, The leader of the Einherjar. Do you remember me?"

The curve of the bowl exaggerated the snake's traits, making the fangs appear longer and thicker. It did not stop looking at me, and I shook nervously when a drop slid to the tip of its fang. The poison plopped at the bottom of the bowl, slowly spreading in a fuming green and yellow circle.

"Of course, I remember Drake," she said with her half-toothless smile. "He was a good man. The last Drake, at least; the others were just brutes who always mocked me."

Sigyn pouted after she spoke, and her arms lowered themselves as she relived the memory of her time on Asgard. She was right. All on Asgard used to tease and joke about Sigyn. None of her people had ever been mocked as much, and most of the time, she seemed not to notice.

Her marriage to Loki had been a punishment forced on the trickster, but Sigyn had lived it as the best day of her life. Yet for all his fooling around, even once married, Loki never spoke a harsh word against his wife, whether she stood nearby or not, which said a lot coming from him. Poor Sigyn, the world would be better if everyone was like her.

I had never made fun of her, though. Not because of my good heart but because I feared Loki and always assumed his promised revenge on all those who crossed him would be cunning and terrible. How ironic that for all my foresight, I was the one bound to his rock.

"Poor Drake," she said then, her hands falling until the bowl almost touched my face.

"Why poor Drake?"

Another drop of venom plopped at the bottom, and an angry hiss followed.

"You know I don't like your plan for him," she said, looking cross. "He's in love, like us, and you want to use that. You wouldn't like anyone using our love against us, would you?" Sigyn was crazy as a blind goat, but maybe I could use it.

"No, I wouldn't," I said, giving my best Loki impression, which wasn't hard since I was him.

"See? So why would you do that to him? Sometimes I wonder if there isn't a bit of evil in you," she said, teasing me with a genuine smile.

"The snake hit me earlier," I said. "I think it got me a bit tired and confused. Can you remind me what my plan for Drake was again?"

"Oh, the bad, bad snake got you," she said before tapping the snake on its head. The beast tried to snap its jaws on her fingers, but she moved so fast they closed on nothing.

"Well," she said, squaring her shoulders as a child about to recite a lesson. "You need someone with the blood of the heroes to get in and out of Asgard unnoticed, so one of those Wolves would do. And you said their leader is driven by passion, which is why you can trick him. His passion is love, so you plan to use the woman he loves to get him here."

"And why do I need an Einherjar?" I asked, playing dumb.

"They can open doors, of course, and the Æsir leave them be."

So, Loki was after our blood and our relative invisibility

among the gods. It made sense, especially since he knew the prophecy. Loki's fate was to guide the army from Hel to Asgard, and since he was banished and trapped in this cave, no one would assume he was up to no good.

"And how do I plan to trick him exactly?" I asked. It wasn't the most important question, or at least the most urgent, but I needed my answer. I needed to know how badly I had been played.

"With the help of Odin's pet," she said, spitting the last word.

"How?" I asked. The snake let another drop of venom end in the bowl, and Sigyn put it on my stomach to shake some blood back into her arms. To think that she had spent the last twenty-seven years doing just that, and all for the sake of her deceitful, piece of shit husband.

"You know I don't like talking about her," Sigyn said as she picked the bowl up again.

"Why not?"

"Muninn is a part of Odin. May he freeze in Hel." She did spit this time.

Odin, mad with grief, had chased Loki to this cave after the trickster had Baldur killed. There, he executed Loki and Sigyn's only son in front of the powerless couple. Some said he used the poor bastard's entrails to chain his father. At least I now knew that part was wrong.

The links tying me to the stone felt more like solid dwarfish iron to me. I barely remember the boy, whose name was Narfi or Narvi, I never got it right, but he had been on the gentle side. He'd shared his mother's intellect as well as his father's bad luck. One of the gods present at the time, a more compassionate one, had left Sigyn a bowl, and that was it.

"She's as ugly as she is beautiful," Sigyn went on. Now

that I had seen Muninn's true colors, I understood exactly what my idled captor meant. Just as Loki had used Sigyn since their marriage, Muninn had made a fool of me for gods knew how long. Now I understood why I'd never laughed at Sigyn; I was just no better.

"I know she does this for love," Sigyn said, "but there are limits to how far you can go. I mean, ending the world just to save one... I mean, I would do the same for you," she said the last part as if apologizing, and maybe my reaction had prompted it, for I can only imagine the emotions written on my face.

There was a time when I pitied Loki. He was a trickster but had been unfairly treated by his people. I once had a conversation with my second Drake about Loki. He had claimed that Loki was playing a dangerous game with the other gods. "*He's testing them,*" the Drake had said. "*He just wants to know how far they're willing to punish him so he can plan his next mischief.*"

For centuries the pattern remained the same. Loki would receive an exaggerated sentence and use it as an excuse to seek revenge. His schemes would increase in mischief, as would the next punishment. And so on, and so on. "*It will end badly,*" my mentor had said.

Baldur had paid the price with his life, Loki had been imprisoned in a small version of Hel, and the end of the world would be his last retaliation. I was certain that Loki's very first trick was something innocent, nothing more than a childlike prank.

"I know you would," I told Sigyn, who looked at me expectantly. She would do anything for her husband, just as I would have done anything for Muninn. And those two tricksters were now free, preparing for the end of the world together. To be honest, what tickled me in the wrong place wasn't the end of the world part, but the image of Muninn and Loki enjoying their victory at this very moment.

"Next time you talk to her in your dreams," Sigyn said, "make sure to tell her I do not like her."

So, this was how they had been communicating; through dreams. I had never known Loki to be a dream walker, but some gods could do such a thing. I wondered for how long the two of them had worked together, probably since Loki's imprisonment. I had never noticed any conniving between them, and it was likely that Muninn was just his way out, or at least I hoped.

Since I was in his body, I wondered if I could use his powers or even dreamwalk. I assumed violating men's dreams was easier than the gods, and maybe I could speak with my men. That, of course, could only happen if I slept. How Loki had managed to do so in this situation was impressive. The threat of the venom was enough to keep me from much needed rest.

"I just—" Sigyn said, then stopped for no reason and looked toward the ceiling as if searching her words or her memory. "I just don't remember how you plan to get Drake here."

That I knew.

It all started when Muninn came to request my presence in Odin's hall. The memory was fresh and still carried the scent of the Asgardian night.

"Drake needed to go back to Midgard," I told Sigyn. "To the place where his and the nine realms' fate would be sealed. Drake knew nothing of it, of course. He was weary that evening, but when Muninn offered to accompany him to the All-Father's Silver Hall, the blind food was only too happy to oblige."

Asgard, one week before Loki's escape

The night air cooled my senses like a bucket of cold water. It was a beautiful night, even by Asgard's standards, with more stars than I could ever count and green beams of light undulating over our heads. On Midgard, folks believed Thor furrowed those lights by riding his chariot. But since Thor roared like a newlywed drunk with Bjorn and a bunch of my brothers, I knew he wasn't responsible for the green lights.

Whatever they were, they illuminated the city and waved a cold light on Muninn's face. She walked fast, and her stride was determined. The pebbles crunched under her feet when we switched paths; we would meet the All-Father in his more private hall, Valaskjálf. An idea I appreciated, for it would take a good ten minutes to get there.

"Do you know what Odin wants?"

Odin's summons usually announced our next mission on Midgard, but we had barely gotten back. He would have to pull his nails before sending us, and they had just grown back. My men also needed rest, though this argument would carry little weight with the All-Father. Between the battle and the brawl, not counting crossing the Bifröst, none of us was in the best of shapes. But Muninn thought otherwise.

"I guess it's about our next journey to Midgard," she said as if it was the most obvious thing in the world. "But I have no idea. Odin seemed preoccupied today, I don't know if it's related."

"When is he not?" I asked without thinking, regretting the words as soon as they left my mouth. She stopped, and the defiance in her eyes was plain. I should have apologized for my words, but I did not. Our gods did not expect our complete submission. I'd even say they usually respected a fiery man more, as long as he wasn't insulting, of course.

"If Father is preoccupied, it means he has reasons to be."

I meant to resume walking first, but somehow, we moved at the same time. "I wouldn't dare think otherwise," I said, trying to smooth the conversation.

"You would be the same if you had to prepare for the end of the world." Her words were unfair. I worked hard to get the men ready for Ragnarök. As far as I knew, I was doing more than Odin himself.

"Odin has known about Ragnarök since he lost his eye; there is nothing new here," I said as we reached a corner near my house.

"The prophecy—"

"The prophecy said that we will win in the most important of ways. Life will go on." I said the last with great shame for using Heimdallr's argument. I did not believe it in the slightest, but like any man, I was ready to use anything in an argument with the woman I loved. A smart move; there was a glint in her eyes. She was impressed.

"Doesn't mean he's happy about losing so much in the process," she replied, her edge gone.

"Neither am I, believe me. There's no mention of any Einheri surviving Ragnarök. Or you, for that matter." I don't know what I expected, but it wasn't the scoff that followed.

"Of course, it tells my *wyrd*."

"It does?" I could recite the verses of the prophecy by heart, and none mentioned Muninn; of this, I was certain.

"I'm Odin's memory. If he dies, what do you think happens to me?"

My heart doubled in weight in my chest. I had not even

thought about it. Odin was prophesied to be among the first to fall, swallowed whole by Fenrir, son of Loki, who had been chained to a mountain when he became too big a wolf to handle. I gulped hard, but now I had one more reason to hate this prophecy. Screw Heimdallr, I told myself; if there was a chance to prevent Ragnarök and save Muninn, I would act on it.

"Don't make this face," she teased me. Her dimples dug deeper, and I remembered what it was like to be a teenage boy again. "We can't escape fate, but it's not like Ragnarök is happening now. We still have time." This *we* had the sweetest taste; it sounded exclusive. "Let's not make the grumpy old man wait," she said with a wink as we resumed walking. Over the last few minutes, I had exchanged more personal words with Muninn than in the previous century, and I felt light-headed.

Then the crisscrossing beams of Valaskjálf's roof slowly appeared atop the hill, soon followed by the glints of the moonlight on the silver-covered tiles. Odin's private hall was both smaller and more threatening than Valhöll. This was no place for feasts and loud manners, but for tranquility and rest.

Twenty Einherjar guarded the hall's perimeter, standing like statues with their massive spears and shields in hand. Guard duty was reserved for good fighters, but not the best. Men fighting around the thirtieth square, which is why we avoided those during the brawl. Guarding a hall at the center of a peaceful citadel had a way of making one wish for Ragnarök.

I don't know what seized me, but before I realized it, my hand went to Muninn's wrist, trying as hard as I could to stop her without using any strength. She did not even flinch, and we both halted. We were still far enough from the guards to speak, but I kept my voice low.

"Do you have any news about your brother?" I asked, taking a risk in mentioning Huginn. "You must miss him."

"Do you know him?" Her tone remained neutral, but I detected a slight tremor in her voice.

Do you know him? She didn't think him dead.

Her creator also often answered a question with another question. With him, it was a way to sound mysterious, but with her, I thought it was a defense mechanism.

"Not much," I answered. "We spoke a few times, usually when I inquired about his sweet sister." *Stupid...* She hid her giggle behind her sleeve, and my heart threatened to burst out of my chest. I was never great at complimenting women. "But if one of *my* brothers just vanished, I wouldn't be able to stop thinking about it. And I have many, and they are dumb as rocks, while you only have one."

"I never stop thinking about him," she confirmed. "Whenever we go down to Midgard, part of me is always searching for him. When I watch you being the Drake, I always expect him to find me. I sometimes feel his spirit flying over my head or his shadow between the trees, and for a moment, I lose my focus and find myself ready to jump into his arms."

A single tear fell from her eye, and I thought at this instant that I had never seen anything more beautiful. I usually hated people crying. The sobs, the quivering lips, the snot, I never knew what to make of it. But the way she did it, with dignity... I would have slayed an *ormr* in her name then. She was good.

"You believe he is on Midgard, then?" This wasn't my story; I should have avoided it. But it was Muninn.

"I know he is on Midgard."

"How do you know?"

"Odin sent him there. I don't know why, but I saw him leave, and he was disturbed." I meant to ask her what Odin had to say about it, but even I wasn't thick enough to meddle in their family's business. "He never came back."

"We'll find him then," I said, trying to sound confident. "I don't know how, but I'll help you. You can count on me." She cupped my elbow, and a chill went from my arm to my throat.

"Thank you," she said before gently pushing me toward the hall. I climbed the three steps leading to the main door, passing between two of my brothers. They probably saw what just happened but made no sign of it, and while I wanted to turn back and watch Muninn go, I managed not to. I pushed the doors open and stepped into Valaskjálf's antechamber.

Torches were lit every ten steps, bathing the room in a dreamlike aura. I had spent many hours waiting for Odin to receive me here despite the absence of any chair. The next door was closed, and two more guards stood before it. I heard a voice on the other side. A heated argument was taking place, though only one of the parties was shouting. I thought I recognized Frigg's voice, but the door muffled it too much for me to understand anything.

"Good evening, brothers. It seems All-Father is being scolded by All-mother," I said. They were not allowed to speak, so naturally, I always made a game of trying to vex or amuse them enough to get a reaction. I usually failed. I was just thinking of entertaining them with the tale of the last brawl, but the door opened from the other side before I opened my mouth.

I was right; Frigg was in the room, though I only

caught a glimpse of her as she stormed out from a back door. Since Baldur's death, my only interactions with Odin's wife happened in the form of those glimpses, which suited me fine. Frigg had never treated me unkindly, and I respected her for putting up with her husband's and son's attitude. But I never saw her smile, and do not think I would have enjoyed her company much.

Odin sat on his majestic high seat, head lost in the abyss of his palms in a pose known to every husband on Midgard and Asgard.

"Thank you for coming, Drake." He had yet to lift his head.

"At your service, Odin," I replied, stopping ten feet from him and bowing my head.

He sat straighter, gratifying me with the sight of his missing eye. He usually wore a patch of some sort, but not this time. For some reason, I had always assumed there was something behind the patch, a fake eye or a stone, perhaps. I tried my best not to show my discomfort, and he played along.

"Were you married?" He had asked this question at least three times over the years, though I could not expect the All-Father to remember all our conversations.

"I was," I replied. "It got me a small farm and two daughters." The same answer I had given him before.

"Lucky man," he said, which would have been his answer no matter mine.

"Did I interrupt?" I asked after a silence that felt too long for my taste.

"Interrupt? You saved me, Drake," he said after an old man's chuckle. "Frigg blames me for everything, I can't stand her nagging anymore. I'm telling you, if she talks to me like this one more time, she'll have to find a husband on Jötunheimr. We'll see how she likes that."

I smiled with Odin. We both knew he would do no such thing. He lost himself in his thoughts for a second, and I knew better than to pull him from them. I observed the floor instead. The light from the torches danced as it embraced the shapes of the silver slabs, twisting and twirling where the hammers had flattened the metal. When I looked up, Odin's eye was on me, serious and sharp. A shiver ran up my spine.

"She's not the only one to blame me for everything," he said accusingly. Not for the first time, not for the last, I felt as if Odin could see right through me. Did he get word of my conversation with Heimdallr? Surely, the guardian would not have betrayed me. Or so I hoped. I decided Odin was just testing me.

"Well, you did make a mess of Bifröst. This having to kill each other when it's time to return home... It's a bitch of a chore. I'm sorry, All-Father, but you botched that bridge." Odin had often heard me complain about the Bifröst; I risked little with this argument. He looked at me even harder, and I had to fight the urge to swallow nervously. His mask of anger peeled off, and he was suddenly a funny old man again.

"That I did, my boy, that I did," he said, untangling the mess of bowels in my belly. "I was quite drunk after a night with Ran's daughters when I conjured that shitty bridge, and I must admit it is not my finest work. But let me tell you—" He leaned forward and threw a glance over his shoulder. "The nine sisters are as wild as the stories say. Wilder even. Took me three days to feel my limbs again. The things they did to me, my boy, you would not—"

"Please, Odin, you are talking about my friend's mothers.

I don't want to know," I said, raising my hand as politely as I could. Ran's daughters were Heimdallr's mothers, the nine of them, apparently, and I knew how bawdy Odin's stories often turned.

His laughter echoed in the hall, and to be honest, I preferred Odin's salacious stories to his earlier stare. "You're not funny. But don't tell Heimdallr I said that."

"I won't, All-Father."

"Ah, how simpler things were back then," he said, his voice hoarse and tired. "Everything was to be built. Asgard was a hamlet more than a citadel, my wife was more beautiful than the stars, and the Einherjar were but a mere band of scoundrels, though that hasn't changed much, I suppose." I took no offense, for none was implied. "Now, all we can do is prepare for the end of everything. I really don't enjoy this part, my friend."

Odin rarely called me as such, and I felt a knot in my throat. I had learned not to trust Odin's acts over the centuries, but this time felt genuine.

"What can I do for you, All-Father?" I couldn't do much for him in the conversation he was pulling me into. The Drake I might have been, but I neither had the talent nor the responsibilities of soothing a depressed god.

"I need to send you and your men again," he said. The Wolves were always *my men* when they had to be sent; otherwise, they were his.

"Is it wise?" I asked. "I mean, my men did not get any rest, and your hands—"

"One night of sleep, and I will give you more nails," he said, curling his fingers inside his fists. They would still be raw from our last trip. He used to recover faster. "And by Muninn's account, your last mission did not take too much from the Wolves. I trust you will be all right. Am I wrong?"

How was I to answer anything other than yes, we would be ready?

"What's the urgency?" I asked. Sending us so soon meant some kind of necessity. A fearsome warrior to recruit, a battle to ensure, maybe even something to do with Huginn.

"A great battle! Of course! Two Norse tribes fighting for a mine of iron. Nothing better than men fighting for the tools to fight more men later. It will bring many new heroes to Valhöll; I can feel it in my old bones." He slapped the arm of his chair, and I marveled at the strength in his "old" bones.

"I'm guessing someone doesn't want to fight?"

"One of the two jarls is young and unbloodied; he will need a push." We would need Snekke this time. This was his kind of mission.

"Anything else I should know about the mission, Odin?"

"No, nothing else," he said, pursing his lips, a habit of his when he lied.

I tilted my head to show that I had noticed his tone. A flashback hit me of a young Einheri meeting the All-Father when he first became a Wolf. My knees shook then, as did my voice. Who would have thought that one day I would throw glances like that to the leader of the gods? And more surprisingly, who would have thought he would give in?

"All right, all right," he said, waving his hands in defeat. "It's just a premonition. Call it a feeling, if you will. I see more than a battle there, but I don't know what it is. I don't see a threat, just... something."

"Thank you, All-Father," I said with just enough sarcasm to avoid being insulting.

"You see why I didn't want to tell you."

Odin had become wise by gouging out his own eye and throwing it into Mimir's well, where the head of an all-knowing god rested. His missing eye could see things that were, are, and sometimes will be, but the latter were not the most accurate visions, as he had explained to me once. It was like waking up from a dream; sometimes all you got from it was a feeling. This was one of those cases.

"We will do our duty," I said more respectfully.

"I know you will," he replied, touching the side of his nose and winking his one eye. I was about to ask for more details, but the sounds of rapid and angry footsteps interrupted us. Frigg was coming back for the second round.

Odin spurted me away with a face warning me to save my skin while I could, which I did without thinking twice. I might have been one of the brave, but no one is that courageous. The door barely closed behind me and already the curses flew.

The two guards kept their composure at the sounds of the second act, and I tried to find something witty to say, but all I found was, "All-Father is going to sleep all-alone tonight." Not my best joke, I admit, but it got me a corner smile, and I felt victorious as I left the hall. I had hoped to see Muninn waiting for me somewhere but was disappointed.

The path to my house was short, but I took my time, enjoying the peacefulness of the moment. Being an Einheri was an honor, being a Wolf even more so, but none of the titles gave much chance for quietness, and I have always been a man who enjoyed it.

My house stood among a maze of narrow buildings built up along a second artery of the citadel. It was an unremarkable place, made of a single room, as we had on Midgard. The center of the room contained a hearth, which I only used for cooking, for it was rarely cold enough on Asgard to deserve a fire for the night. There was a squared table, three stools, and a chest under my bed stuffed with my few and most precious belongings. Not much, but a luxury for a human on Asgard.

My bed winced as I sat on it, but I welcomed the feeling of the mat under my ass and let out a long sigh of relief. I could hear the noise from Valhöll and cursed myself; I would have to get back there to inform my men we were going in the morning. They would not be happy, and neither was I, but we had no choice in the matter. I had been lucky to meet Odin during one of his good moments. Nothing guaranteed he would be the same on the morrow.

I drew the chest from under the bed and lifted the latch. The cover dropped with a cloud of dust as it leaned back to the end of its hinges. The man I had been, and the Einheri I had become had filled this chest with dozens of items.

The Thor amulet I used to wear as a young man was somewhere in there, probably at the bottom. It felt silly to wear an amulet dedicated to a being I saw every day, especially since this being was far less worship-worthy than the legends made him. Most of my brothers still adored him and wore their carved hammers, which, of course, pleased the god of thunder immensely.

A heap of silver rings also littered the chest. I added two to my arms, knowing I would have occasions to give them away soon. Everything had a price on Asgard, and men always wanted more silver. Some had the ambitious idea of buying a house too one day, but mostly, it served to acquire things like water, meat that wasn't boar, or the company of a Valkyrie. The practice wasn't common, but I knew firsthand that it happened.

What I was looking for waited right on top. A long knife made from a dark metal sheathed inside a leather scabbard of exceptional quality. The handle was carved with runes of protection, while a black, angular stone was encrusted in the pommel. It looked like onyx but was said to be unbreakable. Of all my gear, this was the only dwarfish item I owned, and I treated it with all the respect due to such a masterpiece.

Dwarves had long stopped forging for the gods or trading with them. One day, they decided they had enough of the Asgardians' haughtiness, and I could not fault them for it. And for all their competence, no god, neither Æsir nor Vanir, could forge like the Dwarves.

Most of our blacksmiths were actually folks from Midgard. I had never met a Dwarf, but I loved their craft, and I often thought to ask for a passage to Nidavelir, the Dwarves' realm, as my gift next time I won the brawl.

There was a time when the Wolves were equipped with Dwarven blades and mail shirts. Even I had been so richly gifted at first. But when a Wolf died in battle and could not be burned, his gear remained on Midgard, and we had lost too many fine blades. So we now brought the most common blades and armor with us. Not this time, though. Odin had a bad feeling, and though I had made fun of him, this was enough to tickle my superstitious side. The long knife, which I had named Wedge, for it could splinter a shield wall like nothing else, would accompany me.

I unsheathed it and reveled in its sharpness.

Just then, my door flung open, and as I drew the knife back, preparing for an attack, I heard two people laughing. One voice was male and the other female. They both stopped giggling when they saw me with my blade in hand.

"I thought you were with Odin," Cross-Eyes said, his voice a mix of surprise and shame. The woman was a Valkyrie, but I did not recognize her; probably one of those who served mead at the back of the hall. She was much prettier than Cross-Eyes deserved, but being a Wolf had advantages.

"I was," I replied, not hiding my irritation. "What, by Njord's smelly beard, are you doing here?" Oh, I knew his purpose, but Cross-Eyes could plow his woman somewhere else.

"Usually, you stay longer..." he said, removing his arm from the Valkyrie's waist.

"Sorry for disrupting your great plan," I said, not particularly liking his accusing tone. "Odin wants us to go tomorrow morning, so I returned here for some rest. You should do the same."

His eyes tightened at the mention of Odin's orders, but I wasn't going to feel sorry for him. "You're lucky," I told the Valkyrie, who was trying her best to be forgotten, "I just stopped you from a grave mistake. It would have been the most miserable twenty seconds of your life."

He flushed red as I said so, and the girl giggled uncontrollably.

"Now get the fuck out of here," I told them as I lay down in my bed. "And, Cross-Eyes?" I called just as he was about to close the door behind him.

"Yes?" he asked, his head popping in the door's opening.

"Go tell the others about tomorrow." His mouth opened like a dying fish, and I congratulated myself on ruining his night.

"Can it wait a minute?" he asked with a nod toward the girl.

"A minute?" she asked before he shushed her.

"Fine," I replied. He would use that minute, anyway. "Wait!" I said when all that remained of him were his knuckles on the door. "How often does that happen?"

There was a long pause during which nobody moved.

"I'll go tell the others now," he said and disappeared in a heartbeat.

I cursed, stood up, flipped the mat, and tried hard not to think about whose naked butt had soiled it since I last changed my furniture.

Needless to say, it was a short and uncomfortable night.

ᚤ

"The Wolves? A bunch of arrogant goat-fuckers, if you ask me. Especially their Drake. Forbidding good fighting shield-maidens from joining them only to add scrawny arses to the lot. If Odin was as wise as he claimed to be, he would put a woman in charge of the pack."

Gunhild, Second Square Fighter.

5

A knock on the door woke me sweating and feeling parched from dreams of fire and violence. I was also breathless, and it took a second series of knocks to bring me back completely.

"Come in or get the fuck out!"

A strong light filled the room as the door opened. It was late already. My eyes quickly became accustomed to it, but not fast enough to realize I had an esteemed guest, at least not before he spoke.

"Is this how Drake welcomes a friend?"

"Tyr!" I cheered.

I stood at once and snatched a cup of ale to flush the night's breath from my mouth. It felt good and helped me get to my senses as the god of war closed the door behind him. We clasped wrists as men who respect each other do, and for once, I had remembered to offer him my left arm.

"Glad to see you among us," I said, meaning my words. I had not seen him in at least half a year. If Heimdallr's role got him stuck on Asgard, Tyr's, on the other hand, did not grant him much time with us. He was our god of war and forever patrolled the realms to ensure none happened, which meant a great deal of diplomacy, stealth, and wits.

Tyr was also our god of justice, and his rare visits back to the citadel were punctuated by the settlements of disputes between Einherjar and occasionally between gods. Some of those disputes were so old by then that both parties had forgotten the origins of their issue, at least with the Einherjar, because the gods never forgot an insult of any sort.

In my mind, no god deserved to be worshipped more than Tyr. He was the embodiment of bravery and fairness, the two qualities that had cost him his right hand. He was as warm as a fireless Yule, but I had learned to appreciate his honesty and valued his friendship dearly.

"Glad to be home," he said in his typical ashy voice. The dark lines under his eyes had grown thicker. Tyr always looked at the brink of exhaustion.

He stood slightly shorter than me and leaner, though he could, of course, kick my ass in less time than it takes to say *Ginnungagap*, even with a single hand. His hair was dark with a bit of gray, as was his beard, which would only grow to a stubble. His eyes had the dark blue of a stormy sea, but the quietness of a lake, and his lips were thin and never opened enough to see his teeth.

Tyr was a handsome man, but in a way only other men could appreciate. And while he did his best to keep the peace between the realms, he didn't shy away from war either. Once unleashed on the battlefield, Tyr was a contender to Thor himself. Had he been more exuberant, like the god of thunder, men would have worn his arrow-shaped rune as amulet instead of Thor's hammer.

"I hope you will stay long enough to share a drink with us," I said while filling up a second cup for him.

"Maybe," he said, nodding in thanks before drinking.

"The realms are quiet, almost too quiet, really. But according to Odin, you might be gone for some time."

"You've seen Odin? How is he this morning?" He tilted his head again, this time with an expression telling me I didn't want to know. "That bad, huh?" I had been lucky the night before.

"He gave me the details of your mission," Tyr said, which explained this early visit.

"All right, tell me."

"One of them is that you're already late. So why don't you get ready, and I'll fill you in as we join your men by the cliff."

I cursed. Being late is one thing; being later than my men another entirely. This day had not started well, and I felt the whole mission would turn horribly. If I ever had an insightful hunch, it was this one, for this mission would be the trigger to Ragnarök itself.

ᛉ

I had learned all I needed to know by the time we passed the wall. The jarl of a village named Hvitiseid, on the Eastern tip of Lake Bandak, claimed an iron mine from another village named Lagardalr. This lake was shaped like a sleek longship, and Lagardalr stood halfway up its northern side, where the mast would be.

People from this village had used the mine for generations until a battle we might have been involved in occurred between Lagardalr and an invading force from the coast. The village had asked for the assistance of Hvitiseid's warriors, but the price had been steep. In exchange for their help, Hvitiseid would earn the rights to the mine at the time of the jarl of Lagardalr's death. At least, this is what the current leader of Hvitiseid claimed.

The term of this peculiar deal had just been met. The old jarl of Lagardalr, Olaf, had passed away a couple of months ago, many years after the agreement between the two villages. If this deal was genuine, the mine was now supposed to be transferred to Hvitiseid.

Of course, no one from Lagardalr seemed to remember this arrangement. And to make things worse, Jarl Olaf had been killed in his own hall, with no witness, leaving a fourteen-year-old boy in his stead. Folks from Lagardalr were accusing their neighbors of Olaf's murder. If they had indeed killed the old jarl, the agreement between the two villages would become obsolete.

No one had proof of anything, whether the agreement or the murder. One side wanted something, the other wanted to keep it, and both believed to be in the right. It was the perfect soil for war to sprout. According to Odin, the whole lake area could be swept into this war if we played our part well. There was only one minor issue; the new jarl of Lagardalr. He was young, unbloodied, and understandably wary of this war. Hvitiseid was using this to their advantage and sent him a new offer: to share the profits of the mine equally for the rest of the young jarl's life.

This was where we had to intervene.

"We need to convince him to fight," I said, resuming my conversation with Tyr as the silhouettes of my men drew themselves near the cliff's edge.

"While trying to engulf the other villages into this fight, if possible, in equal parts for both forces," Tyr finished. He hated war, and his tone left little doubt about his thoughts on our mission. Yet his role was to keep the peace between the nine realms; what happened within those realms was none of his concern.

I heard Tyr had argued with Odin when the All-Father announced the creation of the Wolves, and even now, their father-son relationship remained frosty at best. Yet there was an end of the world to prepare, so he remained obedient.

"Odin spoke of a *premonition*," I said, insisting on the last word. "Did he mention anything to you?"

Tyr reached for his chin, thought about it for a second, and, to my disappointment, shook his head. "Not really. But from what I hear, he has had an awful lot of them recently. Father needs rest. I wouldn't read too much into it," he said, which made me feel better.

We came close enough for me to see Bjorn and Ulf's back as they relieved themselves down the cliff. I hoped they were not aiming at Heimdallr, who was more than likely down there by the Bifröst. But just then, the gatekeeper of Asgard appeared from the Snake Path. He yelled at them, but by then, my two friends had emptied themselves and were packing everything back in.

The others had gathered more or less around them. Einar was checking the strap of his son's lamellar, tugging so hard that Eigil coughed. Cross-Eyes kept his back to me, and Snekke elbowed him in the ribs. The previous night's story had been told already. Karl stood slightly on the side, massaging the hangover from his forehead. Crossing the rainbow bridge would help with that. A little farther still, Titus was demonstrating the proper form for a thrust to Rune. The boy seemed bored and waved at me with joy.

"Finally!" Karl barked. "We were about to elect a new Drake."

"Drakes aren't elected," I reminded him. "Not that it would help you become one."

"That bad?" Ulf asked, a finger pointed at my dwarfish long knife.

"Odin has a feeling," I replied, which made Tyr's tongue click in his mouth. I wasn't supposed to speak sarcastically about the All-Father with my subordinates. "Odin sensed that it might be a long mission, with some unexpected duties required of us," I explained more respectfully, though the damage was done by now.

"Where do we go?" Bjorn asked.

"Lagardalr, near Bandak Lake," I replied. Heimdallr's massive head nodded at that, but the exchange of looks between Ulf and Bjorn called my attention.

"What is it?" I asked.

"It sounds familiar," Bjorn replied.

"It does," Ulf said. They both frowned and retreated into their memories. Not just them, several others seemed to search for a recollection of the name, except for Rune and Titus.

The first because he had not been one of us when we went to Lagardalr, and the second because Norse names were too complicated for him. Titus had long given up trying to remember them. At least he had an excuse. I, on the other hand, while boasting an excellent memory for faces, could not recall a name with an axe on my neck.

"We went there to stir some Viks to fight with the people of Lagardalr," Karl said, receiving more than one appreciative glance.

Karl had the memory of a whale, and despite being the oldest Wolf, never forgot a battle. He looked smug, with his thumbs tucked in his belt, staring at us with sorrow. "Snekke, Ulf, and Bjorn went to Lagardalr to suggest an alliance with their neighbors to increase their chances. While the rest of us took care of the Viks. Arn broke his leg in a bear trap, and we had to dispatch him. Remember how we had to force-feed him his nail through his whimpering?"

That triggered it. The memory of this mission resurfaced. It had ended in a great battle in which I had been slain quite early on, something I hoped none of them remembered. Ulf and Bjorn snapped their fingers at the same time and looked at each other with big grins spreading across their beards.

"Thurid!" they both called before slapping each other on the back and bending over with laughter.

"Thurid?" I asked. "Do I want to know?"

"The jarl's lady had it big for our champion," Ulf said. "So, when Snekke accompanied said jarl to negotiate an alliance with their neighbors, Thurid was less than shy with Bjorn."

"And being the great comrade that I am," Bjorn said, "I did not feel like enjoying such a bounty by myself." Both of them chuckled and adopted that stupid, satisfied look men muster at the sweet memory of a woman's embrace.

I was right; I didn't want to know.

"Oh, Thurid," Bjorn lavishly called, stretching the breeches by his inner leg for some room. "She was great. Now I'm all excited by this mission."

"That was a good fifty years ago," Karl said. "If she's still alive, she'll have fewer teeth than Einar here."

"Eh," Einar spat. "I have two more teeth than you, you old flea-ridden goat."

"I can change that," Karl replied.

"All right, all right," I said, putting myself between the two old warriors. "Snekke, do you remember anything about an iron mine in the negotiation between the jarls?" My question cut him halfway through a yawn.

"I barely remember that mission," he answered.

Tyr coughed in his hand. It was taking too long.

"Try to remember while we get to Lagardalr," I told Snekke, though I knew he wouldn't try much harder. "It seems we're going to stir more mess on top of the one we did last time. Check your gear one last time; we are gone for some time."

Heimdallr pushed through the group to join his half brother and me, removing the horn from his belt.

"It seems you were right," he said, frowning.

"About what?"

"You're going to fight again where you've fought before."

"Is that a problem?" Tyr asked, probably sensing the tension rising in me.

"Not really," I answered. "It's not the repetition which bothers me, I just have—"

"A bad feeling," Tyr teased me, using the same mocking tone I had used for Odin's premonition.

"Yes," I agreed. "I can't explain it yet, but something has been bothering me."

"You sound a lot like Father," Tyr said.

"Arf," Heimdallr scoffed. "Just need our little raven to scratch that itch, and you'll be as happy as a flea on a dog's back."

I flushed like a beardless boy, which was the stupidest of reactions and the best way to admit he was right, though how he knew of my feelings was a mystery. Of course, Heimdallr had not spoken of love, just of lust, and if I had simply agreed with him, things would have stopped there. Tyr did not miss my blushing.

"Is that true, Drake?" he asked, sounding more concerned than curious.

"Our Drake just wants to poke the little bird; nothing wrong with that. I have also entertained the thought," Heimdallr replied.

Tyr was not convinced.

"Be careful who you choose to associate yourself with. Some of us are more dangerous than you think, and all of us are more selfish than you know," he said.

"Don't listen to Mister Sour over here," Heimdallr said. I could not take my eyes away from Tyr's, knowing a warning or a threat, when I heard one. "I'll slip a word to Muninn next time I see her."

"No need," I replied.

"Suit yourself. Where to?" Heimdallr asked, changing the subject.

"See if there's a river pouring into the lake somewhere between the two villages. Drop us in that river, about an hour from the lake."

"By my hairy ass, that's specific," Heimdallr said as he closed his eyes. The heat from his *seidr* compressed my heart, and Bjorn twisted his head in pain. "Got it," Heimdallr said a few seconds later.

Immediately, his finger traced golden runes on the side of the horn, the famous *Gjallarhorn,* prophesied to be used by Heimdallr to announce the beginning of Ragnarök. The guardian god blew in it, producing a low and disturbing note. The ground shook, and if I had been watching the pond of Bifröst at the bottom of the cliff, I would have seen it shining with all the colors of the rainbow. A path had been opened for us.

I clapped Tyr on the shoulder as he moved between my

men to distribute Odin's nails. They still dripped with blood. No wonder the All-Father's mood had soured overnight.

"A horn of mead is waiting for you upon your return," Heimdallr said as we approached the cliff's edge.

"One piece of hack silver one of us doesn't make it," Titus said greedily, and though he was talking about the jump into Bifröst, I took it as a bad omen for the mission itself.

"I'll take that bet," Bjorn said just before he jumped, tucking his massive axe against his chest.

It took a long time for someone to fall all the way down to the pond, and though it's quite a wide one, it looked rather small from up there. Bjorn made it, nonetheless. His massive body disappeared under the water as if the pond had swallowed him. The rest of my men followed, none of them missing the jump, which seldom happened anyway. As usual, I was the last one.

"Wait," Tyr said. He grabbed my wrist and dropped my right hand, palm up, on what was left of his right forearm. I once again felt the sensation of the *seidr*, followed by a great but not painful heat on my arm as he drew his rune. It glowed black for an instant and vanished under my skin. I didn't know what to make of his blessing, but it couldn't hurt, and I thanked him.

"Good luck, my friend," he said before attempting and failing a reassuring smile.

I nodded to both of them and jumped to join my men.

6

Heimdallr had chosen a perfect place. The forest was thick, rich in shrubs and enough short pines to cover the sight of ten men struggling out of the water. A low bank of sandy earth gently rose from the river, allowing us an easy way out. As I had been delayed, my men were all out by the time I came out of the water and were already gathering wood for a fire.

"No one," Ulf said, appearing through two thorny bushes and pushing an arrow back in his quiver. Snekke conveyed the same message from his observation of the other side of the river, his hay-colored hair pitifully stuck to the side of his head, reminding me of a wet deerhound.

I preferred us to land in rivers rather than lakes. Fewer potential witnesses, enough water that we didn't hurt ourselves, but not too much that we could drown, especially with our mail shirts and leather lamellar. It didn't make us look less ridiculous, but it was safer.

"What now?" Karl asked as he removed his socks to expose his bare feet to the young fire.

"We split," I said, which silenced them completely. I

could even hear Rune's teeth chattering from the cold. I understood their surprise. Splitting the group was usually my last option, and they knew how much I resented the idea under normal circumstances.

"Two groups of five. I take Snekke, Rune, Titus, and Eigil with me to Lagardalr; Ulf leads the others to Hvitiseid." Of course, they complained; they wouldn't be the Wolves otherwise.

Einar wasn't happy to be parted from his son, but I thought it would be good for Eigil. Karl would not like to be under Ulf's command, but I had enough to worry about without dragging the old man with me. It was cruel to Ulf, but he would have to deal with it. Bjorn wasn't happy about missing Lagardalr, and I wondered what he would have done if his old trophy still lived.

"Shut up!" If I let them, it would have gone on for a very long time. "Ulf's group will have to keep the fire of war going in Hvitiseid while suggesting rallying other villages to their cause and hiring mercenaries. We will do the same on our side. In three days, at noon, one of you will come back here to let me know how things are going, and we will plan the battle for two days later." I made Ulf repeat my words to make sure he would follow them.

"Odin said this battle could involve a couple hundred warriors, so I don't need to tell you how important it is to him." They cared little about Odin's pleasure, so I switched strategy. "Which means we may have a pass to visit Sessrúmnir if we succeed." Now, that got a more positive reaction.

Sessrúmnir was Freyja's hall, where the most beautiful Valkyries lived, the sweetest prospect for an Einheri. Odin had mentioned nothing of the sort, but it couldn't hurt to give my men some motivation.

"So, try to stay as sober as possible while we are here. That means you, Bjorn," I said, knowing my friend would play along. He raised his hands as if to say the thought of getting drunk had not even crossed his mind. "And if any of you doesn't listen to Ulf, he will spend the next year in Valhöll."

"That means you, Karl," Rune said with a wink at the old man.

"Mind your beard, boy," Karl replied.

We waited another ten minutes or so to make ourselves ready to travel. Bjorn tied his hair back into a bun, Karl slipped his socks back on, and we were about ready. And that's when Rune asked a question that had been on my mind for some time. Somehow, it felt worse coming from him.

"Did you guys used to come down so often?"

"What do you mean?" Cross-Eyes asked as he rearranged the rings of his shirt.

"I mean before I joined. It's just that I feel like you were more often in Valhöll back then. For example, I knew some of you well, even before I became a Wolf, but I don't think I could name more than three or four recruits from the past year."

He was right, and the others agreed. Besides young Thrasir, I had not taken much time to get acquainted with my new brothers, something I used to do thoroughly in the past. *When had I stopped?*

"And even since I joined, I feel like I spend less and less time on Asgard. Not that I'm complaining about it," he said the last to me. "But in the last few months, we've been more often on Midgard than on Asgard."

Now, that was an exaggeration, but not by much.

"Well, it is summer. 'Tis the season for war," Einar said as he kicked some earth on the fire.

"Is it?" I asked. "I mean, is it summer?"

"Of course it is," Einar replied.

I knew I could trust him, yet fresh snow covered the base of the surrounding trees. I was not bothered by any insects, as would be the case in summer, and I thought the sun was going down very early for a summer day. But Einar must be right; it was still summer.

One of the first things Einherjar lost was the sense of time. There were no seasons on Asgard. The sun remained the same every day, it rained regularly no matter the time of the year, and the temperature was always milder than on Midgard, at least where the Norsemen lived.

On Asgard, we followed the seasons according to the new brothers joining us. Summer battles involved people from different parts and raids at every corner of the Norsemen's world. Winter meant fewer, smaller battles between neighbors. Since the Wolves came from different regions of Midgard, we all had different views on what winter was.

This current summer weather was worrisome for one reason; the prophecy claimed Ragnarök would follow a harsh winter, the likes of which men had never experienced. Fimbulvetr, the great winter. Until now, I thought it would be great because of its violence, but what if its uniqueness came from its resilience? What if we were already in it? I wondered if the others thought the same, and as if he could read my mind, Karl spoke next.

"Maybe Fimbulvetr is coming, and we're truly fucked," he said in an attempt at what he considered humor.

I would need a word with Odin, I thought, but it would have to wait. Fimbulvetr, Ragnarök, and all those mystical shits would have to wait. First, we had a war to ensure.

"See you in three days," I said to get us moving. "And if anything feels remotely dangerous, eat those nails. I don't care if it's a false alarm, and you need to dig through your own shit for the damn things later. Understood?" They nodded, Ulf more strongly than the others. This was why I had put him in charge; he would sense the danger before any of them.

There were no last words or heartfelt goodbyes; warriors don't need them. We parted without a second glance, them going against the sun and us with its weak light on our backs. My men were the best of Asgard; they could handle themselves for a mere three days. Or so I hoped.

ᛣ

We followed the river for half an hour before crossing it on a tree trunk turned into an improvised bridge. My four comrades remained quiet, which might have been a response to my worsening mood. Rune opened the march, his head twisting left and right with great focus at any sound from the woods.

He had darkened my thoughts with his question on our comings to Midgard. Though I could not fault him for that, it wasn't the first time he'd brought up a heavy subject with a seemingly light question or comment. The young warrior could sharpen his focus to a deadly edge during a fight, but in most situations, he tended to speak before thinking. Unless it was an act and he was, in fact, aware of his influence. For the first time since he had joined the Wolves, but not the last, I wondered how much I truly knew about Rune. Even his name meant *secret,* after all.

The lake appeared shortly after the tree-bridge. A lake like hundreds of others on our lands, filled with pristine water stuck between high, lush hills covered with pine trees, ash trees, and oaks. From north to south, the lake was narrow enough that I could see the other side in detail, and a *faering* would only need six or seven minutes to cross it. But from west to east, it would take a long day of walk. Lagardalr stood halfway through the northern shore, just at the bottom of a hill shaped like the back of a walking bear.

"It is a beautiful place," Snekke commented. His spear swayed on his shoulder as a farmer with his tine after a long, arduous day in the fields. I agreed with him. There was a farm across the lake, but it looked empty. Those folks must have sensed the first tremors of war and fled to the main village.

"It looks a lot like where I grew up," Eigil said.

"Didn't you live by the sea?" Rune asked.

"We did," he answered, "but our house was just after the mouth of the river, behind a cliff. We could hear the waves but not see them."

Eigil stood straighter than usual, and I congratulated myself for taking him from Einar for a few days. After decades with his father by his side, it was maybe time for him to be his own man. That he had spoken at all was proof of it already.

Maybe, I told myself reluctantly, it was time to leave Einar in Valhöll and increase our fighting capacity with a better warrior. I would be glad to welcome Arn back with us. This was the thought entertaining my mind when Snekke lowered his spear to point it at a group of men coming our way.

"That was fast," he said before I told him to stop pointing that thing. He was right, though; they had spotted us fast. They were also prepared. Ten men, all armored, with even one of them wearing a mail shirt and a shining helmet. Black and yellow shields hung on their left arm, and most carried spears, though a few came with an axe. The tension must have been high in the village for ten men to be battle-ready, and I told my men to halt and drop their weapons.

"Who are you?" the man clad in mail barked at us when they stood but a dozen steps from us. He was a gray-haired, white-scarred warrior. Had he been a little older, one of us might have given him those scars.

"Mercenaries," I said, "from Jutland."

"Danes, huh," he replied, spitting the name. "I sure as Hel never saw a Dane like that one," he said, pointing his mean-looking axe at Titus.

"Aye, well, we've fought in many places and gathered all kinds of scum," I replied, which got a raised eyebrow from Titus.

"Even some Jötunn, it seems," the old warrior said, nodding toward Eigil, who didn't look that much like a Jötunn. Of course, this man could not know what a Jötunn actually looked like.

"We heard you might use a Jötunn," I said.

"You've heard that, did you?"

"Aye, we did. Rumor has it a great battle is about to be fought for some mine and that the offenders are getting ready to crush the mine owners. Just on the way here, we've seen a couple of groups like us heading for your enemy." This was all a pile of horseshit, but it would give the man enough thoughts to munch on while he considered our presence.

"And why would you come here if so many men are going there?" he asked.

"More silver to be gained from a losing side," I answered. A couple of them spat in my direction, yet they did not even fight the obvious. I gave them a few seconds to find something to say and decided to try another approach.

"Look," I said, "whether we fight for you or against you is the same to us. We'll leave richer men or on our way to Valhöll." Eigil chuckled at my words, and I guess his show of confidence helped a bit, as the old warrior tucked his axe in his belt then. His men picked up the signal, and they relaxed all at once. We grabbed our weapons and walked toward our new hosts.

"What's your name?" the old man asked, grimly smiling as we clasped arms. About half his teeth were missing, and one of his eyes had turned white and useless, but there was no mistake; he was or had been a great warrior. His grip confirmed it.

"Thorstein," I replied. Men trusted someone whose name contained a *Thor* in it more easily. I did not like this borrowed name, but my men were used to it and were thus less likely to make a blunder.

"Halfdan Halfdansson," he replied before offering a courtesy nod to my men. "You'll want to talk to our leader," he said, hesitating for a heartbeat before the last word.

I had guessed the boy-jarl would not be highly respected by his men, but coming from the man in charge of his warriors, this was less than encouraging. Men only fight if they trust or fear their leader.

"The rumors you heard are true," Halfdan said as we headed to his village. My men fell behind and mingled with the warriors. "Unless something is done, blood will spill soon."

"I heard a treaty was being considered to maintain peace."

Halfdan scoffed. "You have good ears," he said. "Our jarl is young. Never fought a day in his life. Mind you, he's smart enough, but I don't know if he'll live to be the man his grandfather was."

"His grandfather?" I asked.

"Olaf, the man I served most of my life. A great warrior, though he was already old when those scum killed him in his hall." Odin had been mistaken in his assessment. The jarl wasn't the son but the grandson of the previous leader.

"Wasn't this Olaf married to a Thurid? I heard she was beautiful," Snekke asked. He shrugged when I shot him my most murderous gaze.

"You even heard about that, did you?" Halfdan asked with a genuine smile. "Aye, Thurid was a beauty when I was but a beardless boy. I polished my sword for the first time thinking about her, if you know what I mean." He said the last, poking my ribs with his elbow. "Her hips were too narrow, though. She died after giving birth to the jarl's only son. Poor Olaf never remarried after that. Didn't stop the old goat from having fun here and there, of course. Half the slaves oddly look the same around here."

Halfdan was warming up to me, and his previous reserve had all but vanished by the time we passed the palisade. I wanted to ask more questions before we faced the young jarl, but curiosity might have raised the old warrior's suspicion, so I listened and still learned quite a lot.

The boy-jarl's name was Hakon. He had a sister whose name I had not yet learned and very little respect from the old warriors who only obeyed him for the memory of the old jarl and the silver the young man possessed.

Lagardalr was a beautiful village, albeit a bit cramped. There were about twelve buildings set in no particular order, but all more or less facing the hall. It was a relatively tall building for such a small settlement, proof that its owner was rich. Of course, the jarl would be in charge of many more families living on the farms spread throughout the neighborhood. This was the center of a fairly vast jarldom.

Folks looked at us with apprehension, especially the thralls, who, indeed, shared a familiar look. I saw no other warriors than the ones accompanying us, though they might have been scouting the territory or simply tending to their farms.

"Not sure about the 'hundreds of warriors,' " Rune whispered as we waited in front of the hall for Jarl Hakon to allow us in. My young Wolf nearly startled me, creeping up on me with such discretion, but he was right; it did not present itself as bountiful as expected.

The door opened, and Halfdan appeared just as I was about to agree with Rune. It had been a short wait; they were desperate.

"Jarl Hakon welcomes you," he said dutifully. "You will break bread with him, share ale and words as esteemed guests. You must leave your weapons outside the hall, though." This was customary and could not be helped.

We dropped our shields and handed our blades to the men who had accompanied us. My sword was an unrefined blade, and I had no issues handing it to the young man facing me. But when he tried to reach for Wedge tucked in my lower back, I grabbed his wrist, and tension rose in a heartbeat. Things could have gotten ugly, but Halfdan cuffed the young man and told him to piss off.

"You may keep it," he said, "but if I see your hand moving to it, I will open your belly from navel to throat. Understood?" I nodded and told myself I liked him more and more.

We stepped into the hall, feeling the air change in the few steps between the light of the sun and the warmth of the hearth. The place was quiet, with just three people by the high seat and maybe four slaves doing their best not to be noticed. Huge tapestries and thick furs hung from the beams, and beautifully carved columns lined the room as yet more proof that Lagardalr had profited from those mines for many years.

I caught Snekke's eyes scanning the place. I thought he was searching for something valuable, but then I realized he had been here before and probably remembered it.

"Here are the Dane mercenaries," Halfdan said as we stopped at the bottom of the jarl's stage. Old furs lined the floor where the jarl sat, and more kept him from the ruggedness of his seat.

I first noticed the woman on his right. She stood tall and beautiful, at the prime of her life, with the stern face of a queen. She had to be the jarl's mother and, as such, the real power in Lagardalr. From what I understood, she was in favor of peace.

Snekke and Titus gasped as one, and I wondered if they also found the woman to their taste. But my eyes finally dropped to the jarl, and I understood their reaction. I, too, gasped at the sight of him. He was a puny young man who, despite being fourteen, could not reach the ground while sitting. Some padding had been added to his garment to give him a better build, but it made him awkward and asymmetrical.

He wore a rich tunic of blue silk, silver beads in his hair, rings on his arms, and a golden hammer amulet hung from his neck. Without a transformative growth spurt, this Hakon would never become an impressive warrior. Every effort to make him look more than he was fell short and instead increased the oddity of his person. But none of this was what surprised us.

Sitting in front of us, shifting uncomfortably under our gaze, was the spitting image of our comrade Ulf. A younger, softer version of our archer. He had the same clever yet discreet eyes, the same mud-color hair, and shoulders that naturally slumped. And if this wasn't enough, he also wore his shoulder-length hair unbound, as Ulf did.

I thought my mind played tricks on me. Maybe I was exaggerating the resemblance, but the girl by his side shared similar traits. She was around ten or eleven years old, twelve at best if, like her brother, she looked younger than her age. Even if Halfdan had not introduced her, I would have guessed who she was. There was a fire in her eyes that was absent from her brother's, and I told myself she would grow to be a difficult woman for her future husband.

"Freyja's tits," Eigil muttered, realizing a bit late what we stared at.

Ulf's grandchildren.

Bjorn and Ulf had enjoyed Thurid's company, and the latter had left his mark in Lagardalr. I had always assumed Einherjar could not procreate. It would piss off Bjorn and destroy Ulf.

"Is there a problem?" the jarl's mother asked.

"Sorry," I said, waking up from whatever spell Hakon had used on us unknowingly. "We did not expect the young man we had heard about to look so fearsome." It was all I could think of, but besides Hakon, no one seemed to believe my words, not even the little girl who rolled her eyes.

"What brings you to Lagardalr?" Hakon asked after his mother dropped her hand on his shoulder.

"War," I replied, "and a chance to offer you our services. We are mercenaries and have fought dozens of battles all over Midgard. I guarantee you'll find no better men than us to crush your enemies." I was boasting, as all good mercenaries do, though I was also being honest.

"We have no enemies," his mother replied in a voice like a whip. Halfdan, standing on my left, scoffed into his beard.

"The men of Hvitiseid beg to differ," I said. It stung her for a second and I thought to use the moment to our advantage. "You do not have enough men," I went on. "Just on the way to your hall, we've seen many men of war, like us, heading to Hvitiseid. Their numbers are swelling; how about yours?"

"I thought you said there were no men better than you," she replied with a smirk.

"Not in quality, no. But quantity can overcome quality."

"We have more men than you know," Hakon said. "One call from their jarl, and they'll come like the wind." This was presumptuous, but I appreciated this rebellious energy. Maybe there was a warrior in this frail boy's shell after all.

"You will need more," I replied. "We can help you gather men before the battle, as well as kill your enemies during."

"And what would be the price for this... abundance of skills?" Bjorn would have loved this woman. She had Freyja's venom. I wouldn't have been surprised if her dead husband had decided to jump from a cliff after one too many arguments with her. I would later learn that he fell from his horse some years ago. I was about to give my usual price in this kind of situation, the weight of my sword in silver, but Snekke beat me to it.

"Food, ale, a roof, and the right to loot the enemy we have killed, my lady," he said, taking a light step ahead.

"You do not ask for silver?" she asked.

"I cannot speak for my comrades," he said, bowing his head, "but looking at you is reward enough, and breathing the same air puts me in your debt."

This was strong, especially for such a harsh creature. But her cheeks reddened, and she looked away rather than show her appreciative smile. I made a mental note to ask Snekke for some advice later, and he had deserved an arm ring for his quick thinking. Except that he had put no thought into it at all; he had just acted.

Snekke had a thing for widows. Joining the Wolves was mostly a chance for him to meet some of them. The silence was turning embarrassing, and Hakon rolled his eyes at his mother's reaction. I swear I had seen this face on Ulf hundreds of times before.

"As my comrade said," I told the jarl, "we only ask to be fed and lodged until the fight happens. We'll take what our blades have claimed, nothing more, and then leave. Your fame will be made for the generations to come and ours too. For mercenaries, fame is worth more than silver."

He liked the sound of that but was clearly uncomfortable. Even among the Einherjar, few could return my gaze, and he did a good job at it for three seconds.

"I already granted you those rights for the night. And the battle—if there is one," he said the last with a look back at his mother, "will be soon." Still half-glancing at Snekke, who had not taken his eyes from hers, she gave a discreet nod to her son. "You are welcome for the time being. At least until war or peace have been decided."

ᛉ

"So, what do you think?" Titus asked as we relieved ourselves in the lake. The sun was melting into the water, turning the surface orange and pink.

"Not much to think," I replied, "a lot to do though." He sneered at that, for it was the mother of all understatements.

We had learned much during a frugal dinner with the jarl's family, and most of it gave us no hope. Hild, the jarl's mother, held a tight rein on her son. Given another few months, he would outgrow her and follow his own path. Of course, if nothing was done, he would most likely be dead before it could happen.

Halfdan, who also sat at the table, claimed that fifty warriors could be called upon from the jarldom. This was the first and best news so far. Those men would not all rally right away, and most would prefer to stick to their hearths rather than fight for a boy tucked under his mother's skirt.

It might have been my imagination, for he said no such thing, but I felt that Hakon was actually eager for the battle. Whenever his mother spoke of peace and marriage, the boy would react one way or another. A tilt of the head, a click of the tongue, or just a sigh. Boys, even the puniest ones, grew up on tales of glory, bravery, and blood. This one, probably even more so, from the lips of the man he needed to avenge.

"The boy needs to man up. We should make him want revenge for his grandfather," Titus said, following similar thoughts to mine.

"Well, not his real grandfather," I replied mockingly as I tucked my package back in.

"At least that answers the question about the possibility of us having children." This question had been thrown around thousands of times at the tables of Valhöll. I looked forward to giving an answer to the men. No doubt, the number of brothers asking to join the crew would increase dramatically. Since only the Wolves came down to Midgard and rarely went to the same place twice, we had never been able to check the results of our *side missions*. I quickly put aside the logical question about the sons and daughters I might have sired over the centuries, for I could see the burden such knowledge would bring.

"Should we tell Ulf?" Titus asked as Eigil and Rune prepared a corner of the barn for us.

"I don't see how we could not. But I don't know how he'll react." It was a lie. I knew how my friend would take it. He was tired of the whole Wolf deal, that much was certain, but he still preferred it to the confinement of Asgard. Those were his two options. Those and Hel, of course.

But now a new possibility offered itself to him; staying with his grandchildren on Midgard. We had no idea how long an Einheri could survive on Midgard, but I was certain Ulf would take his chance. And from my point of view, it was his right. Odin would be furious if I left a man down here, but for Ulf, his rage would quickly fade.

"What do you think we should do next?" I asked Titus, who immediately struck his thoughtful pose, an arm on top of the other and his chin stuck between thumb and first finger.

There were few men I asked for advice. I have always trusted my instinct and sense of logic, but I had been a Drake long enough and knew the importance of a second opinion. And among all my men, there was none I appreciated more than Titus's. He was not only a man of logic and a sound military mind, both of which had turned him into an unbeatable *tafl* player from the day he had learned our game, but more importantly, he was a foreigner and approached things from angles I had not considered. Though, from what he said next, we were on the same page this time.

"Fifty warriors won't cut it. It will be a massacre and not even a worthy one for us. We need many more men. I guess we need to split our efforts."

"I don't like it either, but I agree," I said. We waited for two warriors to walk past us before resuming our conversation, which gave me time to think about our different tasks and how to share them. Thankfully, most of them were easy to distribute.

"You will convince Halfdan to call those fifty warriors he mentioned," I told Titus. He had a natural authority with other soldiers and had formed the beginning of a bond with the old man. It frequently happened that veterans of many wars befriended Titus. "It needs to happen even before Hakon asks for it."

"I guess you will work on the boy in the meantime," Titus said.

"Me and Eigil," I said.

I had first caught the boy's interest, if only by my role as a leader of our little band. But it was Eigil who sparked the warrior sleeping in Hakon's heart when he told the boy-jarl he'd been the same age for his first battle. He handed the arm ring he won during that raid to the boy, and Hakon observed it as if Dwarves had forged it.

This new Eigil was proving an asset, and together we were to accompany the boy on a hunt. Hakon had candidly mentioned it while his mother crooned under Snekke's gaze, and I was glad to accept.

"Snekke will probably be tasked with keeping Hild busy," Titus said with a saucy smile.

"He won't be hard to convince. As long as he keeps her away from her son, I don't mind him plowing her until—"

"I think your man is already hard at work," a little voice said behind us.

Her name was Lif, and she was by all accounts the best thing to come from Ulf. Rune had tried some of his charms on her all evening, probably thinking that even a twelve-year-old could be an ally in our situation. But she had ignored him and kept her dignity throughout the meal. She was a child destined to become an exceptional woman, the kind who marries a jarl and leads in his place. Even now, standing like a mountain in front of us two warriors of Odin, she looked as if she expected us to bow.

"What do you mean?" I asked, leaning on my knees to reach her level.

"Your man, Snekke, he's having sex with my mother right now," she said with no shame and just a hint of anger.

"*Deum meum*," Titus murmured.

"My apology for my man's behavior, young lady," I said, fighting a tear of laughter.

"It is fine," she replied in her adult fashion. "I also want Hakon to spend some time away from her."

"Oh, why is that?" I asked, truly intrigued.

"He needs to fight those swine of Hvitiseid," she said, giving an edge to the insult I had never heard before. Titus let an impressed whistle pass his lips.

"You want your brother to go to war?"

"I want Bove and all his men to die," she replied through her teeth. Bove was the leader of Hvitiseid, and as far as his reputation went, he was a snake and a bully. Lif had loved her grandfather and wanted revenge in his name. But there was more.

"Your mother spoke of marriage," Titus said. Judging by her reaction, my friend had guessed the heart of the problem.

Hild had mentioned marriage to seal the peace between the two villages, and I thought she was speaking of herself. She was still young enough to remarry and have more children, but it seemed she meant to marry her daughter to a son or grandson of this Bove. It wasn't a bad plan. Being twelve, Lif was three or four years from marriageable age. During this time, there would be no trouble between neighbors, and young Hakon would have time to grow. Lif, however, did not seem to like that plan.

"I will never marry anything that came from that filthy pig."

"Peace is not in our interest either," I told her.

"Good," she said as if we had struck a deal, which, in a sense, we had. "We understand each other. I will see you tomorrow then."

I sighed with delight as she turned and headed back to the hall. My daughters had been much younger than Lif when I had been slain, but I hoped they had turned as fierce and genial.

"Ulf will love her," Titus said, arms crossed over his bulky chest.

"Yes, he will."

7

When the gods created human beings, they must have given us their thirst for blood. How else to explain the thrill of a fight, the pleasant savagery that accompanies the fear of battle, or in that day's case, the lust for the kill? We had risen at dawn, shaken from our sleep by a timid thrall. The jarl expected us to break fast with him before heading into the woods.

Eigil and I found him clad in a thick fur cloak, chewing on a piece of bread buttered with honey. He had the expectant look of a child on Yule's Eve, and I wondered if taking the boy into the woods was such a sound idea. Should something happen to him, this mission would be over before it even began.

Halfdan, who also ate with us, put me at ease when he claimed Hakon knew the woods better than anyone and was a decent hunter. Knowing how little the old man respected his leader, this was mighty praise, and I became curious to see it for myself.

Though Halfdan was technically on our side, I did not want to collide with another authority figure, so I hinted that he should have words with Titus. He understood I had something in store for him and accepted to miss the hunt, though not before calling two of his men to join us, something Hakon agreed to with a grunt. There was no lost love between the boy and the old man, and it had not taken much to separate them.

I told Snekke when he finally joined us in the middle of the night that he should do his best to keep Hild busy all day long. And that, too, had taken little persuasion.

"I'll need a bath first," he had said as he dropped on a heap of hay. "So will she."

I had no clue what Rune would do for the day, but I guessed he would keep himself busy.

"What are we hunting?" I asked Hakon after washing my bread down with a gulp of ale.

"Elks," he answered as he squeezed the buttery juice from his piece of bread.

A thrall gave the boy his favored hunting weapon, a light bow, and a quiver full of arrows. I smiled, thinking that, yet again, the apple had not fallen far from the tree.

To hunt a beast as big as an Elk, a hunting spear was a better choice, but I could hardly imagine Hakon throwing one with enough strength to kill, let alone carrying it all day long while trailing the forest. Eigil and I were given one, though, and I kept Wedge in my belt.

"How do we find them?" I asked.

"There's a clearing near the river. They usually gather there around noon, when the sun is high, and the predators are asleep," the boy said while examining the goose feathers of his arrows. "In spring, we use the scent of a female in heat to attract a big buck, but it's too late for that now, so we'll just have to be patient."

He did know his hunting, I told myself with the same

pride as if he'd been my son. If I already felt so for him, it would be a question of heartbeats for Ulf to connect with the boy.

"I know a trick that still works this late in the season," I said. Hakon suddenly abandoned his quiver, eyes shining with curiosity.

Late summer and early autumn is a time when beasts abandon their mating madness to that of fattening for winter. I remembered an old trick taught to me by my father, or maybe he was an uncle. I had never tried it because, from a young age, all I wanted was to become a warrior, but it was worth mentioning.

"I don't know why they do this, but elks and reindeer chew bones before winter. They probably find something in it to get stronger for the bitter days ahead. They seem to prefer the shins, and more specifically, that of humans." I could almost hear the knowledge carving itself in Hakon's brain. "That's why in my village, when a slave dies, we keep the bones of his legs for hunting." The closest thrall to Hakon gasped in horror, and Eigil chuckled.

"You have elks in Jutland?" the boy asked, making me regret my words.

"We do," I said, hoping my reaction had been quick enough to mask the fact that I had no idea if those beasts roamed Jutland. "But not as big as here."

To the thrall's great relief, Hakon ordered her to fetch some pig bones, and with that last piece of item, we went hunting.

ᛉ

Hakon was light on his feet and made me feel like an old bear in comparison. Every twig and dead leaf of the forest was intent on finding itself under my feet. But more surprisingly, Eigil was nearly as discreet as Hakon himself, even though he towered me by a good head and was made from equal parts fat and muscles.

The two other men fared little better than me, though, judging by their heads shifting left and right nervously, they cared more about their jarl's safety than bringing some venison back to the village.

"Your men seem nervous," I told Hakon, breaking the most important rule of hunting, never to speak.

"We're getting close to the mines," he whispered back. "Bove often sends men to disrupt the miners. No doubt they would only be too happy to bring my head back to their jarl."

"Just as they did your grandfather," I said. I thought to sting his pride a little, see where he landed on the question of his grandfather's murder. But all he did was shrug.

"You don't mourn his death?"

"Of course I do," he said. "I just don't think Bove had him killed."

"You don't?"

"Olaf was a rich man and liked to show it. But when his body was found, he was still wearing all his silver and jewelry. Only his jarl torc was missing, and, to be honest, it was far from being an impressive one. Its value was more emotional than monetary. They even left the easy looting in the room. Do you really think a murderer could resist stealing so much silver, even if instructed to?"

His question was more rhetorical, and I must admit he made a good point. The torc had probably been taken as a token of the deed, which meant a rather professional assassin had been sent.

This was a point I should not have cared about. It

stretched far from my goal on Midgard, but part of me was intrigued, and I could not stop thinking about Odin's premonition. It might have been nothing, but I, too, felt the beginning of doubt tingling in the back of my mind.

"Who do you think did it then?" I asked Hakon.

"No idea. Besides Bove, I don't see who would benefit from the old man's death."

"Is that why you don't want to fight?" I asked. I was playing with fire, but I needed a bigger reaction.

"I do want to fight," he said louder, a spark of burning rage in his young eyes. "It's just that—" He did not finish his sentence; I knew what he meant.

"You're afraid," I said for him, making sure not to make it sound like an accusation. Of course I understood. I had fought hundreds of battles, knowing that if I failed, I would still wake up somewhere, and I still started every fight with a ball in my stomach. I do not remember exactly how I felt before my first battle, but I guarantee that I was more scared than excited. And I had been two years older and a great deal stronger than Hakon.

I could have given him some encouragement, some words from an old fighter. I could have told him that bravery can only be reached when a man surpasses his fear. Or that between life and death awaits the bliss of savagery. But words are cheap. It might have been enough at this instant, maybe even the next day, but the moment the fight began, Hakon would run back to Hild's skirt. And if he showed cowardice and died, Asgard would close its doors to him, and we would next meet during Ragnarök, as enemies. I did not want that for Ulf.

No, Hakon needed to find his courage on his own, and he needed to do it fast.

"Show me a man who isn't afraid, and I'll show you a fool or a liar," I still said.

He waved us forward, and the rest of the way passed silently. I used this time to send a prayer to whichever Æsir or Vanir was willing to intervene, hoping for some opportunity. I asked for a sign for Hakon to interpret, or a dream maybe, anything to let him know he was supposed to fight. Of course, if it was that easy, Odin wouldn't need the Wolves in the first place, and I had never heard of a god answering a prayer, or being aware of them, for that matter.

And yet, despite my usual skepticism, there was a miracle of sorts.

It happened shortly after we reached the river. We hid behind low shrubs close enough to the river that bows and arrows could be used. Eigil tossed the pig bones in several places near the water, and we knelt, each of us trying to find a position we could keep for a long time and breathing as lightly as possible. There was no wind to be careful of, and I was getting comfortable with the idea that we might be here for a couple of hours when, out of the complete silence of the forest, I heard a light twang followed by a loud shriek.

One of the two men accompanying us, the one on the far right of our small line, fell face-first, shrieking as he tried to reach the arrow sprouting from his lower back.

A second arrow brushed Eigil's head, but by luck, he ducked when the first man was hit and flattened himself on the ground like a badger. I turned in time to see two men, a good fifty steps from us, bows in hands. One had an arrow pointed at me. While stopping an arrow with a shield is manageable, it is nearly impossible to dodge one coming straight at you.

I jumped toward the wounded man before the archer released and put him on his side so that he could shield me.

He moaned and cried, his face so close to mine that I smelled the mixture of iron and ale on his breath. This was not a fatal wound, as far I could tell, but I'm sure he thought it would be.

Hakon had frozen on his spot, his eyes wide-open in terror at the sight of his man tensing like a dying spider. I snatched him by the collar and dropped him right next to me in the mud. Another arrow passed a good head above us, and I cursed for not having brought my shield.

"Eigil," I called. The men attacking us had the advantage of a fair slope, but by lying as he did, Eigil made a difficult target. If we did not move, though, our doom was on us. The other man accompanying us had run behind a tree, but he was white with fear and shook like a leaf.

"Eigil," I called again. This time, he looked at me. "Your nail," I told him, showing my small pouch in case he couldn't hear me above the sound of the shrieking man. Eigil's eyes turned round and sorry. I cursed at his stupidity. He had not taken his nail with him.

"Frigg's ass, Eigil, you idiot," I said while snatching the purse from my neck, which I tossed to him. "Take it," I yelled.

Now, I had no choice; I had to be brave or risk Helheim. To be honest, even if I showed enough courage to deserve Valhöll again, I doubted the Valkyries would notice this skirmish. I reached for my fallen spear and used this chance to see the two archers approaching slowly. One of them aimed at me when I retreated behind my human shield. There was another twang, followed by a thump. The arrow lodged itself in the neck of the wounded man, its tip jutting from his throat a hand length from my face.

If Hakon had been afraid before, the gargling of his man as he drowned in his own blood made him livid. I unsheathed Wedge and slid it across the man's throat, ending his torment in one smooth line. The light was out of his eyes before the next arrow thumped into his back.

"Hakon," I called, shaking the boy by the shoulder. "He's dead. Stop looking at him, look at me." With effort, he removed his eyes from his man's throat and blinked when he saw me. "I will drag their attention. When I do, you shoot them, you hear me?" I said, waiting for his nod. "You pick your target, wait until you're sure you have him, and you kill the goat-fucker, all right?" His hands shook, and I would be lucky if he didn't shoot me by mistake.

Eigil's eyes told me he understood what was going to happen. But the last of us was helplessly standing behind his tree, mouthing a prayer to our gods with quivering lips. The taste of bile from a hard fight flooded the back of my mouth, even though the first arrow had been shot less than a minute ago.

I raised my head, which nearly got me killed, but used the time it would take one of them to knock his next arrow to make my move. I was no archer, but I knew how hard it is to hit a moving target, especially one as fit as I was.

Not looking back at Hakon or Eigil, I ran as if Fenrir's jaws were closing on me and only stopped when I was confident my comrades had had enough time to do their part. I heard a scream above the sound of blood thumping in my head and knew that at least one of the two archers had been hit. I first checked Hakon, who was nocking his second arrow, then Eigil, his spear still in hand, and an arrow sprouting out of his left shoulder.

I stepped out of my cover to deal with the second archer, reversed my grip on my spear, and took the time needed to register the scene before throwing it. The closest man was on the ground, hands on the shaft planted between shoulder and neck. A fatal wound, by the look of it, even though he still had the energy to wriggle like a worm. But the second man was drawing his arm, almost ready to release an arrow at Hakon.

I bellowed as I threw my spear. The archer turned but was taken back by the impact of my spear lodging itself in his abdomen. He fell three or four steps away, eyes and mouth wide-open in surprise. I don't think he understood he was dying. Wedge, still in my left hand, reminded itself to me. One of them yet breathed.

"Drake!" Eigil called. I was about to curse him for using my Asgardian name, but then I saw why he had called me.

Two more men were running at him from the side, axe and knife in hands. They had timed their attack wrong or maybe had hoped the archers would take care of us. Our last man ran for his life a couple heartbeats before they reached him, leaving my comrade to fend them off by himself.

Coming down the slope as fast as my legs let me, I saw Eigil running toward them, holding his spear with both hands. He lifted the tip of his weapon at the last second, catching one of the two men under the chin. The second one brought his axe down on Eigil at the same moment and drove its blade deep at the base of his neck.

Even after two centuries of being a Drake, even knowing that Eigil had taken Odin's nail, I could not suppress a shout born of fear. I never got used to seeing my men killed in the middle of the action. Frankly, I had forgotten about Hakon at this point, so I almost stopped running when he showed up in my sight, rushing toward Eigil with a spear in hand.

The man with the axe was trying to remove his weapon from Eigil's body, but my warrior grabbed him by the wrist and gathered enough strength to keep his killer where he stood. Hakon used this chance and all the energy of his frail body to drive the spear into the assailant's face.

It was a terrible lunge, not worthy of a warrior, but it was enough. The spearhead caught the man in the eye and buried itself in his brain. A stronger warrior would have pierced the back of the man's skull, but Hakon still put enough force to end his life. The boy let go of his spear, which fell with the dead.

I ignored Hakon and knelt by Eigil. He was still breathing, but not for long.

"Don't tell my father," he pleaded when I took his hand.

"Of course I'll tell him," I said, not holding back my anger. "And here I was, thinking you were better off without him."

"I think I prefer when he's here," Eigil said, his lower lip quivering with sorrow.

"Do you want me to send you?" I asked.

"No need, it won't be long," he replied. "Hakon," he then called, a red bubble popping from his lips. "This one's for you." He pointed at the highest of his silver rings, the one he had earned in his first battle. "You deserve it."

I expected to find Hakon shivering, sobbing, or emptying his stomach, but he impressed me then, looking every bit the jarl he was. He knelt next to me and dropped his hand on Eigil's shoulder.

"Thank you," he simply said, and with that, Eigil left. Then Hakon did sob. Not long. He gracefully removed Eigil's arm ring and placed it on his thin biceps, though he had to bend it so much that I thought it would break. I stilled his hand just as he was about to let go of his new possession.

"As soon as you wear that thing," I said, "you're a warrior, and warriors don't cry."

A new resolve bloomed in his eyes, and we both let go of the arm ring. Eigil had made a mess of things, but his last gesture had sealed the region's fate. Hakon was a bloodied warrior now and had made his decision.

He knew none of the four men we had killed, but they had to have been sent by Bove. The man who had run was now back, shame drawn on his face. If Hakon's eyes could kill, the poor bastard would have joined his friend.

Despite his cowardice, he would serve our purpose. To mask his shameful deed, he would tell the story of Hakon's first and second kill, and just for that, I was glad the coward had survived. The boy-jarl's fame would spread, and men would fight for him. I still made him carry Eigil's body as a punishment.

We looted those men, and as I showed Hakon where to look, I had a feeling of being watched from farther up the forest, but when I turned around, all I saw was a raven taking flight. The bird would have to wait a bit longer for its feast. My mind went to Muninn for a second, but I dismissed the idea that it was her. If she was here and did not want to be seen, I would never have noticed her.

"Eigil was right," I said as we neared Lagardalr again. "You were brave today."

"Not at first," Hakon replied. By then, the thrill of surviving had passed, and he was shaking.

"You pulled yourself up," I said, speaking louder to make sure the other man heard. "Next time, though, aim for the throat. Much harder to dodge." Hakon nodded with a little grunt of approval. I knew he was revisiting the events of the morning. He observed Eigil's body dangling over the third man's shoulder as if it were the trophy of our hunt.

"Why did he call you Drake?"

"Just an old nickname," I said, dismissing the point with a headshake.

"It suits you better than Thorstein."

Lagardalr drew itself between the trees, quiet and at peace. It would soon change, for the boy-jarl had become a man and would claim the blood price from his enemy in the days to come.

ᛉ

"I guess it means my time in Hild's bed is over," Snekke casually said as I cleaned the blood from my hands. Eigil was being washed by Hakon's slaves, preparing him for yet another funeral.

"You're right," I replied. "She won't have any more say in the boy's life."

"Good," Titus said. "At least he won't mind Halfdan having called for the levy." My foreign friend had managed his task with success. This ordeal was shaping up better than it had started, except for Eigil, of course. "Lif will be happy too," he went on, and for some reason, this thought pleased us both.

"I bet we'll soon go for some allies," I said, regretting having used the word bet in Titus's presence. But since it was as safe a bet as one could be, he did not even bother pressing on. "We'll volunteer to accompany the delegations, especially you, Snekke."

"Aye, sir," Snekke replied, mimicking the military salute Titus had taught us ages ago.

Pressing on one nostril, I blew the other one in the bucket of pink water and did the same with the second before spilling its content in the lake.

"Where is Rune," I asked, suddenly remembering our

young comrade. The two others shrugged, but just then, as if he'd heard, Rune called for me, walking so fast that he appeared to run. His face betrayed a look that did not bode well, and I wondered what other unpleasant surprise this day had in store for me.

"I've found something," he said. "You should see it."

Ү

"What were you doing over there?" I asked as Rune led me on a beaten path cutting through the land from the back of the village.

"I wanted to find a vantage point. Get a better grasp of the land and maybe find a good place for the battle. Plus, I had nothing else to do," he said, a hint of reproach in his tone. The path was barely enough for a man to tread without scratching himself over the thorns of the blackberry bushes, and it was turning rockier as we walked.

"Did you tell Titus where you were going?"

"Not really. He was busy talking to that old goat Halfdan," Rune replied. I hadn't noticed that Rune disliked the old warrior, but it's in the nature of the young to dislike the old and vice versa.

"You still won't tell me what you found?" I asked, annoyed at being taken so far from our mission without knowing why.

"You'll see when we get there," he replied again.

I had left Titus and Snekke there to avoid raising suspicion, but now I regretted not having sent my foreign Wolf in my stead. Rune had insisted it should be me, and I indulged him. If it wasn't worth it, I told myself, he would buy me a new mattress back on Asgard.

Ten minutes later, we reached the bottom of the steep

hill Rune meant for us to climb. A thick forest of old firs replaced the shrubs and bushes, and the ground was covered in brown, crunching leaves.

"That's when I felt it," he said.

I was about to ask him what he was talking about, but then I felt it too: *seidr* magic. This was the first time I heard Rune could sense the dark art, but from the way he put his hand on his chest, I guessed he sensed it the way I did.

"What on Midgard?"

The beaten path died, leaving us to trek the dark forest of the hill.

"I just kept following this... thing," he said. It drove us through the trees, getting stronger or weaker according to the direction we took. It was like trying to find the source of a tune, but with your heart.

"You went after someone who can use *seidr* by yourself?" I said, not even trying to mask my anger. "I'm sure you didn't even take your nail."

"I did," he replied, "as soon as I felt it. And I'm not sure *someone* is using *seidr*."

"What do you mean?" I asked.

He pointed at a space between two firs thicker than the others.

The growing darkness made it difficult to notice what he pointed at, but when I saw it, I immediately went for the small pouch hanging on my neck. Odin's nail, the one Eigil had left in the village, rested at its bottom.

A cave.

I swallowed the damn thing, and had I been wiser, I would have fetched the rest of my men. Gods knew I wanted to. A malicious *seidr* poured out of the cave, so thick I felt it at the tips of my fingers. I grabbed Wedge, and Rune reached for his axe.

"Did you go inside?" I asked, whispering.

"I did," he answered similarly. "Not long, just to get a glimpse. There was no one, but I think someone was there recently. It's not empty." Whatever Rune had seen inside, he had not liked. I refrained from asking what awaited us; we were too close to speak, and the *seidr* kept our mouths shut.

We stood on both sides of the entrance, waiting for something without knowing what. I nodded, Rune nodded back, and we went in.

If it was getting dark outside, inside was like the night of a new moon. The dripping water made me nervous, but not nearly as much as the increasing feeling of dark magic filling the place. The pressure in my chest increased with each step, and though I had not taken more than twenty into the cave, I was having difficulty breathing. It was a blessing in disguise, for the place smelled terrible. Something between the stench of a three-day dead fish and that of a wet dog. Five more steps, and I felt more than I saw the walls widening and forming a round-shaped room.

"I could see a little better earlier," Rune said.

The pressure of the walls vanished as we stepped into the room. A dead-end, judging by the echo. I barely stepped in when my knee bumped into something made of wood and quite edgy, which in turn made a multitude of rattling sounds. I bit a curse and palmed the object I had knocked, recognizing a small table. My fingers caressed a blunt knife, then a bowl, and finally something smooth and circular; its surface felt made of skin, but solid.

"You have a flintstone?" I asked Rune, recognizing that I was touching a candle.

The first spark from the friction gave me enough light to see that I was indeed peering over a table, albeit a terribly made one. It took me six more tries and a curse to Freyja's private parts to finally light the candle. The flame was weak, but the sudden light blinded me for a few seconds. I blinked it away and got a better look at the room.

The walls glittered like a night sky, and the candle revealed a place as big as a large pantry, high enough for me to stand, but just barely. The room was round, except for the flat wall at the end, which, unless I was wrong, was carved in a different stone.

The small table I had hurt myself against was a makeshift piece of furniture, done with whatever the person living here had found outside. I had felt everything on it, an old rusty knife, a bowl, the candle I now held, plus a small pile of small bones, mostly from birds and rodents. On the other side of the room lay a pile of pelts serving as a mat.

But the most amazing sight of the room was its floor, covered with dark feathers, hundreds of them. They crunched under my feet as I walked toward the piled furs. I picked up one of them, examining it carefully with the weak light of the candle. It could have belonged to a raven or some bird of prey, perhaps, but it had to be huge, for the feather was nearly as long as my forearm.

"What kind of bird has so many feathers?" Rune asked.

"It can't be just one bird," I replied, placing the feather inside my shirt for a later inspection.

"You said that Odin had a bad feeling?" Rune then rightfully asked. Whatever this place was, whoever used it, it must have been linked to the All-Father's premonition.

"I didn't say *bad* feeling," I replied. "But it looks bad, indeed."

And it was about to get worse.

I patted the pelts and passed my hand between each layer, looking for whatever clue could lead me to understand the mess I now knelt in. Those pelts were fairly fresh and crudely cut from their previous owner, so it was not an agreeable feeling at all. But between what I assumed was a deer's skin and a fox's fur, I felt something colder, made of metal. From the familiar twist of metal strands, I knew what it was before I saw it. A jarl's torc.

Hakon had been right; this was a most common torc. There was no doubt in my mind I now held Olaf's torc, and his killer lived here.

"Loki's arse," Rune cursed, making me wince, for this was the last place I wanted to hear the trickster's name. He took the torc and reached the same conclusion I had.

"We can't tell anyone," I told him. "If they realize the person who has killed their jarl isn't from their enemy's ranks, the war will be called off."

"It doesn't mean the killer hasn't been sent by Bove," Rune said, which was true enough. Hermits were aplenty, and Bove might have hired one.

"Let's keep it to ourselves anyway," I said.

"I don't even know what I'd say."

The candlelight flickered, giving more gloom to the place, and my courage wavered. I put the torc back, not wanting to betray our intrusion, then dropped the candle on the table, sent Rune back to the entrance, and snuffed the light before following him. Halfway through, I told myself I should have checked the wall at the end of the room, for it looked so peculiar in contrast to the rest of the cave, but at this point, I did not have the will or the guts to go back in there.

The sun was very low when we got out. Neither Rune nor I spoke for some time as we rushed down the hill. There was too much to reflect on, and from where I stood, too little of it was connected to our mission. I felt like a piece of *tafl* on a playing board. The question was, who were the players?

The dark feather in my tunic made me think of Muninn, though it could have come from a huge crow, or a raven, or a merle even. My mind raced to Huginn, Muninn's long-gone brother, but he was no killer. I could be wrong, for I had not known him well, and he had disappeared twenty years ago. People change in twenty years. It was thin, but I would keep it in mind, and when the time came, I would show the feather to Muninn.

Rune seemed as lost in his mind as I was in mine. I had nothing to give voice to the doubt gnawing at me, but I had been a Drake long enough to trust my instinct, and my instinct warned me to keep my eyes on him. Something was off in his demeanor. Everything just came too easy to Rune. His sudden fighting skills, his spot within our ranks, and now his finding of a small, hidden cave in the middle of an unknown territory. It was thin, but I did not like it.

For the second time that day, I went back to Lagardalr with a head full of disturbing thoughts. Two large piles of wood had been erected by the lake, away from the other structures. One of them supported Eigil's body, his hammer, and his shield. We had only spent a day here, but one of us was already gone. We also found ourselves dealing with *seidr,* a mysterious killer, and I would have to get Odin's nail back at some point.

I envied Eigil.

8

The cave...
3 days after Loki's escape.

I resisted sleep for three days. Three days of listening to mad Sigyn's babbling about the life she and I would have once out of the cave. She spoke of the children we would make, the servants who would do our bidding and the peace that would follow Ragnarök. I listened and responded as best I could, for it made her more careful with the bowl and prevented the snake from dropping acid into my eyes.

Once a day, she had to leave the cave to empty the bowl. If she dropped in on the cave's floor, foul-smelling fumes would rise in a thick, yellowish fog that stung the eyes to painful tears. I dreaded her absence when nothing stood between me and the beast. I swore it waited for those occurrences.

As soon as Sigyn was out, the fattest pearls of venom emerged from its fangs, and it's a wonder I was only burned once in those three days. Sigyn, I suspected, also used this time to relieve herself, breathe some fresh air, and do whatever a woman does when she gets some privacy. She could be gone fifteen to thirty minutes at a time, then would show up as she did the first time, scurrying to my help. Well, really, to Loki's help, for she would not acknowledge I was Drake.

I learned more when playing her game than when resisting it, anyway.

As I suspected, Loki and Muninn's association had been fairly recent. At least not older than the trickster's presence in the cave. According to my new friend, Loki had worked on his plan from the beginning of his punishment. I took it with a grain of salt, for I doubted Sigyn had a clear sense of time. Loki explained little about his plan to his wife. She wouldn't help him much, and I guessed he still preferred me not to know the details.

As I gathered, my blood would give access to Asgard, from where he would trigger the beginning of the end. His plan, however, would take time. He needed to weaken the Æsir and the citadel before leading the full force of Hel and Surtr on us, and this would not happen in a day. Sigyn did not know why her husband worked with so much dedication on Ragnarök, but it was clear that getting me here was more than a means to escape.

I prayed that the time Loki needed would also give my men a chance to notice the difference in their leader and somehow come to my rescue. It was thin, but I counted on them being such pains in Loki's ass that they wouldn't let the trickster behave as he wished.

It was a detail, but I finally learned about the cave near Lagardalr and the flat wall. It was a piece of Asgard's cliff, dragged from the sacred island by Odin himself to serve as the door to Loki's prison. The idea that the All-Father had just forgotten about it was ridiculous. Muninn, being the only creature in the nine realms with charms that worked on memories, must have had something to do with it. I also guessed this was the origin of Odin's *bad feeling*. A part of him remembered the name Lagardalr and how the village neighbored Loki's jail.

The cave sat on top of a high mountain at the border of several realms—none of them being Asgard or Midgard—a place of desolation where nothing grew but thorns, some poisonous ivy, and a wind to chill the balls of a Jötunn in summer. When I asked why she never returned to Asgard, Sigyn said she could simply not. The mouth of the cave gave way to a narrow path dug in the mountain's rock. But after a few steps, the path stopped, and then it was a flat cliff of sharp rock and emptiness. She could not spot the ground and assumed there was none.

"If you can't open the door, you need wings," she told me. "And I don't see any slain hero to open the door here," she giggled. "Plus, it's a one-way door." My heart sank when she said so. Loki could fly, or so I heard, but I doubted he could fly between realms as Muninn did. This point had made his choice of ally easier.

Those were details, but I had decided to learn as much as possible during my time in Loki's cave. Not that it mattered. I would die here, as Loki. Not of hunger, for it seemed hunger and thirst ignored the existence of this place. I would just die. Ragnarök would take place without me by my men's side, and the worlds would end, and that would be it.

I succumbed to sleep with this idea on the third day. I had waited as long as possible until Sigyn woke up from a brief nap. She stood and held the bowl even while asleep, but my faith in her was thin, so I waited.

Once certain she would keep me safe, my mind went off, letting go of the last piece of resistance. I did not know exhaustion could be so painful. I dreamt of that not-so-far-away day when my most bothersome problem was telling Einar that his son had gotten killed.

ᛉ

"He did what?" Einar's eyes threatened to pop out of their frames, and his nostrils could not bring air into his lungs fast enough.

"Your son almost got me a ride to Helheim; that's what he did."

"You saw him eat the nail, though, right?" This was the second time he asked.

"Yes. He ate *my* nail, since he had forgotten his, and died bravely. He's fine."

"And while we freeze our asses here, the big oaf is enjoying the warmth of Odin's hall," Bjorn said, his mood even worse than mine.

They insisted I gave my report first, but from the look on their faces, things had not gone well on their side either. I had asked for one of them to come, but all five were here. At least all of them had survived. I went on to tell of Rune's discovery, not leaving any detail besides my growing suspicion regarding the young Wolf.

"I have to ask," I said. "Did Bove really order Olaf's murder?"

Ulf exchanged a look with Bjorn before deciding that he was the one to answer.

"He claims he did not," Ulf said. "But he's clearly capable of it, and Olaf's death does help him."

"Crazy as a blind horse, that one," Karl spat as he rubbed his hands near the fire burning between us.

"What happened after the pyre?" Ulf asked.

I told them how the next day had seen things moving in Lagardalr, or at least out of it. Hakon sent messengers with a call to arms to all the nearby villages. In the message that was to be repeated, the young jarl claimed he would pursue the fight to the door of his rival's great hall and share the spoils with all his allies. Naturally, I sent Snekke, accompanied by Rune, in this effort to bolster our ranks.

"Why Rune?" Karl asked. A fair question. Rune had a big mouth with a mind of its own. Sending him on a task of this nature was an odd choice at best, a risk at worst.

"I didn't want Snekke to be by himself, not after the attack in the forest," I answered, making it up as I spoke.

"What about Titus?" Ulf asked over the sound of Cross-Eyes chewing on a mouthful of nuts. "He could have gone with Snekke. No risk of him blabbering something he shouldn't."

"He's busy in Lagardalr," I replied, truthfully this time. "He has a jarl to train and only two more days to do so." Hakon had suddenly realized his lack of martial practice, and though I warned him four days would not suffice, he had insisted.

For once, Hild and I agreed; he should not join the fight. But Hakon had tasted blood and thirsted for more. Poor Hild saw all her influence on her son vanish with the last of his innocence. She had let a boy go hunting, and a man had returned. Lif was delighted by her brother's change, and to mark her appreciation, she gratified me with a wink during the funeral of the two slain. Truly, she would become an amazing woman, I told myself again.

"How is the boy?" Bjorn asked. "Every bit of the weakling Bove makes him sound to be?"

"Actually," I said, putting some excitement in my voice. "Despite being so lowly born, Hakon has the making of a great leader. A bit weak in the arms, but a mind of steel."

"Lowly born?" Bjorn asked. "I thought his grandfather was a powerful and respected jarl."

"Olaf was indeed a great man, or so we've heard," I replied, "but he's not Hakon's real grandfather. Though none of them know that."

Ulf tilted his head like a rooster checking a worm.

"Ulf is," I said.

"He's what?" Karl asked. His voice had reached heights I did not know it could approach. Sven Cross-Eyes nearly choked on a handful of nuts, and it took Einar patting his back to get him breathing again. Ulf's reaction was worth his weight in silver, too. His mouth hung open like a dead fish, and I saw more white in his eyes than I knew existed.

"What in the—" Bjorn said.

"Are you sure?" Ulf asked. His hand reached for my knee. "Drake, are you sure?"

"As sure as one can be," I replied, smiling at my friend's reaction. "You have a grandson and a granddaughter in Lagardalr."

I was taking a risk here. Ulf was a good man, a tired Einherjar, and had never been a father, something he often mentioned with regret. He might very well ask to remain on Midgard, and if he did, I would grant him his wish. Odin would punish me for it, but Ulf deserved this shot at happiness. That was still down the line, and in the meantime, I took pleasure in his dumbfounded face.

"How is it possible?" Karl asked, in control of his voice again.

"We never knew it was," I replied. "But we never knew it wasn't possible either."

"What about me?" Bjorn asked, sounding like a boy expecting the same toy as his brother.

"What about you?" Ulf asked.

"We enjoyed the same woman."

"Well, I got her pregnant."

"So?" Bjorn asked.

"You do know two men can't get a woman pregnant at the same time?" Einar replied, one eyebrow raised higher than the other.

"Of course they can," Bjorn said with a scoff. His face turned blood red when he noticed our head shakes.

Even Karl, who by his own admission knew little about women, mirrored our expression. Keeping ourselves from laughing at Bjorn's expense took all we had, and we only managed until Sven burst out, sputtering chunks of walnuts all over the fire.

"I have a grandson," Ulf said, the only one not partaking in the guffaw.

"I'm guessing we all have," I said, which quietened them all. "This is the first time we have proof of it, but if it happened once, I don't see why it wouldn't have happened before. For all we know, Midgard is littered with our pups."

"Freyja's tits," Bjorn said. It was him I was particularly thinking about when I said so. All of us may have descendants living on Midgard, but supposing it and knowing it are two different things. Ulf blinked back to the present, a thousand questions in his eyes.

"I'm afraid your son died from a horse fall," I told him. Surprisingly, it did not seem to bother him that much. He had yet to realize that it meant we would face him during Ragnarök. This kind of death, even if it happened during a battle, did not qualify as brave.

"How about the girl?" he asked.

"You'll love her," I replied. This conversation had to end here if I wanted to know about their side of the mission. "Now tell me about Hvitiseid and Bove." They exchanged sorry glances, silently arguing over who would speak first.

"It did not go well," Sven said.

"Oh really? I didn't expect that at all," I replied with enough sarcasm to get his crossed eyes looking away.

"This fantasy you've told Hakon about Bove hiring mercenaries left and right," Karl continued, "that's no fantasy at all. He's been gathering men for months, the promise of the mine attracting them like flies to horse shit."

"How many?" I asked.

" 'Bout two hundred. And more are coming."

"Fuck," was all I could reply. Snekke's tongue would have to be even sharper than usual.

"Even with even numbers, I wouldn't fancy our chances against Bove," Einar said. "He's a sick, sick bastard." The others nodded, and it gave me a chill to imagine the kind of men who could cower the bravest of Valhöll.

"It's just the way he goes from bad to worse," Ulf explained. "I've never seen anything like it. One second, he's drinking and feasting; the next, he rages as if someone had pissed in his mead, and it takes blood for him to quiet down. A lot of blood."

"Four men died while we were there, and we barely stayed a day," Sven said. "Two of them were thralls, but still."

"If he has so many men, I'm sure you could have blended in," I said. "Maybe crack some heads to make your place known, as usual."

"Well, that's exactly what some of us did," Karl said with an accusing glance at Bjorn.

I guessed what happened before they told me.

This was our usual pattern. We'd find the loudest mouth in the village, smack it shut, and earn our place at the jarl's table. Our champion was often charged with the smacking, of course. All it took was just a bit of brain to distinguish a proper target from an untouchable one. For example, beating a prow man to a pulp served us well; a jarl, not so much. It shames not only the man, but his whole band as well.

"How was I supposed to know he was a jarl?" Bjorn said, slapping his knee. "He was so big. The big ones are never the jarls, you know that?" he asked me, looking for help. Jarls were *sometimes* the strongest of their men, and it happened to be the case for a guest of Bove, who also led the biggest band among all of Hvitiseid's new army.

"Did you kill him?" I asked. I was actually amused by this turn of events. Things going bad when I wasn't around justified my rank, and while this mission had a sour taste since the Bifröst, it was just that, a mission.

"He was breathing when we left," Bjorn replied.

"Barely," Karl said.

"Well, at least we won't face him in battle." Bjorn opened his hand in my direction as if I had just agreed with him on the whole story.

"And it gave a good laugh to that goat-fucker of Bove," Einar said, enforcing what he thought of the man. "We were safe as long as the jarl approved of Bjorn's zeal, but we didn't stay to see how long that would last."

"We heard a rumor that Bove plans to fight in a fortnight," Ulf said. This was the one piece of good news in all of this. Bove was not ready, though we had no clue what he was waiting for.

"Well," I said, standing up, "at least the Wolves are together again. Most of us, anyway. And as long as it is so, we have nothing to fear." The Wolves had gotten themselves out of worse situations, and I was sure we would once again prevail, somehow.

The battle would take place, and we would recruit many new brothers. We'd then find ourselves on the benches of Valhöll and forget all about it. I had Ulf to worry about but otherwise trusted us implicitly. I don't know if my words helped, but I sensed a regain in their energy when they, too, stood.

"What do we tell Jarl Hakon?" Karl asked.

"I already told him I had men in Bove's camp. Though I didn't mention that five of them would come back with me today."

"Hopefully, none of them will notice how one of us looks so much like their little lord," he replied, and I cursed myself for not having thought of that.

I told Ulf to tie his hair in a bun, as Bjorn did, and to keep his beard as wild as it was now, hoping it would create enough of a difference with the boy to fool Lagardalr's folks. So far, none of the few elders had recognized Snekke, but Ulf and Bjorn, especially, were more noticeable.

Muninn had most likely wiped their memories clean back then, but it was a risk. There was nothing to do about it now except maybe keep the two of them out of the village. But since one of them had two living grandchildren in the village, I don't think he would agree to remain out of it.

"Drake," Ulf softly called on the walk back to Lagardalr.

"What is it?" I asked.

"I've heard Bove say what he would do to Hakon. And I can guess what he would do to…"

"Lif."

"Lif," he repeated with a smile on his lips to melt my heart. It vanished in a heartbeat. "From what you said, I don't see us winning this fight."

I could only agree. So far, it was two hundred men against fifty-something.

"If I sense the tide turning against us, I will protect my children."

"We're not there yet," I said, not wanting to expand on what my friend actually meant. "We'll cross that bridge when we get there."

"I've already crossed that bridge, my friend."

Nothing was added to this conversation, nor did it need to be. What else could I say, anyway? *You should let the bastard turn your grandson's skull into his next drinking cup and share your granddaughter with his men?* I didn't have it in me, and neither did Ulf.

ᛉ

Snekke and Rune came back with better news. In one day, they had visited three neighboring villages whose chiefs or jarls had promised good fighting men. And those leaders had been good to their word when, just the next day, warriors started pouring in, cramming Lagardalr to its limit.

Hakon announced the battle for the next day, hoping to catch Bove by surprise. By this last evening, he had gathered a force of one hundred and twenty men, plus nine Einherjar. It wasn't enough, but our presence would tip the scale, or so I hoped. More were to join us in the morning and during the march, and for a moment, I wondered if we should postpone the fight so that they could all arrive. But two things made me stick with the plan.

First, the men already present would be the best and bravest. A weak man in a shield wall is more damaging than anything. It only takes one man to step back for the entire line to lose its fighting spirit and start running for their lives.

An extra thirty cowards would not help. Bove had more men, but mercenaries had fewer reasons to die and turned their heels more easily. One hundred and twenty warriors defending their homes would overcome two hundred ill-motivated men.

Second, changing plans on the eve of battle would confuse our fighters and weaken their fighting spirit. They might even see Hakon as a coward, and, in truth, the boy might lose heart as well. Bravery and cunning would have to do.

Bove expected Hakon to hide behind his palisade and believed he had another two weeks. He'd never see us coming, and the more off-balance we caught him, the better our chances. So we would leave the next day, shortly after dawn, and march straight to Hvitiseid. Hakon's men had named three sites from here to there where we would have the land advantage should Bove notice our advance and decide to meet us.

A little voice in my head reminded me several times on that last day that this was just a mission and whether we won or not wasn't the issue. But the closer we got to it, the more I cared about giving Hakon his victory.

It wasn't just that I liked the boy and his sister, but I'd grown to accept that Ulf would remain here. A victory would be a worthy farewell present for my brother. I had no more doubt on that evening, as men drank, sang, and ate in Hakon's hall, Ulf would not return with us. The candles lighting the feast glimmered in his eyes as he watched his grandson entertaining his guests. He loved the kid already.

He kept his word and mentioned nothing of their relation to the boy or the girl, who, he admitted, had the making of a fearsome woman and a very annoying wife. If any person in Lagardalr thought Ulf and the jarl looked alike, none of them mentioned it. Ulf kept himself quiet around Hakon, but managed as much time near the boy as possible. Titus, who was training him, offered Ulf to practice a bit of archery with his grandson. My archer returned from the training session with a wide grin that had yet to disappear.

"Hel of an archer," he said, probably for the fifth time that evening.

"Good," Titus replied, "because he's one of the worst swordsmen I've ever trained. No offense, Ulf."

"I think he still intends to be in the wall tomorrow," I said.

"He'll change his mind when he sees the enemy," Titus said.

Bjorn emptied cup of mead after cup of mead with whoever would knock his cup, while Snekke stayed as close to Hild as ivy to a trunk. It did not even occur to him that a mother would have other ideas for the evening before her son went to war. Einar was already lying on his heap of hay, Sven was busy with a young slave somewhere, and the rest sat around me as if we'd been home. But something was missing, I told myself, something I could not identify.

I thought about the cave, the torc, the feathers, and all it could mean, then shoved those thoughts from my mind. The battle was too close to worry about those things. Muninn would have some answers, maybe, and if not her, then Odin. We would go home the next day, and I had enough to worry about until then.

"What do you make of our chances?" Titus asked, shouting the words, for the hubbub of the feast was at its peak.

I looked at the bottom of my cup, stirring the remaining ale to clear the foam as I thought of an adequate answer. "Of making Odin happy? They're excellent."

It had been a long time since our last large-scale battle. There was a time when we Norsemen fought in great battles involving many kings and jarls, but those days were gone. With nearly four hundred warriors, this had to be our biggest fight in a decade, at least.

"And of victory for the boy?" Rune asked, dragging Ulf's ears back into our conversation. Damn him, I thought. *Does the boy have no filter?*

"Fifty-fifty," I answered, not so honestly this time. In fact, no matter my hopes, I could not see us as victors. Simply put, I hoped for victory but had no faith in it.

"That's oddly optimistic of you," Karl replied, his few remaining teeth munching on a piece of hard meat.

"Drake is just being considerate," Ulf said. "He doesn't want to say that my grandson and granddaughter will most likely die tomorrow. At least not in front of me."

"Why do you care?" Karl asked. "As Drake said, you probably have a good dozen of them on Midgard."

"Like you would understand," Ulf replied.

"Of course I do," Karl said, honestly looking hurt. "I'm a grandfather too, you know."

"You are?" Rune asked before I could. My question would have contained just as much surprise.

"Well, I was. I had six living children and fifteen grandchildren by the time I became one of Odin's soldiers."

The looks we exchanged at the table were worth a barrel of Heimdallr's mead. Even Titus, who was something he called a Stoic, which apparently gave him the power to deflect the feeling of being surprised, remained baffled beyond words. I had known Karl the longest, almost three hundred years, and this was the first time I heard about it.

"I'll be damned," Ulf said. "If grumpy old Karl was a grandfather, then it's indeed nothing to think too much about." He rose from the bench, belched, and claimed he had to take a piss.

"What's wrong with him?" Karl asked, his eyes never leaving our comrade as he left the hall.

"He never was a father," I replied. Karl grunted and went back to his cup. He seemed to understand. Or maybe he just didn't care that much.

To be honest, I was tempted to agree with the old man. I had two daughters when I was alive, but I rarely thought about them. It might have been different if they had been boys or had I seen them grow up before finding myself on the wrong side of a shield wall. But as it was, I could not completely sympathize with Ulf. I understood, though, and sometimes, among friends, that is enough.

Snekke gave us a couple of minutes to appreciate the hall's atmosphere before he took Ulf's spot on the bench. He reminded me of a dog kicked away from the fire as he grabbed the pitcher of ale and filled his cup without a word.

"No luck, huh?" Rune said with feigned empathy.

"Mothers," Snekke simply replied, which got Karl to raise his cup in approval.

Bjorn's laughter boomed from somewhere farther down the hall. At least one of my men was enjoying himself. Two, since Sven Cross-Eyes remained absent. It always amazed me that despite his odd gaze, Sven could charm women so easily. Truly, confidence could do miracles.

I was about to let the noise drown me, hoping to catch

another few minutes to get lost in my thoughts. There, I'd be with Muninn and dream of a time when she would know and reciprocate my affection. Whatever time was left until the end of the world, in my mind, I always spent it with my dark little raven.

I conjured the memory of her fingers on my elbow and remembered her laughter. The hall ceased to exist; it was just Muninn and me under Asgard's sky, the green beam of light undulating over our heads. I would see her the next day, and things would be fine.

Then, someone faked a cough to catch my attention, and the hall came alive again. Lif stood by our table, a pitcher of honey-smelling mead in her arms.

"This hall hasn't been so noisy for years," she said as she poured some of it into my cup, as graceful and proud as the Valkyries back in Valhöll. As if to say: *I'm serving you because I want to, not because I'm supposed to.*

"Thank you," I said, lifting my cup.

"It is I who is grateful. Much has changed since you arrived." She went on to fill Karl and Titus's cups but avoided Snekke and Rune. The first, for what he had done with her mother, and the second, just because she did not like him.

"Let's hope this change will last," I said.

"You will win tomorrow. And when you return, I will have more of this for you," she said, shaking the now nearempty pitcher.

"If you do not mind," Karl said. "One of our comrades is outside for some fresh air, and his cup was empty." His face harbored more wrinkles than I had ever noticed, and it took me a couple of heartbeats to realize it was because Karl was genuinely smiling.

"The archer with the sad eyes?"

"That's the one," Karl replied with a wink.

"All right, I will bring him some," Lif said before padding to the door.

I did not leave Karl's eyes as he checked the girl on her way out, and I could easily see the grandpa in him. The mask fell the second she was out the door.

"Don't tell him it came from me," Karl said.

"I don't think he would believe us," I replied.

"So you *do* have a heart," Rune said, earning him an elbow in the ribs.

"Thorstein!" I heard someone call. "Thorstein!"

Titus snapped his fingers in my face to remind me I was Thorstein. Lifting my head, I saw young Hakon hailing me from his high seat, a horn in his hand and an unmistakable grin on his face. His cheeks gleamed from too many cups of mead, which was not that many at his age.

"Thorstein," he called again. "Your man here tells me that no one on Midgard is to be feared more than your band." Bjorn stood at the bottom of Hakon's dais, surrounded by a large group of warriors. The room got suddenly silent, as if waiting for my answer.

"Bjorn is right," I said, loud and clear. "You've never met another group of warriors like mine." I tried to sound as boastful as I could. Warriors respond better to arrogance than to timidity. "No one is more worthy of fear than the Wolves of Asgard," I said the last with even more strength, and, on cue, my men howled like actual wolves.

"Never heard of them," a man said, which got several others to laugh.

"Another crew who thinks themselves like the mighty Jötunn Slayers," someone else added.

"We piss on the Jötunn Slayers," Karl barked, which was funny to us because we had indeed pissed on some of them.

The Jötunn Slayers had been a large group of mercenaries with a blotted reputation and not one pair of balls between them. Odin had even sent us after them, their fame having traveled as far as Asgard. The All-Father's disappointment was great when we told him how they had turned their back on the first occasion.

"No, Lord Hakon," I said. "I guarantee you've never met better men than mine."

"Well," Hakon said, using someone's arm as he climbed down from his dais, "I've seen you fight, and I've seen Eigil fight—may he be sharing mead with the gods as we speak now." *You have no idea how right you are*, I told myself. "But I have never heard of the Wolves of Asgard. Maybe you could share some tells of your exploits?"

It was actually an excellent idea. I shifted to Snekke. His wolfish smile told me he was of the same mind. He emptied his cup and slammed it on the table.

"You ask about the Wolves, my lord," he said. His voice grew in strength and clarity, as if each pair of eyes staring at me made him an inch taller. "A fair question. One we've heard before. Last we did was, if I recall, in King Ingjald's great hall minutes before it burned. His last words were—"

"Cursed be the Wolves!" we yelled with him.

"The same words were heard from Ivar's lips as his boat in the river tipped. The old ring-giver, mad with fear, looked us in the eyes and said—"

"Cursed be the Wolves!"

"One summer night, Jarl Jorund the Tall meant to visit his fair lady, only to find her already busy. 'Who are you?' he asked, *seax* in hand, blood in his eyes. And though of our spears, we only wielded the poles, we faced him, and he said—"

"Cursed be the Wolves!"

The hall roared with laughter, even Hakon. Snekke climbed down the bench in a theatrical leap, snatched a horn of ale from an old warrior, and regally walked toward the jarl.

"From Ladoga to Frisia, we've fought. From Helheim to Asgard, our fame reaches. Widows curse us, defeated jarls as well, but for as many men who wish us dead, the same number revere our name."

"So do their wives," Bjorn said.

The following laughter gave Snekke a few seconds to drink, and I to marvel once again at how fast he could enthrall a room full of warriors.

"Shield-breakers, Men-shamers, Worm-feeders, we've heard them all, the names our foes give us. Or so we assume, for it is hard to tell what they say when they run the other way," Snekke said the last with a mocking wave of the hand at imaginary men fleeing from him, and once again, men cheered. Even sullen Hild smiled. Maybe Snekke was not out of luck after all.

"But to the men sharing our wall," he said after a short break, during which the room got quiet again. "I say: drink, eat, and laugh tonight, for tomorrow, you either dine in Valhöll or in this hall. Fame is upon you, silver even more. But none of this is worth more than knowing that you've fought alongside Asgard's Wolves!"

My men and I howled again, and it was a chilling sound. It was the sound of coming death and a cry of pride. We howled until our lungs emptied and many a man joined us while others cheered, enjoying this well-practiced show. Snekke received his share of pats on the back, but his eyes remained on Hild. We, too, at our table, were given more attention than before. Our cups seemed to fill themselves, our plates as well, and even Rune was greeted by seasoned warriors as if he were Thor himself.

Hakon regained his seat, but not before banging cups with Bjorn and Snekke. A knot in my bowels formed as I looked at the young jarl. He was so young, I noticed, so very young. His place was not on the field of battle, and yet he had to lead men on it. Had it been another mission, this would not have given me any second thoughts, but I couldn't help worrying about Ulf's grandson. Surrounded by so many grizzled warriors, the contrast was too great.

Seeing all those old fighters, I suddenly realized what had been missing: Halfdan. Hakon's champion was nowhere to be seen in the hall, and though it is not uncommon for men to choose a good night of sleep before a fight, I doubted Halfdan was one of those. I thought about the last time I saw him. It had been a couple of hours ago. He was putting an edge on his axe then, nothing unusual, but there had been something odd in his eye as we nodded to each other.

I thought about asking some of his men if his absence was normal but stopped myself from ruining the mood and possibly insulting a man respected in Lagardalr. *What harm could he do in such a short time, after all?* I asked myself when another man slapped my back as if we were long-lost brothers.

How much I would regret not having done anything about this gnawing feeling. If I had listened to my instinct, all my men would have made it back to Asgard, and Lagardalr would be more than ashes.

9

For the first time in ages, I had pleasant dreams. A soothing wind caressed my cheeks as I savored the sight of a grass-covered plain bathed in the light of a gentle sun peering between perfect clouds. I was lying on the grass, oblivious to any thought of war. I wasn't alone in this dream. There was a woman. I do not believe it was Muninn, but I cannot say it wasn't her either.

It was just a woman, and her presence was like balm to my tormented spirit. It was boring, and it was amazing. Even there, I felt it was time to wake up soon. I was lucid, counting the blades of wind combing the hills in waves, refusing to let go of this perfect picture. War awaited me on the other side. I needed this a little longer.

Someone tripped over my foot and woke me in the blink of an eye.

"Fuck, I'm sorry, Drake, got to take a shit," Bjorn said as he stepped over my legs, his still shaky from the night. We had slept in the barn even though most of the guests slept in the hall. It was still dark, though already a faint light could be guessed in the sky. I had yet to fully emerge and thought of returning to my perfect, boring dream. My eyes shut by themselves, and I was already falling into the comfort of slumber.

"Drake!" Bjorn called, his voice like a horn of war.

I sat up before I knew it.

"Fuck," I said. It had to be mighty important for Bjorn to yell and wake me up twice. He stood by the lake, one hand working on his belt, the other pointed at a ghostly orange light growing behind a hill east of the village. Not growing, no, it was moving.

"What is it?" Titus asked, one eye still closed.

"Torches," I answered, realizing what they were as I spoke. A lot of them, coming straight from the direction of Hvitiseid.

"They'll be here soon," Bjorn said. I gave us twenty minutes at best.

"Wake up the others," I ordered Titus. "Finish what you were doing and get ready," I told Bjorn, who simply grunted. I shook the remainder of sleep away in the few steps separating me from Hakon's hall.

The door opened just before I reached it, and a scruffy middle-aged man stepped out of it with haggard eyes. I shouldered him away and ignored his curse. The smell of vomit flooded my senses as soon as I passed the door, making my eyes tear up. The floor and the tables were littered with sleeping men. They would sober up pretty fast.

"War!" I yelled. "War is here! Wake up, you goat-fuckers!"

It did the trick, though I had to repeat myself. Some of them jumped to their feet and understood immediately, while others could not be bothered to do more than roll over and fart.

"What is it?" Hakon asked as he surfaced from the back room, his hair a crown-looking mess.

"Bove's here," I said. Now that achieved to stir the room to activity.

Men rushed to their weapons, shoes, and shields. Hakon looked at me with big eyes full of his old self, paralyzed by what he had heard. "You need to get ready," I told him, dropping my hand like a hammer on his shoulder to snap him out of it. He nodded and went back to his room.

"Where to?" someone asked as he laced the side of his leather jerkin above a thick padded gambeson.

"East," I replied. "Gather with my men by the palisade."

This was bad. This was fucking terrible. Waking up to the horns of war saps the morale and sucks bravery right from the belly. A sneak attack would have been worse, but not by much. *What was Bove doing here this morning?*

Even if I had all those men ready for the fight, we would never have made it to the closest battlefield in time. It would have to take place here, by the village. At least it would make the few men from Lagardalr fight with more vigor, knowing that their women and children stood behind.

I did not ask if anyone had seen Halfdan, for I was certain I knew already where to find him and did not want to tarnish whatever hope those men still nurtured. Instead, I made a joke about Bove making it easier for us. It did not get a significant response. I could do nothing more here and decided to check my men.

"What's the plan?" Einar asked as soon as I stepped out of the hall, startling me in the process.

"You stay here," I told him, pointing where he stood. "If any of them looks like they're going the other way, you kick them toward us." To my dismay, I realized the night had fled in the short time I'd spent in the hall. Time always chooses the worst moments to speed up. I preferred to fight at dawn, but not like that. I was already out of breath, and that was just from waking up.

Thirty men had gathered in front of the short palisade, just where the floor was covered in grass and not mud as the rest of the village. Among them were all my men, except for Einar, who would be hard at work keeping the cowards from fleeing.

"What's the plan?" Rune asked as he handed me my shield and helmet. I gripped the first and put on the second.

"The plan?" Karl scoffed. "We fucking kill as many as we can, that's the plan."

"Karl's right," I said, and I don't know which of the two was more surprised. "No time for grand plans and refined strategies. We fight like we've never fought before and take as many of them as we can."

"What about the kids?" Ulf asked, driving a blade into my stomach with his pitiful stare. He knew what I meant with my last order; we would lose. We had already lost.

"I am sorry," I said, using whatever patience I had in me. "You have more of them on Midgard; be sure of it."

"Drake," he pleaded.

"Ulf, you want to save them? Get your fucking bow and stick as many of the ugly bastards as possible, all right? Now, all of you, eat your nails."

Ulf did not like my answer, and I waited until he swallowed his nail before I let him go from my sight. I had gotten mine back the previous afternoon and had spent a considerable amount of time cleaning it. Even then, its consumption was accompanied by some gagging.

Hakon then joined the mass of men, his short frame walking nervously between two large warriors carrying solid shields. The boy in him had disappeared again, and he now looked the part, eyes breathing a fire as hot as Fafnir's.

"Where?" was all he asked me.

"Behind this hill. They should show themselves in five minutes."

For once, I had been optimistic. They appeared from the woods on the next hill a few minutes later. Our ranks started grumbling as one. If we stayed put, we had a very slight height on them, not enough to gain a proper advantage, but enough to see them clearly.

"One hundred and eighty, give or take," Titus said as I was getting to one fifty. Less than expected, which wasn't surprising. Mercenaries tend to disappear between the feast and the fight.

"Still more than us," Karl grumbled.

Not even half of our men stood with us; with those too drunk to care, we would be lucky if we got to one hundred. The realization that we would gather maybe sixty warriors for Valhöll hit me for a second, and the Drake in me sighed at what the All-Father would consider a failure.

Bove's men stopped a good hundred paces from us, their heap of bodies slowly forming a shield wall three men deep. Some of them left the ranks for the wood, working on their belts. It's funny what a man might consider a priority at times like this. For many, just like those men running for the woods, it was as much a question of pressing need as it was of dignity. They knew they might die soon, but they did not want to soil themselves in the process.

I took a good look at the back of my hand, where Tyr had traced his rune, and sent a prayer that whatever he did would help in the coming trial.

Bove appeared through the ranks of his forming shield wall, and even from this distance, I saw the man for what he was: a brute. He was neither tall nor short, but his frame was impressive. He handed his shield to the man on the left and stomped toward us, his massive axe in the other hand. Another man walked with him. Halfdan.

The traitor could not possibly have gone all the way to Hvitiseid and back with an army in less than a night. Bove and him would have been working together for some time and this was the fruition of their plan. Halfdan's absence should have tipped me off more than it did. I would have seen it coming if I had not spent so much time worrying about Ulf's progeny and the seidr-filled cave, and I could have prepared the men for what was about to happen instead of letting the enemy fall on our sleepy heads.

Hakon walked past me and nodded for me to accompany him. The men facing us would grow more confident at the sight of Hakon meeting their jarl. If life had given the boy another four or five years, he would have been capable of great things.

"What should I do?" Hakon asked, his voice betraying the fear growing in him.

"Don't waver," I replied. "He will stare you down, but no matter what, do not break contact. This is the first engagement of the battle, understood?"

Hakon nodded and swallowed hard.

If I had been impressed by Bove earlier, I was downright apprehensive now. He was bald as an egg, which made his red and gray beard appear all the more savage. His eyes were green, like the mossy water of a swamp. His shoulders were powerful, and they had to be to wield that barbaric axe of his. It was so thick that I doubted it had any edge. The torc around his neck was made of good twisted silver, and the beads in his beard were of gold.

But the worst was his aura. After hundreds of battles, I

had developed enough of a sixth sense to recognize a great fighter, and Bove was one. In Valhöll, he would be a second or third square fighter without a doubt, but on Midgard, he was the worst kind of man to face in the shield wall.

Bove smiled when we came to face him, flashing two rows of well-maintained teeth. "Hakon, good morning," he said. His voice took its roots deep in his barrel of a belly and carried the diction of an educated man.

"Bove, thank you for making it easy for us," Hakon replied, using my previous words. Bove had not expected this kind of reaction.

"I was just eager to sit in my new hall," Bove said, scratching his beard.

"You will sit in a new hall, all right," Hakon replied. "Valhöll, if you're lucky. Though I would bet on Sessrúmnir. That's the one for women, right?" The question was meant for me, and I did not even try to suppress a chuckle. Hakon was no warrior, but he spoke like one.

"That's right, and for men with particular tastes," I said.

"Ha," Bove boomed. "You are much more of a man than I've been told."

Halfdan blushed at those words yet had the decency to remain silent.

"You, on the other hand," I said to Halfdan, "will go nowhere but Helheim, and your body will become a target practice for your jarl." I don't know why I said that.

Halfdan had merely done what he had thought smart. He had been a warrior of Olaf, not Hakon. Oaths are important to us Norsemen, but sometimes not as much as the opportunity to rise in the world. His face reddened when my words hit him and even more so when Hakon spat at his feet. I saw his hand move to the handle of his axe, but that's when Bove chose to end the charade.

"All right, there will be enough of that in a minute. You must be this Thorstein I've heard about."

"I am."

"Nice trick to send your men to my hall," he said, sounding genuinely appreciative. "I will look for you in the wall, and I expect you will help me today."

"Help you?" I asked.

"Of course. Look at all the men I brought," he said, gesturing to the thick wall behind him. "For any of them you take down, I will keep a good amount of silver in my hoard."

"Oh, don't you worry about your hoard then. It will remain intact, though not for you to enjoy."

"What do you want?" Hakon asked, a bit too fast for my taste.

There was always a pretense of negotiation before a battle. A game to show our opponent a way out and an excuse for later tales. Hakon had broken this tacit rule of engagement. Bove did what I had warned Hakon and stared at the boy. I did not look at Hakon, which would have distracted him, but I prayed for him to fight Bove's stare. He did, and he did well, for a time. Bove's smirk told me when Hakon had broken.

"What I want is your mine and your people," Bove replied. "I will need your head, too." He waited for Hakon to reply, but the boy did not, so he continued. "Your sister will be well taken care of." I shivered at those words. "And your mother will be married again, to Lagardalr's new chieftain," Bove said the last with a slap on Halfdan's back, and I swear I saw shame on the old man's face.

"She would cut your balls off," Hakon replied, and I was in complete agreement that she would.

"I would treat her well," Halfdan said. He said *would*, not *will*. Bove might be confident in his victory, but not all his men were.

"If you accept my terms," Bove said to bring the conversation back on topic, "there will be no bloodshed today." Hakon pretended to think on it, adopting a thoughtful pose that reminded me of his grandfather.

"I'm sorry, but I have to refuse," he said, looking everything but sorry. "It conflicts too much with what I want."

"And what is that?" Bove asked.

"Revenge for Olaf."

Bove's sigh was deep and long. For a second, he looked tired. "I know you won't believe me, seeing how I came all the way here with a war band and what we plan to do to your women, but I swear on my honor, Olaf's death had nothing to do with me."

Even if I had not thought beforehand that it was true, I would have been prone to believe him. Hakon was not so inclined.

"What honor?" Hakon asked, his nose wrinkled like a snarling dog.

"Boy," Bove said, and I knew then that we had lost the exchange. "Talk to me about honor after you grow a beard. Not that you'll have the opportunity to." Hakon was about to say something, but at this point, I felt like his next words would harm us more than them, so I interrupted him.

"Each of my men carries a purse of hacked silver," I said. "Tell that to your boys; that will make them fight like real men." Bove looked at me with an eye almost shut, studying me as if I was half-mad.

"We know some of them; how do we recognize the others?" he asked.

"They're the ones who will be smiling over a heap of bodies," I answered, and finally, I saw some doubt on Bove's face, just a twitch of the lips. We were no typical band of mercenaries, and he now knew it.

"I will tell them and add some from my own coffers."

Good, I thought, at least they will fight bravely.

This was as far as it would go, and from an unspoken signal, the four of us broke apart. Men still poured from the village to our shield wall. I should have tried to make the parley last longer.

"I'm sorry," Hakon said.

"Don't be. You spoke well."

I was talking to a dead man, and it saddened me because the chances that a Valkyrie would pick him were slim. I glanced toward the woods, where Muninn must have been watching, but of course, did not see her.

"Stay with Ulf," I said. "Stand tall, shoot as many as you can, and praise your men. Never stop raising their spirit." I thought he would refuse and claim his rightful place in the wall, but he simply nodded.

Despite their reputation, archers have one of the most dangerous spots. They have to stand on something to have enough height for their shots, at least if they intend to aim, and thus make great targets for the enemy's spears. Ulf was a master at shooting and ducking, but I doubted Hakon would do as well.

Seeing his face as we regained our shield wall, I clapped him on the back and roared with a big, fake laugh. Hakon was completely taken aback by my gesture.

"You should have seen their faces," I said loud enough for all to hear. "They thought they were meeting a boy but left holding their asses. By Thor's hairy balls, Hakon might be young, but he has enough imagination to make Odin blush." I saw some smiles through the beards of scared warriors facing me and decided to push a bit farther. "If he does everything he told them, not even the crows will want to eat what's left of them." Some of them laughed this time, a good sign.

"What did you tell them?" one warrior asked.

"I told them we'll offer their balls to the fishes of the lake and feed the rest to our pigs," Hakon claimed, getting more cheers. "As for their women and their silver, well, I'll only tell those of you who survive, but there will be plenty of both." A hundred men raised their blades and cheered, showing a united front to our foes.

This cheer, I thought, would resonate all the way to Asgard, and the Valkyries would have no choice but to notice us now. Bove was doing more or less the same with his men, but his task was a lot easier. I curled a finger at my men, and they formed a circle around me. Einar was there as well now.

"We will take the brunt of the attack," I said, thinking of how I had goaded Bove. "If one of you kills that tree-humper Halfdan, I give him my house for one night. Two, if he dies pissing himself." Their grins and chuckles were things of beauty.

My Wolves, most of them, had no fear crippling them. Some thought they would die anyway, the others thought they would make a difference, and all knew they would dine in Valhöll tonight.

"How do you see it?" Titus asked.

"We have two lines where they have three," I replied. "Cracking that nut will be a bitch and a half, but I didn't see archers among them."

"They wear leather," Karl observed. "Only a handful of mail shirts among them."

"And they seem to gather in crews," Titus said. "There won't be much unity. Not like on our side."

"Bjorn on the front line, at the center," I ordered. "Einar and Rune left and right of him, Sven and Snekke behind them. Titus on the far left, I take the right end. Karl, you're behind me. Ulf, you stay with Hakon and shoot the bastards who try to flank us." I said all of it in a straight line and nodded to myself in the end.

Fighting near Bjorn was a tricky business. He left many gaps and needed one of us to constantly pull him back. Einar would do it this time since he did not need to take care of his son. Rune was more of a gamble, but at this point, all I could do was trust him to manage by himself. Titus would handle the defensive side, the left tip of the wall, by himself, and I trusted his cold blood to manage such a task. Karl would help me with the most dangerous part of the wall, the right, where there was no shield to protect my flank.

"See you soon, brothers," I said as the circle split. "Ulf, if the situation gets desperate," I told him, whispering to make sure no one else heard, "take care of Lif."

He said nothing, but he got my point.

I laced the thong of my helmet under my chin, feeling the comforting pain of its rim on the back of my neck. At the back of our line, Ulf and Hakon climbed on two barrels and took a similar side stance. The resemblance could not have been more striking. I saw a man drop another quiver full of arrows between the two archers' feet. No one else was coming from the village.

A horn blew from the enemy's ranks, making my belly tense. A man stepped out of their ranks, a black and red shield dangling in one hand and a broad axe in the other. He wore no other armor than a bear pelt draped over his shoulders. I knew what he was, but the way he slapped himself and bellowed like an animal confirmed it. A berserker, challenging us to a one-on-one. I thanked the gods. This would prove helpful, for we had two berserker killers among us, and the morale of our shield wall would increase soon.

"Cross-Eyes!" I called from the depths of my lungs.

"Ha," Karl coughed behind me. "You want to shame them."

He was right. I did not just want a victory; I wanted to shame the enemy. Bjorn would have been just as good a choice, but Sven Cross-Eyes was small and thin. His victory would be all the more resounding.

Sven came out of our ranks, spear bouncing over his shoulder. He strolled to the berserker as if this was just another practice bout, and his foe roared with rage.

I've always hated berserkers. They were less than reliable once they summoned the beast, as dangerous to their own as to their opponents. And that's if they could summon it. Sometimes, they pushed themselves for hours before anything happened, especially if they did not have the needed mushrooms or leaves. This one, obviously, had none of those issues, and I thought he would charge Cross-Eyes before my warrior reached the center of the field.

The contrast was so great between the two fighters that for a second, I worried I had made a mistake. The next moment told me I had not. Cross-Eyes said something to that beast, and I guess it might have involved his mother, for he bellowed like a wounded bear and threw his shield at my Wolf.

Cross-Eyes ducked under the shield and rolled to the side just as the axe came down on him. He sliced the tip of his spear at his opponent's thigh as he recovered his balance and was up on his feet before the berserker could roar in pain. It did not look like a deep wound, but it stung the man's pride.

Sven then hopped on the spot, one foot after the other at first, then two feet together. His grip on the spear loosened a bit, and he let it slide down until he caught it from the very end of the pole. Then he did something I had never managed to parry and which I found particularly annoying. He waved the spear up and down with his arm extended, with a counter timing to his jumping.

From where I stood, it did not look much, but for the man facing him, the effect was devastating. You just could not discern if the spear or the man was going up or down, while the way he held the spear at arm's length gave him a far greater reach than usual. For the berserker, the spearhead must have looked like the head of a snake about to strike. After a brief hesitation, the berserker decided he did not care about Sven's tactic and charged.

That was exactly what Cross-Eyes expected. In one smooth motion of the wrist, the spear darted forward, faster than an arrow, and sliced the man's face right under his left eye. He still pressed the attack and lunged his axe as if it were a sword, but the attack came short by a good arm's length.

Sven skipped back and cut at the berserker's hand in the same movement. The axe fell to the ground, its owner having released it to grab his bloody fingers. Another shallow wound, but the berserker now realized the direness of his situation. Cross-Eyes had fought dozens of men like him, while he had never met any like Cross-Eyes.

The crowd's silence was deafening.

"He should finish it," Karl said, and I agreed, but I knew how much Cross-Eyes enjoyed those moments. And the bigger his opponent, the more pleasure he took from shaming them. Sven let the spearhead drop on the ground when the berserker took his axe back. His arm must have been killing him after bobbing the pole like this for a minute.

But this, too, was a feint, and when the berserker charged once more, the spear came up in the blink of an eye. Sven's foe impaled himself on the spear, right at the left shoulder, and while the men on our wall cheered, I knew this was bad news. Sven's style relied on movement and cuts, not on stabbing. He meant to retrieve the spear, but the berserker grasped the pole, and in terms of brute strength, there was no comparison between the two.

"Let it go, you moron," Karl grumbled as if talking to himself.

This was another reason I have always hated berserkers; they feel no pain, or at least it doesn't bother them. This one had half a spearhead stuck in the shoulder, yet it barely slowed him down. He removed it and pulled the pole in one short and mighty yank.

Sven, refusing to let go of his weapon, was immediately dragged toward the berserker and found himself trapped in a bear hug. He screamed as the berserker crushed him against his chest. It lasted for five or six heartbeats, and then it was the berserker's turn to scream in pain.

I first thought that Cross-Eyes had head-butted him, but what he had done was far worse. They were immobile, Sven's face against the berserkers, the two of them chest to chest like lovers, and I did not understand what was happening. When Cross-Eyes's head rocked back, the bottom of his face was covered in blood, and he spat something.

"He bit his ear off," Karl said with a faint tremor of amused horror in his voice.

People assumed that Cross-Eyes was a polished fighter relying on technique and speed. They were wrong. Sven was a fucking animal.

To his opponent's credit, he did not let go, even after his ear had been crudely torn from his head. He should have let go; his end would have been quicker. Cross-Eyes brought his teeth back on his target, this time aiming at the neck. He pulled his arms from the bear hug, and seeing those two spider-like limbs savaging the berserker's face brought the taste of bile to my mouth.

Sven's head shook while his teeth remained in the beast's throat, and the shrieks went from painful to pitiful. Sven finally let go and spat a piece of flesh. Blood gushed from the man's neck for a few heartbeats. Besides the big warrior's plaintive wail, the battlefield got quiet. The berserker dropped to his knees, letting Cross-Eyes stand on his feet.

He looked down at his opponent and gave him a nod of recognition. Then he jammed his hand inside the neck wound and yanked on whatever he grabbed there, spreading gore in a wide arc when he pulled it out.

A man threw up somewhere down our line. Maybe sending Cross-Eyes hadn't been my smartest idea. I am not sure how many of our men still had a fight in them at this very moment. At least the enemy must have felt the same.

Sven returned to us, teeth flashing bright in the middle of so much red. No matter what happened next, this must have caught the Valkyries' attention. A man clapped his axe against his shield as my berserker-killer grabbed a skin of water from Rune, and the rhythm spread in our wall.

Cross-Eyes raised his hand. "If that's their best, you have nothing to worry about," he said. The ensuing laughter was nervous, I could tell. Sven avoided my gaze as he took his place back in the wall, for which I was grateful because I did not know if I should have congratulated or cursed him.

"I guess they got the message," Karl said, nodding toward the shield wall across the field. They moved as one man, slowly sweeping the plain in an approximate line of shields bearing many colors.

We braced ourselves; shields clapped as they overlapped. None went over mine, for I was the last of the line.

The warrior on my left was a solid man with the arms of a farmer. He wore no helmet, an old padded tunic, and a worn-out leather jerkin that wouldn't protect him against a spoon. His wood-chopping axe had seen better days, but he had kept a good edge on it. And more importantly, he was steady in his breathing. He'd seen other battles and would perform well, even near the end of the line. He noticed me measuring him and offered a half-toothless grin. This was the kind of man I expected to meet again on the other side of the Bifröst.

Bove's shield wall walked over their dead champion. Our opponents appeared more in detail now. Their far left in front of me was made of men carrying yellow shields with some kind of red mark like the scratch of a bear in the middle. All of them wore good metallic helmets, and the one closing their line was covered in arm rings.

Bove would have put his most solid crew of mercenaries at this spot and I thanked him in my mind for the honor. I had not noticed, but the battle lust was already in me, and I found myself craving the next moments. I was usually a slow starter; the frenzy would take me after a man had swung an axe at me or after I had claimed a life, but not this time.

Maybe it was the nature of the man we fought for, maybe it was my loathing of Bove and Halfdan, or maybe

Cross-Eyes had put me in the right spirit. Whatever the cause, I was ready and about to do what I did best.

"Thor, make me strong," the farmer on my left whispered. "Odin, watch me."

The handle of my sword felt rough in my hand. I made small circles with it to test its balance, which was as good as I could expect. My shield, white with a snarling red wolf painted around the boss, was already tiring me, but it would get much worse.

Wedge waited against my lower back, ready to run havoc when the fighting turned to an entangled mess of pressing bodies, where it would be more useful than a long sword or a clumsy axe. I did not expect to die today, or at least not before the fight was lost. Our enemy moved from a walk to a trot, and in the last ten steps, they rushed with a great bellow.

"Brace yourself!" someone shouted in our line.

The last thing I heard before the two walls crashed was an arrow passing close to my head. It buried itself in the eye of the warrior backing my most direct foe. I did not hear him scream.

The warrior facing me, a man well in his forties, made two big, round eyes when the arrow barely missed him. This one second of stupor was all I needed. I feigned a vertical slash. As expected, he raised his shield, leaving his legs unprotected. Using my many years of experience, I reversed my slash to a thrust, and the tip of my sword stabbed his thigh in the next second. His scream was muffled by the tumult of battle, but I guessed his pain as I twisted my blade to make sure I severed the big artery. He let go of his axe to grab his wound, a big mistake, even though he was done for, anyway.

Karl's spear flew by my cheek and ended the man's

suffering, burying itself in his mouth. Another man took his place and met me with a fast spear lunge. The attack had been feeble. This man was not ready. Ten heartbeats ago, he was in the third line, praying for the men in front to end the battle before he had to replace one of them, and suddenly he faced me. I did not envy him.

He was younger than my first kill, but he was not stupid. He planted his spear in my shield and then let it go, almost making me lose my grip with the sudden added weight. The spearman used this moment to pick up his fallen comrade's shield and axe and still managed to parry Karl's blade. It was done with little grace and a fair amount of luck, but it worked.

More men took the empty spot behind him. Those men knew their business. Now, I faced another wall of three men. I hammered my sword again, and this time, it was no feint. My opponent blocked it with his shield, but my blade bit into the rim, and I gave him a taste of his medicine by letting it go. The extra weight made him drop his shield, just a little, but enough for my most experienced warrior to thrust his weapon. Karl's aim was deadly in this attack, and our opponent only had time for half a gasp before the spear pierced his brain through the eye.

I drew Wedge while he fell on his knees, dragging Karl's spear with him.

"Odin's balls," Karl cursed when he lost his weapon.

The farmer grunted; blood gushed from a neck wound threatening to blind me. He covered it with his shield hand, but his face was paling fast. He was a goner.

"Karl, on my left," I barked. The farmer fell to his knees, then on his face. Karl was on top of him to prevent a breach in the wall. He had grabbed a shield and his long knife, and expertly used both to keep the two men in front of me at bay.

We had done well in the first moments of the battle, but our advantage was vanishing fast. My two opponents were good, and I had no one at my back now. Worse, now that I had thinned their ranks, our archers would target a bigger group. I was truly alone here.

My direct opponent shouted with each of his blows, but such was the chaos that I couldn't hear him at all. He used his axe with the apparent purpose of hacking my shield to pieces. I thought he might succeed, for the planks were giving away, only staying together because of the metallic rim and boss.

But just after he blocked a stab, he used the barb of his axe to pull my shield down. It was a neat trick we often practiced on Asgard. If the warrior at his back wasn't stupid, he would time his next lunge just as my shield left my face open. I counted on it.

Finding the exact moment the spear would come, I crouched and let it pass a mere inch above my head. I let go of my useless shield, dropped my knife, then caught the second-rank enemy's spear pole with both hands and pulled on it with all my strength.

Had the spearman been smart and fast enough, he would have let me have it, and I would have been a dead man, having no shield and the wrong end of a spear in my hands. But he was neither smart nor fast enough, and I was gratified with resistance at my yank. He bumped into the man between us, and both landed flat at my feet.

I don't know why, but the spearman didn't move once on the ground. Maybe he had knocked himself on the head. I kicked the other one in the face as he looked up at me, and I knelt to grab my long knife, now lying in a mix of spongy earth and blood.

It took me a couple of breaths to find it, but when I did, I wasted no time and buried it deep in the first man's exposed chin. It's funny how I had not heard him yell earlier on but could now clearly distinguish the gurgling blood in his mouth. I think it was this sound that made me lose my rage and made me feel suddenly exhausted.

If I hadn't been an Einheri, I would have slit the last one's throat, but this would have given him a dishonorable death. Instead, I left him to regain consciousness and resume the fight or wait for another battle in the future.

"Taking a rest already?" Karl said angrily.

I looked up, ready to curse him, but the blood trickling from his mouth told me this wasn't the time for that. His tunic was turning red under the armpit, and I guessed his lung had been stabbed. The pain must have been excruciating.

I picked up one of the yellow and red shields near me, and that's when I realized that five men lay at my feet. It could not have been more than a minute since the fight began, but already death surrounded me. The man behind Karl's opponent noticed me as I was about to stand, and his spear nearly ended me. It took a great deal of strength for me to raise my new shield in time to stop his strike.

The man who should have been guarding Karl's back was on his ass, hands clutching his belly. I had no clue how a second-row fighter could have gotten hit in the belly, but I left him to his whimpering and took his place, ready to relieve my comrade. It takes skills and experience to trade places with a man in the front row.

I tapped twice on Karl's shoulder to let him know I was ready and saw his head nod. The man in front of him hammered his axe down. Karl blocked it, then it was his turn to attack. He gave a mighty push with his shield to gain some space, then stepped to the right so I could take his spot. I did so with a vicious kick aimed at my foe's shield as if I meant to break a door. He fell on his ass, but the man behind managed to stay on his feet.

Karl coughed painfully. He wouldn't be with us much longer.

A sudden shout of victory came from the center of the wall, far on my left, and I shifted my attention just long enough to see Einar's head on a pole.

"Fuck," I said, fighting for my breath.

My heart froze for a beat. Einar had not been there when I ordered my men to swallow their nails. He'd been making sure none of the warriors fled the village before the fight, and for the life of me, I could not remember him taking the nail later on. Einar had died a mortal. Already, I saw myself announcing to Eigil that his father would not be coming back this time.

Losing your attention was the best way to get yourself killed. However, we were reaching that moment where men stopped trying as hard and spent most of their effort on keeping the pressure and waiting for someone to commit a life-ending mistake. The two walls were shields against shields, tired men on both sides. Someone would slip or lose his grip, and the warrior in front would use the opportunity. The madness would rekindle itself for as long as the breach needed to be exploited or plugged.

Sometimes, it would be enough to tip the battle, sometimes not, but it would never last long. The man who had not fallen from my kick saw this opportunity in my dumbfounded look and decided to shorten our wall with my death. The tip of his spear appeared as big as a fist, and I only had time to curse.

It stopped a finger length from my face. An arrow had grazed my earlobe and ended its course in my opponent's throat. The man fingered the shaft with a surprised look, and when he meant to speak, nothing came out. I think he meant to ask me for help.

I looked back to Ulf, sure that my archer had saved my life once again, but young Hakon had his eyes on me and his bow empty. We nodded at the same time, and he took another arrow from his quiver, which still contained a good number of feathers. No doubt he had killed more men, for he looked very natural on his barrel.

Grandfather and grandson were reaping death, and they looked formidable. Ulf would love to see this scene from my spot. And just then, in front of my eyes, Hakon vanished. He went from the barrel to nowhere in the blink of an eye.

His shriek, high-pitched and strident, sucked the air out of me. I understood what had happened before Ulf did and rushed to the spot where Hakon had landed, a spear pole jutting from his belly. My friend jumped from his barrel, and we both knelt to the wriggling shape of the boy.

"Hakon!" Ulf screamed, his hands shaking.

I had given no thought to the man I had kicked earlier and whether I had condemned the one on my left by running from my spot. All I could focus on was the paling face of the young jarl as pain dug wrinkles worthy of an old man on his face.

"No, no, no, no," Ulf said, panicking.

I don't know what Hakon was trying to say, for the sounds coming out of his mouth made no sense. From experience, he was either cursing the gods or calling for his mother.

"Take him to the hall," I told Ulf, shaking him by the shoulder. His eyes were livid, but he nodded and lifted the boy under the legs and neck. Hakon whimpered like a wounded dog when taken off the ground.

The clatter of metal on wood increased again, but even if Heimdallr had been blowing his horn by my ear, I would not have been able to take my eyes from Ulf as he trodded back to Lagardalr's great hall. His steps were short and low to avoid worsening the wound, but seeing how the spear pole waved, Hakon must have been in agony. Ulf moved slightly to the left to avoid a body lying on the ground. It was Karl's.

Rarely had I felt the jaws of defeat about to snap on us more keenly than at this moment, and though it would usually spark my fire, on that day, it extinguished it.

Climbing on the barrel Ulf had been using, I immediately saw that it was as bad as I had foreseen. The two shield walls were barely moving. Most men kept their heads low behind their shields, but while ours was a one-man line, Bove's still boasted two rows in most places. He carried the pole mounted with Einar's head, pacing back and forth and shaking it up and down for us to see.

Bove saw me and crooked his head to drink the blood pouring from Einar's neck. He stepped over many bodies on his morbid walk, especially at the center, where Bjorn was still swinging his axe as if chopping wood on a beautiful spring morning. By my estimation, we had given more than we had taken, but Bove still held the advantage and was now waving his men to the sides of our wall. We were about to be surrounded. It was time to retreat.

"To the hall," I yelled. "Step back to the hall."

A couple of men made the mistake of running back instead of moving with the line, and one of them received a spear between the shoulder blades for his haste. The rest slowly took the first step backward, shields still connected. I came down from the barrel and took my spot back at the far right just in time to prevent the man I had unwillingly left in charge from being overrun.

Picking up the shield of a dead man from our side, I made the connection just as my comrade blocked yet another axe blow and, with perfect timing, punched my shield in the axeman's face before he could register my presence. It was not a mortal wound, but would make him hesitant.

Fatigue was plain to see on our opponent's faces, and despite having the advantage, they did not press much as we stepped back into Lagardalr. I saw the first house on my right and remembered another should be fairly close on the left. For a second, I thought of making a stand there, using the two buildings to protect our flanks.

Had it been another mission, this is what I would have done. We would still lose, but we would take more of the enemy beforehand. I dismissed the idea and let the men walk back. Another plan was taking root in my mind, and though it may have been the madness of the fight speaking, I knew this was our last chance to satisfy Odin and take Bove down. At this particular moment, the latter was my priority.

"Snekke!" I called.

"What?" he asked, his voice still strong.

"Take Karl back to the hall," I said. Two seconds later, Snekke peeled from the wall, and I was pleased to see him unscathed, or at least not too much.

"Keep the line," Titus barked from our left. It said a lot that I could hear him.

The man facing me was pretending to fight more than

anything. Every few steps, he would jam his knife under my shield, but there was no heart in his attempts. Bove boomed orders to his men, cursing their mothers or promising silver to the man who would break our wall.

From the corner of my eyes, I saw the women of the village fleeing their huts with baskets full of whatever they did not want to be looted. The smart ones would run into the forest, the others would go for the hall. They wouldn't have if they knew my plan.

"What do we do?" Snekke asked behind my back a minute later, breathless.

"Keep the hall doors open; clear the space inside," I barked, closing my eyes from the pain of my shield receiving a mightier blow.

"We fight in the hall?" he asked, a bit too loud for my taste. "It ain't Valhöll, you know?"

"I know," I said. "I know what I'm doing." In truth, it was a bet even Titus would have refused, but it was the only plan I could think of.

Snekke tapped on my back to tell me he was leaving, but before he did, he gave me the first good news of the day. "By the way, you owe me a night in your house." His tone had been nonchalant, and I laughed a guttural sound from a parched mouth.

"Just one night?" I asked, remembering that I had promised two if Halfdan died pissing himself.

"He died fast," Snekke replied, not masking the regret in his voice. He left then but did not have to go far, for the hall was less than forty paces away.

"Thor's arse, who the Hel are you?" the man on my left asked, and I guessed it was indeed a curious conversation he had just witnessed.

"You'll soon know," I replied.

The most complicated part of the retreat was the next, getting everyone in the hall. We could not just rush in; the door was not nearly wide enough for it. And we could not wait too long in a line, otherwise we would just have been one long row of men with an actual wall at their backs.

"Titus!" I called this time. "Into a column!"

"Yes, sir," Titus replied.

"Follow my lead and tell the men next to you to do the same," I told the man on my left. The frown he gave me was more curious than angry, but it was enough to make me want to kick him in the balls.

The hall was less than twenty paces away now, and I had no time to explain myself, so I just moved and prayed for him to be less of a dumb oaf than he appeared to be. When I took my next step back, it was a wider one. With each following step, I also changed the angle of my progression. In a few seconds, instead of having my back to the building, I was moving perpendicular to it.

To the man in front of me, it must have looked as if I was opening our shield wall to him. He could have chosen to stay in front of me and walk to the side as I did, but he made the mistake of keeping the line, and I smiled at his confused glare when the distance between us increased.

The angle of our shield wall narrowed until Titus stood at my back, and we formed a two-man column with our shields on the sides. Our timing was impeccable, and I could almost touch the hall door when Bove ordered his men to charge. He had been outfoxed this time and had taken too long to react.

Titus and I stepped inside, each on a side of the door, and helped the men get in the building as well. Most of them did so without needing to be pulled. Cross-Eyes was panting like a dog and looked ten years older than he had when the sun rose.

I had hoped Ulf would be ready to keep the enemy at bay with his arrows while the rest of our men joined us in the hall, but he was nowhere to be seen. Rune and Bjorn closed the retreat and were now side by side at the door, and I must admit they made a formidable team. The young one worked the shield Bjorn did not carry and protected our champion in the brief moments between two swings of his axe.

"Ready when you are," Bjorn said, and for a second, I wondered if he was talking to us or taunting the men facing him. He stood an arm's length from me, heat evaporating from his body in clear steam.

"Well, why don't you do something then?" I asked, because as long as he stayed by the door, I could not close it.

He cocked his head in a way that told me where I could shove my tone, but within a few heartbeats, he gripped the sides of the door, took a step back to gain momentum, and threw his foot forward in one of the mightiest kicks I have ever witnessed. Not waiting to see the result of his battering, I slammed my side of the door, and Titus did the same.

Bjorn had to duck a spear as we did, then Snekke dropped the latch between us, and we kept our shoulders against the door as men on the other side rammed it. The blade of an axe appeared an inch from my face, and I felt a cold sweat drip down my back while men on our side brought tables and benches to bolster our defense.

"The back door, too," I told a couple of warriors after they dropped Hakon's high seat against the door.

"What now?" Rune asked, hands on his knees and sweat dripping in fat pearls from his mane.

"Chop the columns in half," I said, pointing at the closest ones to us. "Not completely; they still need to hold."

"Ah, fuck," Rune said, standing straighter.

"That's going to make the roof collapse on us," a grizzled, blood smeared warrior said.

"Trust me, I know what I'm doing," I told him in a tone intended to be reassuring.

He was right, of course, but I could not tell him that. The sound of axes cleaving at the door stopped for a second and was replaced by the more distinctive boom of a ram of some sort.

"Go keep the bastards at bay," I told the old man before leaving for the back of the building, where I knew I would find my archer. "Get a fire ready," I told Cross-Eyes, who sat against one of the poles that would be weakened. He nodded and struggled to his feet, the blood smeared around his mouth, giving him the look of a *draugr*.

Ulf did not notice me when I stepped into Hakon's chamber. The quiet of the room was in full contrast with the chaos of the day. The boy lay still on his bed, a piece of red linen over his stomach instead of the spear. His mother and sister wept on his left, and his grandfather on his right. None of them seemed to care about the smell coming from the boy's body, but it had already flooded the small room.

Lif stabbed her angry little eyes at mine when I approached the bed. She blamed me for the death of her brother. I let her wrath wash over me. I traced the Valknut on Hakon's forehead and sent a prayer to Odin, though I had little hope. Archers rarely made it to Valhöll. Not that they lacked courage, but their particular skill did not give them much chance to show it, and Hakon certainly had not been given much of one.

When he finally looked at me, Ulf wore a face saying he

thought the same. We exchanged no words. He knew—or at least I assumed he knew—that I was sorry for him, had no time to waste here, and needed his help.

He swallowed hard and let go of Hakon's hand. The sound of axes chopping the poles supporting the roof could be heard from the chamber, and it probably told Ulf all he needed to know.

"What's happening?" Hild asked, her voice more gentle than I would have assumed.

"We lost," I said, and if she was surprised or saddened to hear it, she did not show it. "This isn't much, but I will avenge Hakon with the lives of his enemies before we join him," I said the last part for Ulf as much as for Hild.

"Good," she said, "make them pay."

I meant to tell her that she, too, would perish. Her daughter, all the slaves, and free folks who found themselves in the hall would. But she already knew. I wondered if she planned to take her own life, as most noblewomen did in that situation and that of her daughter.

The ram battered the door once more. I could hear the splitting of the wood from here. Some of our men cursed, though I didn't know if they were insulting the enemy or the Wolves axing the poles of the building.

"Let's go, Ulf."

"Just one second," Ulf said as he went around the bed. He knelt by Lif's side and put his callous hands on her thin shoulders, which earned him the girl's defiant look we had come to expect and love.

"I'm sorry for Hakon," he said. "He was a brave young man and made his grandfather proud." Ulf fished the small pouch in which he stored Odin's nail from under his shirt.

"Ulf, no!" I barked.

I had seen him eat his Odin's nail before the battle. Of all my men, I had made sure *he* did it. But when he raised his other hand to silence me, I noticed the bandage wrapped around the little finger. I cursed him for having tricked me. Ulf had eaten his own nail and had kept the real one for one of his grandchildren.

"You knew I would not be coming back," Ulf said without looking at me, and I swear I was about to force the nail down his throat and kill him on the spot. Instead, a great sorrow flooded my heart, knowing that I was speaking with my friend for the last time.

"Little girls can't go there," I told him.

"We don't know that," he replied. That it never happened didn't mean it couldn't, especially with this gift. "Lif, I know it looks disgusting, but you will eat this, and everything will be better after."

The girl looked at me with a face like a thousand questions, then turned to her mother, who nodded again. And Lif, the first girl in our history, ate a nail of Odin.

Another crack. Bove's men were getting close to breaking the door.

"Drake, your mushrooms," Ulf asked. "I know you use them as well." I was beyond arguing with him, and I wouldn't need them, anyway.

"There is enough for two," I said while looking at Hild as I handed the white and brown mushrooms to my archer. It might have been my imagination, but I saw a glint of gratitude in the woman's eyes. "Make it quick," I said to Ulf this time.

I left the room, giving Ulf some intimacy in his last moment with his granddaughter. Ten men had their backs and shoulders against the door, bouncing back with every boom of the ram. Another three faced the back door, spears ready to fly. Half the poles looked like they'd been gnawed at by beavers, and it wouldn't take much to break them completely. And though there was more to be done, Bjorn was arguing with one of Lagardalr's men who refused to let go of my champion's axe handle.

I snatched the lit torch Cross-Eyes was holding and climbed onto the last standing table in the room.

"Hakon's men!" I called. The room fell silent, and about forty pairs of eyes turned to me. "Your jarl is dead. You are dead as well; your body just doesn't know it yet."

"If Hakon is dead, we can negotiate," someone said.

"What kind of man are you?" I spat with all the venom I could gather. "You would negotiate with the man who had your ring-giver killed? Shame on you." His face reddened, half from shame, half from anger, I assumed. "Bove will let none of you escape, and even if he did, is that what you want? Are you men, or are you thralls? This is the moment warriors live for. This is your chance to show Odin your worth and earn your place in Valhöll. Harden your heart, make yourself strong, and kill as many of the bastards as you can as an offering to the Æsir. Men of Lagardalr, be brave; Odin is watching!"

The cheer was much louder then. A raven perched on a beam, cawed and looked at me with human eyes. It had to be Muninn. She had timed her presence perfectly, giving flesh to my omen, and when I looked down, I did not see forty men; I saw forty Einherjar lusting for blood.

The raven flew from a gap in the roof, and I raised the torch to spread its flame to the hanging furs. The beams were made of old wood; they would not resist for long. In a matter of seconds, the furs started fuming, and soon the thatched roof did too.

I placed six men with big axes by the most fragile poles with orders to finish the job as soon as the enemy stepped inside. The rest were to fan out as much as possible, especially toward the back, where I stood, to give space for Bove's men to swarm the hall.

"Thank you," Ulf said as he took his place beside me. He had no more tears to shed, but their passage marked his face.

"Odin will kick my ass if you don't show up, so try to die well," I told him. This is not what I meant to say. I wanted to tell him how stupid he was, how much I would miss him, and that his name would not be forgotten. But I guessed he knew all of it.

"You will tell her who I was," he said. He was certain Hakon would not be among us on Asgard.

"I'll tell her you were a pain in my ass," I said. He chuckled, clearly not believing me, and I think it was what undid me. Realizing this was most likely the last time I'd hear my friend laugh after two hundred years of him being like a brother to me broke my pride, and I let the tears roll down my cheeks. I pulled him into an embrace that only men about to die can pull without shame.

"It was an honor," he said, his face against mine.

"I'll see you back home," I told him.

The door gave out then. Big splinters burst inside the hall, and I signaled for the axe-men to finish the poles. Bove's men pulled the furniture out of their way, and the first of them rushed to his death. Ulf loosened his arrow, which ended its course in the man's throat. He then dropped his bow and pulled two long knives from his belt. His victim was trampled by his comrades, many of whom were greeted by a thrown spear.

For a second, I thought we could repel the assault, so strong was our counter-attack, but we just did not have the numbers.

The hall winced like a wounded animal. Its body leaned to the side, a sure sign that a couple of poles had been severed. It might have been the heat from the flames playing with my eyes, but I believed my plan was working and prayed for more men to step into the hall before it collapsed.

"Odin!" I yelled.

I charged, shield against my chest, ready for impact. Oblivious to any thought of safety, I simply rammed the first man in front of me and took him plus another two in my fall. Even Bjorn would have been hard at work to do better than that.

"Get up," Ulf said, offering his hand as I lay there like a drunk struggling for balance.

I looked up at his face, extremely pale compared to the burning beam on top of us. The roof was leaning dangerously, and I heard the beam collapse before I saw it.

"Watch out!" I said as I shoved Ulf backward just in time for him to dodge the beam. I did not feel any pain as it crushed my skull, and before I knew it, I was crossing the rainbow bridge.

I was going home.

Ý

"Why do many Einherjar choose the bottom of the cliff? Simple, the back of Valhöll is worse than Hel. Not that any of those in front seem to care."

Knut Ormson, back-hall fighter

10

Asgard,

When I emerged from the Bifröst, I remembered nothing for a few heartbeats. There was no pain, no worries, not even the memory of what had just happened. My face remembered a kind of pain, the phantom of it anyway. It was a blissful moment, like the morning of a sumptuous feast that leaves you by some miracle without a hungover. Then men gasped for air, and I was no longer by myself.

"Frigg's ass!" Bjorn spat as he regained the edge of the water.

Everything came back in a sharp, icy splash of memories and pain. The burning beam, the cave with the feathers, Hakon, Lif, Einar, Ulf.

"Ulf!" I called.

Asgard's sky was as beautiful as ever, spotted with perfect, fluffy clouds and a gentle breeze to keep them moving.

"Where's my da?" a voice I knew well asked somewhere

behind me. Eigil was on the brink of panic, so said his trembling voice. He was helping Snekke out of his soaked *brynja*, and for once, the latter wasn't speaking.

"He died like a moron," Bjorn said as he raised himself on the muddy ground. "Basically gave his head for the taking. Next time, you stay with us; this way, if he dies, your side will be shieldless."

Eigil jumped from Snekke to Bjorn, caught him by the collar, and threw him out of the water and flat on his back. Besides Thor, I had never seen anyone toy with Bjorn like this. Bjorn gasped as Eigil straddled him, his large hands closing on Bjorn's throat.

"Don't you talk like this about my da, you hear me, you dumb...goat-fucker," Eigil barked in a flash of anger. I got on my feet and locked my arm around his neck. It took all I had to drag Eigil off my friend.

"Your father died on the field," I said as Eigil tried to find a gap in my armlock. "We could not get him in the hall, where we all burned. It might be days before he's here. So why don't you calm down until then, huh?"

I was sick of violence at this point. I was tired, angry, sad, and without patience. The truth was, I did not know if Einar would ever be back. If he had taken his nail, it could still take him days to cross the Bifröst, the time needed for crows or some other beasts to eat his flesh. Unless his body was offered to the flame by a gracious enemy or a surviving ally, though neither seemed likely.

Even if he had not taken the nail, the Valkyries might have chosen him if he fought bravely enough, and he would be waiting atop the cliff. From where I stood, the slain being carried to the top of the cliff looked like one of those green lights illuminating the northern nights.

After dropping our new brothers, the Valkyries would

then fly back to their hall, and for the life of me, I have no idea who among those we see in the citadel was tasked with carrying the new Einherjar. Eigil tapped on my arm to tell me he understood and lacked air. I dropped him and let him breathe, then helped Bjorn up.

"That was a mess," Bjorn said as he massaged his throat.

"The roof collapsed just after you head-butted that beam," Cross-Eyes explained, answering the question I was about to ask.

"At least that part of the plan worked," I said. Bjorn cocked his head with a nod to tell me he agreed, then he gave his hand to Eigil.

Rune emerged from the water, and then Titus came right after him. The younger beamed with pleasure at what could be seen as a success from someone else's point of view. Not the way I saw it. Ulf would most likely not appear, and half of me wanted to run up the path and find out if he and Einar waited among our new brothers. I could already paint their dumb faces in my mind. Ulf would joke about having taken the easy way up, and Einar would immediately scold his son.

The other half of me wanted to wait here. Karl had yet to show up, though it would happen any second now. But it was the last nail-eater I was anxiously expecting. Never had a girl, or a child for that matter, crossed the Bifröst. My skepticism was at its peak. I dreaded that a child could not withstand the rainbow bridge, and my friend was now in Hel for nothing.

"Here you go, as promised," Heimdallr, who had just emerged from his hall in the cliff, said, offering me a bullhorn of his mead.

Spontaneously, I took his gift, and his wonderful sight

must have spotted the misery in my heart, for he immediately hid his golden teeth behind his lips. "What is it?" he asked gravely.

I took a long sip of his mead, the best in the nine realms. Its taste was amazing, as always, but it did not wash the lump stuck in my throat. "Odin's feeling proved true," I told him and could tell no more, not in front of my men. They would soon notice Ulf's absence.

"I have seen many chosen ones ascending just now," Heimdallr told me. "Even though your man said it wouldn't be as big a war as we thought."

"Eigil told you that?" I asked, remembering he had been back for three days already.

"He didn't say much, but he spent the last three days in my hall. Not that I invited him. I sent him to give his report to the All-Father when I could not take his sulking anymore, but he came back a couple of hours later."

Karl's head jerked from the surface at this instant, greeting us with a limitless flow of curses. Rune and Sven were on their knees to help him out.

"So, what could have gone wrong?" the Æsir asked.

"We found something," I whispered, my chin nodding toward Rune. "I don't think it belongs there."

Heimdallr's fiery, golden eyes stared into mine, searching for the meaning of my words. All his joviality vanished. He'd never looked more like his father. I thought to tell him about the girl, or at least to ask if such a thing was possible, but just as I opened my mouth, he looked away, like a cat hearing the squeak of a mouse.

"What in the realms?" he asked, turning his whole body toward the pond.

My men must have felt the god's tension rising, for they

all stopped bickering and stared in the same direction, even Karl, whose legs still dangled in the water. A heavy silence fell on us as we waited for whatever had bothered Heimdallr. Knowing what to expect, I was ready to jump back in the cold water to help Lif out of it. Unless Einar showed up, in which case he was on his own.

"Oh," Heimdallr said, stretching the syllable. "It went wrong indeed."

And just as he finished speaking, a small, blurry shape bobbed to the surface. We saw Lif's back and the back of her head, but the rest of her was underwater, and she was not moving.

I had been ready to jump, but I did not. None of us did.

"Frigg's ass," Bjorn said, speaking the words we all thought.

Then Karl waded to Lif's body.

ᛉ

"Move," Heimdallr said not too gently, shoving me aside with just as much care.

Lif's unmoving body was turning blue in front of my eyes. I remembered the pain of my daughter's birth as I watched the god kneel by her side and rub her chest for some reaction. He pulled his sleeve and put his thumb on her forehead.

The pressure from his *seidr* compressed my heart, and I saw Bjorn close an eye and turn his head for the same reason. Heimdallr mumbled something, which I would not have understood even if he had been shouting, for it was in the forbidden language.

The eight Wolves gathered around Heimdallr and Lif,

the futility of our presence made even more pathetic by our silence. I could barely breathe when his incantation ended; so strong was his magic. But the pressure stopped when a golden flash traveled through his arm and vanished into the girl's forehead.

She coughed hard, first to spit out the water in her lungs, then for air, and the collective gasp of relief changed the mood instantly. Heimdallr was the son of the nine goddesses of the waves; he knew how to save folks from drowning, of course.

"Steady, girl," he said, patting her back as she struggled to calm herself. "Small breaths, take it easy."

"What happened?" she asked, her voice hoarse from the effort. "Where am I? Where is my mother?"

"You are on Asgard," Heimdallr replied as if it was the most natural answer in the world, and though it might be hard to believe, the sight of him helped her settle a bit. "As for your mother," he continued before turning his eyes on me, "I don't know." I had rarely seen my Æsir friend so menacing, at least toward me, but I had been through enough on that day to meet his gaze.

"She isn't here," I answered, breaking contact with Heimdallr to give her the comfort of a familiar face. "I am sorry."

"Drake, a word," Heimdallr said, not as a question. I pointed at Eigil's cloak and snapped my fingers to make him understand he was to share it with the girl, then I went after the Æsir. Bjorn fell in behind me, and I would not turn him away.

"Care to explain?" Heimdallr asked. The fire dancing in his golden eyes shivered with his ire. "The Bifröst was not built for little girls, you know that."

"Hasn't been made for us either," Bjorn replied.

"Oh you, shut up, or I'll show you Thor isn't the only one who can make you feel like a woman!"

"I wasn't given much of a choice," I said. "Ulf gave her his nail when he knew we would all die." Bjorn, who had not known, sighed when I said as much.

"Why, by Freyja's tits, did he do that?" Heimdallr asked.

"She's his granddaughter," Bjorn replied, which made the god scoff.

"No, she isn't. Einherjar can't have children. You are dead, so you can't give life. Your seed is...dead."

"Look at her," I replied, not hiding my irritation. "Use your famed sight and tell me she isn't Ulf's blood."

It wasn't only his words that bothered me but also that his knowledge of our kind seemed so obvious to him and yet had never been explained to us. Heimdallr checked over my shoulder and took a good look at the girl, whose color was slowly coming back as Karl massaged her back. She was confused and had lost her usual bravado. She was a child surrounded by a pack of wolves in a foreign land.

Heimdallr's face widened in shock. "By the Norns," he said, blanching from gold to blond. His right hand moved by itself to the horn at his belt. "This cannot be."

"Apparently, it can," Bjorn said, taking a little revenge.

"You and I will have a word with Father," the Æsir said. I had already guessed we would. How could we not?

"First, I must check if her brother and grandfather are up there."

"I doubt it," Bjorn said.

"Which is why we won't tell her anything about it," I told him. "Are you coming?" I asked Heimdallr.

"I'll join you later," he replied. He was pissed and

confused equally, but I had no space for that, so we left him there.

If I knew him, Heimdallr would spend the next few hours bent over the Bifröst, looking for any trace of malfunction, or spell, or curse, or anything that could explain how a child had survived the crossing. And if I knew him better, he would more than likely be considering the presence of Loki in all of this.

"I am sorry for Ulf," Bjorn said as we walked back to the group. I did not ask why he thought Ulf would not be there when we climbed the cliff.

Truth was, if he had been, he would be climbing down the path by now, and I, too, was losing hope fast. They had been close friends too, and as Lif's grandmother could testify, had shared a lot through their time under my command. Bjorn and Ulf had been my right and left hands for nearly as long as I had been a Drake, and losing one was a pain I had yet to register.

"I am sorry, too," I said.

Shoving Rune aside, I knelt at Lif's height. She was barely holding it together. With all the gentleness my rough warrior's hand could muster, I squeezed her arm, which only served to bring her tears to the surface. She drove herself against my chest and sobbed with heavy spasms for a long time.

Noticing my embarrassment, my men disbanded into smaller groups, and some even began the climb. I stroked her hair; she locked her arms behind my neck, and without shame, I must admit I was tempted to use this moment to let go and behave as she did. I did not, knowing that my men were still close by and that Lif needed me to be strong. But neither did I try to stop her.

"My name is Drake, by the way, not Thorstein," I said when I thought she might have fallen asleep against me.

"I know," she said, still not moving. "The big man called you that earlier." Then she showed me her puffy eyes. Lif had regained a bit of her proud self, and I marveled at the strength of this little girl. "Is he—"

"—Heimdallr? That he is. He's a bit grumpy right now, but he's a nice god."

"Is Freyja one as well?" she asked. Freyja was to young girls what Thor was to men, and I did not have the heart to take it from her.

"You'll soon find out," I said. "But first, I will introduce you to Odin."

"Odin," she repeated, not capable of saying more. It only occurred to me that women grew on Midgard without believing they would ever meet the gods unless the said gods came to trick them into sleeping with them.

For men, it was the opposite. We lived our lives believing we would come back to life as an Einheri, never doubting our bravery until it so happened that we had to prove it. "You see this path," I told her after she rubbed the last tears from her eyes. "We call it the Snake Path. It leads to the citadel of Asgard. We need to climb it, but I will carry you since you just crossed the Bifröst."

I thought she might reject my offer, but I guessed she knew it was better to accept it now rather than ask for it halfway up. I barely felt her on my back; she was so light.

"You look more like a Drake than a Thorstein."

"Thank the gods for that," I said with a heartfelt laugh. I think it infected her, for without knowing why, she laughed too.

When Lif recovered from this sudden outburst, she asked questions about the gods, the Valkyries, the Elves, and the Dwarves. Enough questions to leave me breathless before I could see the end of the path. For most of her questions, I either had no answer or chose not to give them, so she grew slightly irritated by the time we heard the first voices.

My back hurt at this point, and I switched her to my arms instead, remembering that I had done the same with my eldest daughter, though she had been much younger. It was a beautiful memory.

Unfortunately, the bliss did not last.

Titus stood at the head of the snake and shook his head when he saw me. I swallowed hard but found my throat dry. Neither Ulf, Hakon, nor Einar awaited there. It was not a final verdict for the last one, but for my friend and his grandson, it meant only one thing, Helheim.

I stooped to let Lif down, and she walked toward a couple of warriors she had known in Lagardalr. They looked even more confused at the sight of their little lady, but they still welcomed her as if she were a queen. At least we had done our task well. It had been a long time since our last round-up of this scale. About one hundred men stood in a confused pack, even as my men moved between them to quell the inevitable quarrel between warriors who had been killing each other mere minutes ago.

To my great surprise, Bove wasn't among those new Einherjar. He might have survived, or maybe he failed to impress the Valkyries. Unfortunately, another face I would have preferred never to see again stood among them. Halfdan, the traitor, waited on the side, as he should, considering how many of them he had betrayed.

I did something then that stood against everything I was supposed to represent; I let my grudge speak. The Wolves were professionals. We brought war to peaceful lands, we got men killed and tested their bravery, then we went home and expected those who had passed Odin's test to forget their lives and agree with their new purpose. But *I* was not agreeing this time. The anger clinging to me after a fight surged as if it had never left, and Halfdan must have sensed it, for he took a step back.

I grabbed him by the collar of his *brynja* and shoved him right by the edge of the cliff. Halfdan's fear widened his eyes, and he flapped his arms in circles as I lowered him backward over the emptiness.

"What're you doing?" he asked.

"Drake," Titus, the closest of my men, said, speaking as he would to soothe a horse. "I know how you feel, but that's not our way."

I looked at my foreign Wolf, knowing that he was absolutely right. I was setting the wrong example. Those men would talk about it, and Odin would blame me for the murder of a precious soldier. *Fuck all of them!* What did Titus know of our thirst for revenge? Let them talk! Let Odin blame me! I had earned the right to kill that bastard in the name of Ulf, Hakon, and Lif.

The girl made me hesitant, looking at me as if she wanted me to drop Halfdan. I was tempted to leave him be, forget his existence as he withered through the squares. Most of us had done worse things than switching sides. With time, everyone would forgive him. But the rage shaking my arm was too strong, and I decided that, for once, I would not lead by example; I would lead by fear.

"Tell Ulf this is for him."

Halfdan did not get the meaning of my words but understood his doom when I released my grip. He fought the fall and almost kept his balance long enough for Titus to grab him. But both failed, and for the second and last time,

Halfdan died that day. His scream was long and brought me no joy, but when it ended, I made myself fearsome for what came next.

"You are now Einherjar!" I shouted as I turned around, ignoring Titus's head shake. The mob facing me was grim and more confused than ever. At least they had stopped their bickering. "You will fight for Odin, the greatest honor a man can aspire to. And when the time comes, you will be in the shield wall facing the forces of Hel, Jötunheimr, and Múspellsheimr. Do you want men like him next to you?" I asked, pointing at the emptiness, the bottom of which was now sprayed with Halfdan's brain and flesh.

Some of them agreed, though not strongly. Halfdan had no supporters here, but neither did I gain many after this little show. And since I had personally slain a few of those men, I did not want to waste more time here.

Fortunately, I would not have to accompany them, as I understood when Muninn appeared through the crowd. She was far from being the godliest creature of Asgard, but her presence astonished them nonetheless. Facing her cooled me down a little, though her eyes had no friendship in store for me.

"Odin wants to see you," she said, her voice loud enough for the men to hear. "And your guest as well." I did not like the way she mentioned Lif, making her my responsibility when she was, in fact, a burden dropped on me by my now-dead friend.

"Bjorn, take them," I ordered my champion, who waved the group toward the white wall. Muninn took a peek over the cliff, registering the sight of Halfdan's remains for her report to Odin.

Lif walked to me, head straight, and no fear in her eyes as she stared at Odin's raven. "Thank you," she whispered when but a step away from me. I admitted to myself then that I had made a mistake. Lif's future was uncertain, and I had set a terrible example for her.

"I shouldn't have done that," I told her.

"No, you shouldn't have," Muninn said. "Odin will not like it."

"Well, Odin did not lose a friend today," I snapped. "Haven't I gathered a hundred men for his army? Haven't I earned the right to choose my brothers as well? Because if the Valkyries are blind enough to choose this piece of filth rather than my brother, then maybe they shouldn't do this job at all."

My blood had yet to flow in a quiet stream, and the way Muninn met my stare poured fire into my veins. I loved her, and my desire for her had never been stronger, yet I was ready to sever any chance of a future with her for the chance of an outburst. She was about to meet my anger. Instead, she breathed out and walked past me, and somehow it hurt even more.

ᛉ

"I'm sorry for your friend." Muninn's voice drowned in the ruckus as the white wall rose back up. At first, I wasn't even sure she had spoken at all, but she looked genuinely sorry, so I accepted this truce offering.

"Ulf," I said. She was Odin's memory, so of course she knew his name. I said it for myself, as if uttering it kept him alive a little longer.

"Ulf," she repeated. "I did not know him well, but he seemed like a kind man."

"He was." Being kind was one of the most useless things an Einheri could be, and the gods did not care much about this trait. "Did you see how he died?"

She shook her head.

"The roof fell, the hall burned, that's all I know."

"Did Bove survive?" Lif asked. She had understood by herself who and what Muninn was. It pinched my heart that Ulf would never know how amazing his progeny was.

"Bove?" Muninn asked.

"The enemy's leader," I replied. "Bald, gray-red beard, thick, and vicious."

"He survived, but barely," Muninn said. "He did not have much of an army when I left. If the villagers react fast enough, he will not have made it out of Lagardalr."

"Killed by old men and women," I said, chuckling.

"I hope they make it slow," Lif said.

My mind had cleared by then. I loved Muninn again and thought of apologizing for my earlier tone. It might have made things worse, but such is the weakness of a loving man that I came close to it. Instead, as if having a mind of itself, my hand went for the inside of my tunic in search of the feather I had retrieved from the cave. I could not find it.

"What is it?" Muninn asked.

"I had something for you," I said, stretching the collar of my garment to take a look inside.

"For me?"

"A feather I found in a cave. The place reeked of *seidr* and old blood. It might be nothing, but I thought it might be related to—" I was about to give her brother's name, but Muninn squeezed my arm and nodded toward Lif. She did not want the girl to hear it.

"We'll talk about this later," Muninn said, and her word was final. Then she came closer and spoke in a lower voice. "Whatever it was, don't mention it to Odin."

This was odd. I always thought Muninn reported absolutely everything to her father. Then again, I had never really asked, so maybe she did have a secret garden. Muninn's secrecy was misplaced on Lif, though. The girl was nodding with fatigue, and each step brought her closer to complete exhaustion. I thought I might very well have to carry her again before we arrived in Odin's hall.

Fortunately, we did not have to go all the way to the Silver Hall. Odin waited outside, near one of his smaller domains, and he was not alone. He sat under a thick ash tree that was said to have grown from a single leaf of Yggdrasil. I often saw him there, contemplating the emptiness from a simple three-legged stool, though usually by himself.

This time, on his left, stood Frigg, the gods' queen. Odin never called himself a king, a title he found belittling. Frigg had no such issue with royalty and insisted on being referred to as Queen Frigg. Despite her age, Frigg was beautiful. Or maybe it was her age that made her beautiful.

Her silver-ash hair was tied in an elegant bun, stretching the skin of her face in a defiant search for youth. She wore a long dress of dark blue waving with gentle gusts of wind. Her posture and the severity in her eyes reminded me she still mourned her favored son. She had never smiled much, but what had been a serious and graceful face now wore a permanent pout. Before Baldur's death, I found Frigg more attractive than Freyja, the latter one being too flashy for my taste. Now, though, I wasn't so sure, and I guessed the All-Father felt more or less the same.

Between Frigg and Odin sat Geri while his brother, Freki, lay down on Odin's right. The two wolfhounds had none of the couple's sullen looks. Contrary to Muninn and Huginn, Geri, and Freki were just animals, though they did not age.

Freki's head rose when he picked up my scent, the two of us having been acquainted for a long time. Geri had more pride, and I did not like him as much. I thought Freki would come to me before I bowed to Odin, but the All-Father only had to open his hand palm down for the wolfhound to resume his position.

"This is Odin and Frigg," I whispered to Lif.

"I had guessed," she replied nervously.

"Do not talk until they ask you a question," I said.

I tried to judge Odin's mood and found him as cold as Helheim's winter. On the one hand, I had fulfilled my mission and filled Valhöll's benches with more soldiers. Muninn's report would hopefully have described the odds my men and I had struggled against. On the other hand, a Wolf had died, maybe two, a girl had crossed the Bifröst, and an Einheri had been sent to Hel by my hand.

A quick analysis of my situation told me I was fucked. Frigg, who had never liked her husband's army of dead warriors, would use my deeds against me, and I had given her enough ammunition to skin me alive. Luckily, Odin rarely listened to his wife and would choose to go against her out of spite more often than not.

I still kept a safe distance.

"Drake," Odin said, his voice betraying no emotion.

"Odin," I said, saluting him with a slight bow of the head. "Queen Frigg," I then said, saluting her in the same manner. I received no reply from her.

"It seems you have encountered some difficulties," Odin said, dropping his gaze to Freki, who was licking his fingers.

I had to be careful; admitting any shortcomings would make my case more difficult. I doubted Frigg would meddle too much in replacing a Drake, but it was no secret I had her husband's favors. Chiding me was chiding Odin; she would like that.

"We did, All-Father. Your premonition was accurate." Odin had not foreseen anything in particular, but I was glad to throw some responsibility back to him. After all, if the All-Father had a vision, what could I, a mere man, do about it? Odin discreetly nodded, and I understood that he and I were on the same boat and were rowing against his wife.

"Your man told us the scale of the war wasn't as Odin had *imagined,* though," she said. It had been several years since I last spoke with Frigg. Her voice still stung like a whip. I laughed inside, imagining Eigil standing in front of either of them to deliver his report. Maybe Eigil's lack of oratory skill was his best defense against Frigg. I don't think she had any patience for blabbers.

"It was off to a poor start," I said. "But we improved the situation as best we could."

"Ah, yes," Frigg said, making me cold in my bones with her stare. "And you performed such a wonderful job that you decided to reduce our numbers a little." There it was, my first blame. I let a tense silence settle between us, a chance to see where Odin stood on the point. The All-Father remained focused on his wolfhound and would not take part in the conversation. I was alone this time.

"I took it upon myself to kill an Einheri, yes," I said, trying hard to sound both apologetic and assertive at the same time.

"And why did you slay one of your *kind*?" she asked. Lif stiffened at the word *kind*.

"Contrary to the Valkyries, I witnessed the man's value for several days. He wasn't worthy."

"Judging is not your mission," Frigg said. "Killing is."

"Killing isn't my mission," I said, matter of factly, which

made Frigg's back straighten even more. "My mission is to give men a chance to join the ranks of Odin's army. Killing is just the final step of what we do." This time, I was certain of Odin's corner smile. Unfortunately, Frigg noticed, too, and it only fueled her anger.

"Judging is still not part of it, though." She was right. When no answer came from me, she pursued her attack. "But maybe Drake is a great judge of character after all. Maybe we should give him a spot within the Valkyries."

Now, she had gone too far. I have nothing against the Valkyries, on the contrary, but no man likes to be called a woman, not even by a goddess. I was about to snap back at her, but Odin beat me to it.

"Enough," he said lazily. "Drake has proven his worth over and over; even you can't deny it." This wasn't a question, but Frigg was about to reply, her face already turning red. Odin simply raised a finger to silence her, and I have to say he did it almost politely. "Why did you kill him, Drake?" He nodded again and expected honesty.

"We've lost two Wolves because of this man's betrayal." I stopped there. Whatever else I'd say would weaken my point. I had often noticed this in my time as a Drake; the fewer the words, the lesser the chance for a rebuke.

"Two?" Odin asked, genuinely surprised.

"Einar and Ulf." I had not meant for my voice to shake.

"Ulf isn't coming back," Muninn confirmed when Odin looked at her. "But Einar is on his way; it will just take more time."

This was amazing news, though I would have liked her to tell me beforehand. It had been a day filled with shit and sadness, so knowing one of my men would be back was like a hot bath after a snowstorm.

"Your archer?" Odin asked. He grimaced in silence,

wrinkling his old skin even more. We had argued for hours when I had appointed Ulf within the Wolves. He had been against it. None of my previous Drakes had prepared me for an argument with Odin, and it had taken all I had to make him understand that Ulf's fear of death was a strength. Odin refused until I won a brawl and earned the right to close the conversation.

"I am sorry," Odin said.

"He loses a man, kills another, and you're sorry?" Frigg asked. She was baffled at her husband's kindness, and so was I.

"He did not lose a man!" Odin thundered, standing up.

Despite myself, I took a step back. Odin's wrath was formidable, and I wanted no part of it. I had not felt it, but Lif's hand had found mine, and her face had suddenly paled.

"His brother has been killed, and he claimed vengeance. I would have it no other way. The Drake is above any other man. If he says one isn't worthy, then I trust him."

Frigg opened her mouth, but Odin spoke faster.

"One more word on the topic, wife, and I will find another queen. Am I clear?"

Frigg clamped her lips and shot me the look she had meant for her husband. She may not have hated me personally before, but she now did. Freki scampered toward me, tail between his legs, and was now using me as a shield. On the other side, Geri was unmoved by his master's voice.

"Fine," Frigg said as her husband cooled down. Somehow, he looked as if he had grown taller during his bout and was now regaining his original height. Even the sky seemed to brighten as his temper returned to normal.

"And who is this?" Odin asked, eyes smiling. Odin looked as if he had regained some energy from his argument with his wife. On a personal level, I felt as if I had aged ten years, and my back was damp with sweat.

"My name is Lif," the girl said before I could introduce her. With a noble audacity, she took a couple of steps and bowed to the All-Father, then to the queen of the Æsir. "I am —was the sister of Lagardalr's jarl."

"It is an honor, Lif," Odin replied, smiling as any grandfather would. "I am Odin, father of the Æsir. And this is my wife, Frigg."

"I am honored to meet you, Queen Frigg," Lif said in the most innocent voice, offering a perfect bow to the goddess. "My mother prayed your name every day, and I now understand why."

"And why is that?" Odin asked, his cunning old self seeing clearly through Lif's game. Frigg was probably not fooled, but who can resist a child who plays the game of flattery? Not an Æsir, that's for sure.

"Frigg is everything a woman, or a girl, can dream of becoming," she replied, not leaving the queen from her sight as she spoke. Odin chuckled, and for the first time in this conversation, Muninn did the same. In fact, they both sounded quite similar in the way they laughed.

"I thank you for your kind words," Frigg said. The frown between her eyes finally took a rest. "This may be the best thing the Wolves ever brought back to Asgard."

"Agreed," I said after a chuckle of my own.

"And why did my Drake bring such a worthy guest?" Odin asked me while still looking at the girl.

"This was not my doing," I replied without sounding defensive. "Ulf gave her his nail."

"Why, by the Norns, did he do that?" Odin asked. I really wished he hadn't. There was no way around it; they all listened, and I had to answer truthfully.

"She's his granddaughter." They all gasped, the four of them. Eigil had not mentioned it then. It was either dumb or very smart of him.

"What?" Lif asked, forgetting her genial behavior from earlier.

"This isn't possible," Frigg said.

"Are you sure?" Muninn asked, her hand touching my biceps.

Odin said nothing, but he did not look any less baffled.

"Heimdallr also said it was technically impossible," I told Frigg, choosing to answer her first. "But you only need to look at the girl to see she is Ulf's blood."

"Could she be a descendant from when he was alive?" Muninn asked a question I had brushed off the first night I met Lif and her brother.

"She could. Ulf was from the Uppsala region, which is far from Lagardalr, but he had been slain more than two centuries ago; his family could have traveled. He always claimed that he never had children, though. Plus," I said, looking at the girl who struggled to keep up with what had been told, "she just looks too much like him. Her brother did, too."

"You're talking about the archer?" Lif asked.

"I'm sorry you learned it this way," I said. "Olaf wasn't your real grandfather."

"This is not possible," Frigg said again. I shrugged.

Until a few days ago, I was as lost as any of my kind on the topic. Then, I had thought that Midgard was littered with the Wolves' pups. And finally, this very day, I learned that Einherjar could not have children. Despite all of this, there wasn't a doubt in my mind: Lif was one.

"Come here, child," Odin asked, opening his hand to Lif. She joined him, but not without shooting me a worried glance. "This will sting a bit," he said as he unsheathed his long knife from his belt. She said nothing, not even when the knife drew some blood from the tip of her thumb.

The All-Father checked the blood pearling at the surface like a seer reading an augur. Then, without asking, he brought Lif's fingers to his mouth. Her arm tensed as she meant to jerk it back, but Odin's grasp was far too strong for her. He licked behind his upper lip and clicked his tongue.

"She has the heroes' blood," Odin told his wife.

"How?" Frigg asked.

"I have no idea," he replied. "It *is* impossible. And when the impossible happens, it can only mean one thing."

"Fate," Muninn said.

"My little pet is right. Fate needed this child to exist, so she did."

"What for?" The queen asked.

"Who knows with those three bloody crones," he replied, waving his hand in disgust.

Odin, and most gods, hated the three Norns who weaved the strands of our lives, for, in the end, they had power over everything, including the gods themselves. "For all we know, young Lif here is a great sign from fate. Are you hungry, child?"

How could she be? I told myself. Her whole world had been turned upside down three times in less than a day. She had died, then found that she had not, and finally had learned the truth of her ancestry. On top of it, she now heard the All-Father and the queen of the Æsir calling her a child of fate. Of course, she wasn't hungry.

"Yes, my lord, I am hungry," she replied. Whether she was pretending to gain Odin's favor, she sounded honest.

"Let's take care of that first, then, shall we?" he replied, slapping his thigh as he stood up. "Muninn, accompany young Lif to the kitchen and get her something decent to eat, will you?"

"Yes, Father." I had not noticed that her hand had remained on my arm.

Lif gave me a last glance as they left, and I must admit I was slightly concerned at being separated from the girl.

"I will speak with Mimir about it," Odin told his wife when Lif was far enough.

Mimir was, or had been, the wisest of the gods. A bottomless pit of knowledge until he had been beheaded during the war between the Æsir and Vanir. Now, only his head remained, dipped in a well carrying his name. Odin's eye dwelled in the same waters, and when the All-Father was bothered with questions or doubts, he would fetch Mimir's head and question his old friend.

Sometimes Mimir replied, sometimes he didn't. When he answered, though, it was in the form of riddles or enigmatic verses. The prophecy of Ragnarök was just another example of the head's taste for claptraps.

"Can you make sure she's comfortable with us," he asked Frigg. I thought she would explode again, not caring to be treated as a common wet nurse, but Odin then said something I had never heard him say. "Please."

Frigg could not have looked more surprised if her husband had sprouted horns, which was why I believe she accepted and left without a second look, Geri on her heels. Odin watched her go, a semblance of love in the eyes. It vanished as soon as the door of the hall closed behind her.

"*Please*," Odin repeated, puffing with derision. "Do you see what she makes me do now?"

"I'm glad to see her well," I said. After she lost her son, bets had been placed on her dying of sorrow. For years, she had looked miserable, on the brink of death. By comparison, she now looked alive.

"Yes, the beast is finally stepping out of her den. And she has grown claws and fangs during her hibernation," he said. "I might send her to take care of Fenrir for me. At least one of my problems will be solved."

Fenrir was the beast wolf prophesied to kill Odin at Ragnarök. Before knowing of his fate, the gods had chained him to a mountain, and now none of them dared approach the monster for fear of starting the end of the world.

In fact, this was the problem with the prophecy of Ragnarök; we all knew how it would end, but no one could tell how it would start. Killing Fenrir, for example, could end Ragnarök before it even began but the attempt could just as well be part of the story and cause the giant wolf to regain his freedom. Which is why the gods had decided to do nothing about their certain death.

"They might team up," I said, which made Odin laugh.

"That will be the end of me for sure," he said.

Frigg would never have done such a thing. She and Odin were like most old couples; their love ran deep, but they did not like each other anymore.

No, Odin was sincere in his appreciation of his death. I think it was his curse to know exactly how he would die, but not when. That he could do nothing about it was the worst part of it. It made him more human than he wanted to be.

"Walk with me," he said after a short but heavy silence. I wondered if he was talking to Freki or me, but we both moved at the same time.

Life was bright and warm in the citadel that day, as if the coming of so many new brothers had roused the energy of its inhabitants. Einherjar never wandered close to Odin's hall, but many Æsir, Vanir, and Valkyries did, some of whom would already have heard that a human child had crossed the Bifröst.

Odin remained silent for a time, which stretched to the lower city where my brothers and I lived. We left it behind as well and walked the meadow separating the citadel from the white wall.

"Tell me of Midgard," the All-Father asked me when no one could hear us.

"What do you want to know?"

"Anything my little crow might have missed."

"I don't think Muninn misses much."

"Oh, she sometimes misses the obvious." Despite my best efforts, I felt heat rising to my cheeks. If I knew him well, he spoke of my affection for her.

"It is cold on Midgard," I said, changing the topic as fast as I could.

"Ah," Odin scoffed. "Thank you, my boy, you are quite the observer."

"No, I mean, it is supposed to be summer, but it is as cold as any winter," I said. Odin hummed from the back of his throat as he drank my words.

"You are thinking of Fimbulvetr, the great winter preceding Ragnarök." This was not a question, and Odin's sarcasm was now a memory. He retreated into his thought cage, leaving me alone on Asgard's plain.

"What else?" he asked, this time with more urgency.

"What do you want to know, All-Father?"

"This *feeling* I told you about before you left," he replied as we reached the wall. We changed direction to follow the structure, which would eventually lead our steps to Valhöll.

"You think it has nothing to do with either a Wolf's death or a girl crossing the Bifröst?" I asked.

"I know it has nothing to do with those things," Odin

said, waving those *things* as unimportant, as one would the mention of snow in winter. It pricked my anger to hear him speak of Ulf's death so lightly, but I kept my ire within.

To someone as old as Odin, an Einheri's death was akin to losing a goat. "No, it wasn't this kind of thing. Did anything else happen?" He asked the last as he dropped his bony fingers on my shoulder. Despite being the leader of the Æsir and one of the most powerful beings of the nine realms, he looked old and fragile.

Maybe I did not want to add more weight on him, maybe I was unhappy at the way he had brushed off my friend's death, or maybe I was keeping my word to Muninn, but I did not mention the cave. I should have spoken. Even then, I knew it was a mistake.

"Nothing worthy of note."

Odin nodded and remained silent. The silhouettes of Einherjar in training drew themselves on the horizon. When he saw them, the veil of doubt slipped from his face, and Odin was strong again. He became the leader about to inspect his troops, the father to us all.

"We will introduce the new men tonight," Odin told me as we marched through this unit. "But the brawl will wait until tomorrow evening. You and your men deserve that."

"Thank you, Odin," I said. My shoulders slumped at the news. Rest. I had not even realized how much I needed it until the possibility hit me.

I thought to ask about Lif and whether I could do anything to improve her stay or if Odin knew what would happen to her, but he acted first and grabbed me by the elbow. He was not a gentle and feeble old man anymore. The tips of his fingers pinched my bones and forced me to wince.

"And Drake." His dark eye suddenly darted into mine.

My heart froze on its beat. "Don't you dare kill one of my soldiers again. I don't think there could be a better Drake, and I don't want to have to find out if I'm right. Do we understand each other?"

"Yes, Lord."

"Good," he said.

Odin left me near Valhöll. My breathing was shallow, and my legs shook for long minutes after he vanished into the streets of the citadel, wondering if he had threatened to replace me or eliminate me from Asgard.

11

Loki's cave
4 days after Loki's escape.

My dreams were normal, sadly normal. They flashed with no control on my part. Dreams are not attached to the body, so, of course, I could not use Loki's dream charms. Instead, I dreamt of war, of fire, of death. The usual. For once, I felt myself waking up. The cold stabbed my toes like dozens of needles, my teeth hurt from chattering in my sleep, and I tried hard to keep my eyes closed for a little longer. But the voice suddenly ringing next to me forced them open.

"Who are you?" she asked. A strong, determined voice to the antipodes of Sigyn's childlike tone. Forgetting the chains, I meant to sit up and, of course, was driven backward by the heavy links, but not before bumping my head into the bowl protecting me.

"Who the fuck are you?" she asked again, and this time my vision cleared enough to see that it was still Sigyn who spoke. It was her while not being her. Her back was straighter, her dumb smile replaced by a scowl, and the shine in her eyes by ice. She wasn't any prettier, and by the gods, she scared me.

"I am Drake of the Einherjar," I said, understanding more or less that I was speaking to another Sigyn.

Some folks behave as such after receiving a blow to the head. Sometimes they lose some memories, sometimes they create some, and sometimes they invent another self. Sigyn, the new Sigyn, hissed when she heard my name, then spat on the table, just far enough from my foot to avoid her husband's body.

"I knew something was wrong," she said. "Loki never snores." I did not speak, for she clearly did not like me as much as her other self, whom I already missed. "So, he's done it," she said. I felt no amazing amount of love in the way she spoke of her husband. "He's gone."

"He is," I replied. "With Muninn. Four days ago."

"Fuck," she said. In her mouth, the word sounded strange, almost foreign. "I was gone four days this time." Sigyn stood up as if her presence served no purpose, leaving me unprotected from the snake. If I had not been completely awakened, this would have done the trick.

"Sigyn!" I called, shaking the chains as I dodged the first drop. "Stay here, please."

"I'm not your slave, Drake." Even her gait was different, full of pride, not so different from Frigg and Freyja.

"I never treated you wrong!" I said, echoing her words from our first conversation. "You said so, remember?"

Above my head, the snake responded to my surge of fear and shook with a renewed frenzy. Its mouth opened wide, darting the first, then the other fang in my direction. I saw deep inside its blood-color maw. Then the snake produced two more drops of venom, and they were all I could see.

They slid slowly to the tips of the fangs, getting fatter as more juice accumulated. They fell, and I knew I could not avoid both. I did the stupid thing of closing my eyes and turning my face. One drop landed right in the center of my ear.

It took the time of a heartbeat for the pain to stab my brain with a new level of suffering, and when it did, my scream nearly made me faint. In my three hundred years of existence, I had been stabbed, decapitated, disemboweled, tortured, skewered, and drowned on several occasions. Still, nothing, *nothing*, came close to the pain I felt at that moment. It was so strong it prevented me from losing consciousness.

Something else got into my ear and rubbed its contour, pulling some of the poison out. It was Sigyn's finger, which she flicked with pain when I opened my eyes again. It still hurt, but in comparison, it felt like a bee sting.

Sigyn came close to my face, spat into my ear, and all traces of pain vanished right away. As she stood back up, she punched the snake with a not-so-gentle "fuck off." It hissed back, but she paid no attention to it. There was no more pain, but the world still spun as if someone had slapped me on the side of the head.

"You never made fun of me, I'll give you that," Sigyn said. She sat next to me and picked up the bowl again. "By the way, the other one doesn't know how to do this," she said, talking of the healing property of her saliva. I waited for the world to stop moving and for the taste of vomit to leave my mouth before I asked her a question I really wanted to ask this intelligent, angry Sigyn.

"What's going to happen to us?"

"Us?" she asked, scoffing. "Nothing. Absolutely nothing."

"What do you mean *nothing*? Loki is just going to leave us here until Ragnarök?"

"Not only until Ragnarök," she corrected me. "Even after."

"After Ragnarök?" I asked, wondering if this Sigyn wasn't as lost as the other one.

She saw my doubt and sighed. "This place," she explained, rolling her eyes to show the cave, "is one of the few places that will survive Ragnarök. For all I know, it could have happened already, though I doubt it."

I don't know if I was supposed to feel relieved at the idea of surviving Ragnarök, but I did not. My existence was tied to Ragnarök. I was to fight the last war, and I was supposed to lead my kind into battle. Facing real death in a mission, I could live with, but being robbed of my most sacred duty pissed me off more than I would have thought.

"I don't know if you still love him," I said, "but fuck your husband. Taking Ragnarök away from me—"

"He is my husband," she replied. "So, I do love him, but I also hate his guts. So, yes, fuck him." We smiled at each other like two old friends who met again after a lifetime apart. "But your presence here," she went on after we got interrupted by the snake, "that's more Muninn's idea than Loki's."

"It is?" I asked, wondering if my anger could rise even higher.

"Of course. Loki wanted one of you, but she came up with your name and how to get you. And to be fair to my husband, I think he would have preferred someone else. He was fond of you, after all." That was a lot to take in, and I doubted Loki had any soft spot for me. "Isn't he the one who gave you your dwarfish knife?" she asked, sensing my doubts. It hit me then. I had completely forgotten how I had been gifted Wedge, but it all came back now that Sigyn mentioned it.

As a newly appointed Drake, I had taken part in a peacekeeping mission in Jötunheimr. Loki and some Æsir had been part of the expedition, and I had, not knowingly, saved Loki from a life-threatening situation. Wedge had been my reward. Had Muninn taken this memory as well?

Even Loki could not possibly have given me the blade, knowing what would happen decades later. It was just one of those twists of fate the Norns have in store for us. If I survived Ragnarök and the three of them did as well, I would have to pay those hags a visit.

"Since we are stuck together for the foreseeable future," Sigyn said as she tried to find a spot to sit on my bed of rock, "how did the mean raven get you here? With love, I suppose?"

"Not just love," I answered. Sigyn leaned a little over to show I had her attention, and since I had nothing better to do, I told her of the night after Lagardalr. "She also used my lust for her."

ᛦ

Bragi had spun a poem about the battle of Lagardalr before sunset. Like the master weaver of words he was, he balanced tales of bravery from both sides, making the names of the most distinguished warriors ring throughout Valhöll.

The fight between Cross-Eyes and Njal, the berserker, took the first stanza, the verses in honor of the vanquished outweighing those for my man to please our new brother. Far from the battlefield, Njal appeared rather shy and friendly, though he was not the brightest of the lot. I feared he would soon join the clique of Magnus Stone-Fists if we did not warn him first.

Bragi enchanted them with his voice, his lyre, and his rhymes. I lost count of the verses, many of them exaggerating such-and-such moments of the fight, but the hall was entranced. We warriors liked to brag about the strokes we dealt or dodged, but in all earnest, we mostly reacted and depended on luck.

Training and experience made our reactions faster, but not our thinking. If a big bearded bastard hammered his axe at you, you didn't strategize about the best way to parry; you got your shield in between or moved aside, then you hacked with desperation. If you were lucky, it looked smooth enough to deserve a verse in Bragi's poem. Otherwise, you raised your cup for the names you knew.

The god of *skalds* did a magnificent and concise job of this poem. Considering the number of new brothers, I had feared an interminable piece, but I found it quite on point and neither too long nor too brief. Even the part about Einar's death resonated with glory for his slayer. Now that we knew our comrade would return, we could relax and cheer with the others. Killing a Wolf was a worthy feat, after all. It got Einar's killer, a certain Gorm Bjarnisson, a silver ring from Odin himself.

To his credit, Gorm came to salute us once the presentation was over and expressed his sorrow to Eigil. As far as my warrior was concerned, it was unnecessary. Still, we appreciated the gesture, and I made my usual mental note to keep this Gorm in mind. Of course, if we had not known of Einar's return, Eigil would have bashed Gorm's brain over the walls. But Eigil was drunk beyond reason that evening.

While his father's body was slowly being pecked out by crows on Midgard, Eigil enjoyed the end of his torment and enjoyed it with a vengeance. I did not share his jolly mood and kept as much as possible to myself and my mead, which tasted bitter that night.

Sensing I had no space for laughter, Sven Cross-Eyes took Eigil and Gorm to our other table, where my old comrade Arn and some others passed the time as well as they could. Snekke almost fell from his bench when Eigil's weight lifted from it.

"Well," Karl said when he recovered from the sight of Snekke spilling mead over himself. "I'm over to some unfortunate bastard or some very fortunate Valkyrie." I was amazed he had stayed with us for so long, but he surprised me even more before he left. "To Ulf," he said, lifting his cup above our table. "A pebble in my boot he was, one I will miss."

"To Ulf," the others said as our cups gathered.

I did not shame myself with tears, but the knot in my throat did not make the passage of alcohol easy.

"I hope they don't have bows in Hel," Rune said.

"Fuck, boy, that was stupid even for you," Bjorn said with more anger than usual.

I could have told the boy to shut his ale hole, but I knew what he meant. We would face Ulf during the great battle, and I, too, would not like to be on the wrong side of his arrows. Most of us believed warriors sent to Hel did not *live* as we did here and existed more like thoughtless *draugr* waiting to be reanimated for the last war. I had seen actual *draugr,* and I couldn't imagine those undead able to shoot a bow.

"It's true, though," Rune defended himself. "Ulf was the best archer I've ever met. I once saw him shoot an arrow between the planks of my opponent's shield." He mimicked how said arrow passed by his cheek, whistling as he did so.

"An amazing shot."

"That's nothing," Bjorn said as he hammered his cup on the table. "I once saw him snap another archer's bowstring with an arrow before a battle in Zealand. He then let the man attach another string and did it again. This archer threw his bow in frustration and just walked away from the battlefield." Rune looked incredulously at our champion, then at me. I nodded; this was a true story.

"I only once saw him miss," Snekke said. Like me, the other Wolves at the tables looked at him with raised eyebrows. We had all seen him miss shots here or there. "With our golden lady there," he explained, pointing his cup toward Freyja on the dais.

The memory came back. Ulf had tried to shame Bjorn by proving that *he* could charm the goddess. The result had been masterful, but not in the way he had hoped. Despite her looks, Freyja is a monster of strength, and her slap twisted his head backward, killing him on the spot.

The look of surprise as his face unnaturally turned to us had been a cherished and retold story for many years. I laughed like never before at the memory and was soon followed by my comrades, except for Rune, who had not been one of us then. It took a while before I regained control of my guffaw, and my eyes were watery when I did. I raised my cup to Snekke in gratitude.

"To Ulf," I said.

"To Ulf."

Bjorn belched, then wiped his mouth with the back of his hand.

"Well, talking of Freyja," he said. "Time for my evening's attempt. Maybe she'll accept some pity sex."

"I bet she won't," Titus claimed, and I think he was being

serious, though not even Bjorn would take that bet. "In that case, I'm off to Astrid."

I had no desire to remain with Snekke or Rune, and I guessed they didn't either, so I also took my leave from the Wolves' table. For once, I would ask Odin's permission to leave the hall. I had to show some respect for his authority, if only to make amends for my actions that morning. It would also give me the chance to get closer to Lif, who sat like a perfect daughter on Frigg's side.

The queen's presence had been a shock to us. I don't know how Lif managed to convince her to attend the feast, but it completely reassured me regarding her life on Asgard. If she could bring the queen of the Æsir to spend some time with us Einherjar, Lif's potential was indeed limitless.

The girl wore a dress of green silk tailored to her size, which was amazing considering how little time she had spent on Asgard. A golden twisted torc adorned her neck, giving her a regal attitude to match what already seemed to be her surrogate mother. Lif would remain twelve for the rest of her second life; otherwise, even the haughtiest Vanir would have fought for her once she grew up.

Swimming against the mass of warriors, gods, and Valkyries, I knelt in front of Odin, something I had stopped doing many, many years before. I waited for some time, then lifted my head just enough to see his finger ordering me to stand. Even then, I kept my head low.

"If the All-Father allows it, I wish to leave the feast and get some rest," I said, shouting the words to be heard above the tumult.

"Very well," Odin said in his most commanding voice. "You deserve some rest."

I brought my fist to my chest. "Thank you, Odin. My queen,

it is good to see you here." Her reply came as a snobbish nod. I winked at Lif and got the same in response. She had lost her mother and brother less than a day before, but handled it well.

I don't know why I always used the back door on the side of the dais to leave Valhöll. The hall had hundreds of doors; any of them would have done. But using this one, so particular in size and position, always gave me a feeling of being done for the day. I was no longer the Drake of the Einherjar when this door closed behind me.

I loved the feeling immensely. Rarely had I walked home with such a clear head and under such a peaceful night sky. The moon's light bounced on the surface of the many buildings in an aura-like halo. The sudden solitude unburdened me of my pride, and I let my shoulders slump. Ulf was not my first loss as a Drake, but he was the heaviest.

"You ass," I told my friend, looking at the moon to address him.

It was an incredibly selfish thought, but as I neared my house, I wondered if another loss among my pack could hurt as much. Titus's death would be hard to swallow, and he would be irreplaceable, and I couldn't picture Bjorn's passing. But, no, none of them would hurt as much as Ulf.

As I opened the door latch, a breeze of air came from within. It smelled fresh, despite being the first time I opened it since Lagardalr, and a scent I knew well and had come to recognize with joy accompanied the freshness.

"Muninn," I called, even before my eyes adjusted to the darkness.

"Drake," she said as she rose from my bed. "I hope you do not mind me intruding."

"Of course not," I said as I closed the door with the back of my foot. I minded a little. Her presence on my bed made me nervous, if only because I knew of its state.

By habit, I went to the small table at the center of the room, opened its drawer, and used some utensils to light a thick, honey-smelling candle. While the moon's light had been white as Asgard's marble, the candle bathed the room in a soothing yellow. In the two blinks it took me to adjust, I noticed the difference in Muninn.

She wore a dress as dark as usual, but it revealed her neckline and did not cover her arms. Muninn's bosom was not ample, yet I had never seen as much of it, and I found breathing difficult. She'd adorned her hair with small black and white feathers, attached with a few silver beads, and had painted her sharp eyes with a line of dark blue ending in a thin curve. It brought the white in them out and made me weak in the knees.

Intertwined circling figures embellished her dress from shoulders to ankles, marrying the alluring shape of her hips. A belt of black leather, whose only purpose was to tighten the garment closer to her belly, ended in a thin buckle of silver, the craft of its making obviously dwarfish.

Every day, Muninn was a beautiful woman in *my* eyes, but this evening, she would be the most beautiful creature to every man.

"Thank you," I said, tripping over those two simple words. "I mean, for coming here," I went on, though too late, the damage was done.

Then she did the only thing she could have done to look more beautiful; she blushed. She pulled a strand of hair back behind her ear, and her cheeks took a pinkish tone. I think she gestured so to mask her smile. At this instant, I would have put my hand in Fenrir's mouth, as Tyr had, if she had asked me.

"I wanted to continue our conversation," she said. "Just the two of us."

Such a sweet sound.

Men are stupid creatures. We never second-guess our luck until the snare tightens. Muninn had made herself beautiful for me, this I knew, for she had not attended the feast. She had sought my company and my company alone. I wondered if seeing me with Lif awakened some jealousy, perhaps. Or maybe she simply meant to comfort me for Ulf's loss.

Thoughts and hypotheses fired in my brain, and I struggled to read them. Muninn was in my house, prettier than I had ever seen her, looking for some time with me. Ragnarök could happen tomorrow; tonight was the night of my dreams.

"I brought something," she said, pointing at a skin of hard leather on the table.

"Water?" I asked.

"Mead," she answered. Water was a luxury; mead wasn't. It flowed without interruption in Valhöll to the point that most men did not care for it anymore after a few years. I frowned, confused.

"Not that mead," she said playfully. "Odin's."

Now *that* was a worthy gift. Heimdallr had the best of meads for himself, but Odin's was the strongest, purest honey wine of the realm and in a limited quantity.

"I did not think Odin was happy with my service enough to grant me this present," I said as I picked up the skin reverently.

"Father is a deceitful god, always hiding his true feelings and meaning. But today, I'm not sure he would have given it to you."

"You took it without asking?" I asked, dropping it back on the table as if it had caught fire.

"Who do you think I am?" she replied with an impish

attitude I did not know her to possess. She stood and removed the cork before I could tell her this might not be the wisest idea ever. If Odin caught me red-handed, with his little raven and some of his mead, the very day I had killed one of his soldiers, I would join Ulf in a heartbeat.

"Well, many thanks for your gift."

The sensational smell of fermented honey made my head turn. The mead consumed by the Einherjar was on the weak side. Still stronger than ale, but not by much. Odin's stood on the other side of the spectrum, and I poured it sparingly into two fairly clean clay cups. Muninn sat back on my bed as I handed the first cup to her, and I took a stool for myself. Our fingers touched as I handed her the cup, a fleeting moment frozen in time. She brought the cup to her lips, keeping me in check as she drank some of the god's beverage. I did the same, gulping more of it than I should have. My head started spinning the next instant.

"You wanted to talk about what I found on Midgard?" I asked.

"I did," she said. "But if you do not want to, I'm still glad for your company."

What do you answer to that?

"It's fine. Let me tell you."

I told her everything about the cave, from the feather-lined floor to the jarl's torc and even the odd-looking wall at the back. I did not mention my guess about her brother, but I told her everything else, even how I felt regarding Rune discovering it.

Muninn played with her cup, twirling it as she listened. The mead's spell was numbing my senses and slowly crippling my capacity to think. So when she tilted her head to the side after a few seconds of silence, exposing her graceful neck, I pictured myself grabbing it with my callous fingers and pulling her to a passionate kiss. I would lay her down on the bed, and we would push those dark tells to the morrow.

"Tell me of the feathers," she said, popping my sweet delusion like a bubble of soap. I shook my head to gather my senses.

"I took one with me, but it must have fallen during the fight," I said.

"If it was Asgardian in nature," she said, "it would have dissolved as you crossed Bifröst. It is the same with Odin's nails." This was the first I ever heard of the nail's mechanism. I had learned more about Asgard and the Einherjar in a day than in the past century.

"So, you think it might be Huginn's," I asked. In a very bird-like fashion, she looked at me without moving her head.

"I believe so," she said before emptying her cup, tilting her head backward and exposing more of her neck as she did. Again, I had to refute the swarming heat from my thoughts. "But I need to make sure." She dropped her cup on the table, leaning so close that I shivered.

"How?" I pushed myself to ask.

"You are not Odin, so it won't be as easy," she said. "But I can also search through your memory. Humans are also Odin's children, after all."

"But how?" I asked again.

"Come closer," she said, patting the mat by her side. I swallowed once and obeyed. I sat as close as I thought the situation demanded and felt her knee against mine. She lifted her hands and was about to bring them to my face, but I grabbed her wrists nervously.

"Can you access all my memories?" I asked. There were a few memories of other women, mostly, as well as some fabricated ones of her, that I would rather she did not discover.

"Only those we both look for," she said. "But you have to relax first. Close your eyes." I let go of her and closed my eyes. With two fingers, she gently pressed both sides of my head. I tensed immediately. "Relax," she said, this time a bit more forcefully.

"I'm trying," I replied. My frantic heart formed a barrier against her efforts. At least, I told myself, she was memory and not thought. That would have been bad.

She sighed, then tried something else.

It came all at once, her movement, her smell, the wetness of her lips on mine. Oh, I was not relaxed, but I stopped stressing out at once. Then, I was back in the cave.

Everything was distorted. The walls were not straight but undulated, as if looking through the heat of a fire. The light from outside as I penetrated the cave was blue and gray, and Rune's face was blurry and his voice echoing.

I had no control over my actions. Everything happened as it had in reality. I found the candle in the cave, noticed the feathers, picked one, checked the pelts, looked at the torc, and noticed the back wall. Even through my memory, I experienced my regret at not spending more time checking the wall. Then it all sped up, and I was whooshed out and down the hill on the way to Eigil's funeral. Rune spoke, and I checked the feather more carefully, as I had done then. Even though my vision flooded in a dreamlike blue, the feather shone white.

"Huginn!" Muninn said as the memory popped and reality returned. She sprang up while I was still waking from the trance and the taste of her lips. "You found Huginn, Drake!" Muninn said. She lost control of her feet and crossed the room once.

"You're sure?" I asked, standing as well.

She planted herself in front of me, her eyes shinier than ever.

"He's my brother, I would recognize his feathers among any."

My excitement sparked at seeing the woman I loved so enthused, and I grabbed her by the arms to keep her on the spot. "This is great," I said, my voice getting higher.

I locked her gaze in mine long enough to notice small stars and my face in her eyes. I could not say who moved first, but her lips were back on mine before I realized. We kissed, just for the sake of kissing this time, and her taste will stay with me forever. Sweet and sour like blackberries.

I do not believe any woman ever gave me so much pleasure with just a kiss. It wasn't the passionate kind that led to sex but the result of sudden joy needing an outlet. So, when our faces broke apart, there was embarrassment. I still had to stretch my breeches when she looked away.

"I'm happy for you," I said after we both suppressed a small giggle. There wasn't much to be happy about. I had merely found a clue of Huginn's presence. A fresh clue, but he could have been gone for some time. And there was the mystery of the dead jarl's torc. If Huginn had anything to do with it, finding him might not have been such a brilliant idea.

"I have a chance to find my brother because of you, Drake. I will never forget it."

"Maybe it's what Odin felt," I said. A shadowy veil passed over Muninn's face, giving it back some of its usual sullenness.

"We cannot tell him yet," she said. "Father has lost too much over the past decades. If we give him hope and it turns out to be in vain, he might never recover."

I should have been suspicious. In fact, I was probably suspicious. Muninn was keeping too many secrets from Odin. But I had just kissed her, and I was still wriggling with the idea that she would be mine tonight and maybe for the rest of my second life.

"Let's find your brother first, then," I said. The look she shot at me was worth all the silver I possessed. Everything was in it: gratitude, surprise, respect, and maybe even a bit of lust.

"You would help me?" she asked, her voice trembling. Her acting was perfect. I was fooled.

"Of course."

"Why?" she asked, playful mischief twitching her lips. She knew why. I had told her with everything but words, and I contemplated the idea of using them. I wanted to tell her everything. My pride prevented me, though. Men just didn't say stuff like this. We prove it.

"I've never seen you smile as much as in the last five minutes. I don't want it to go," I said. "It would also please Odin to get his Thought back, and after this morning, I need to get back into his good graces. So how can I help?"

"Well," she said, looking at the floor while she gathered her thoughts. "Odin isn't going to just let me go to Midgard, not after what happened to Huginn."

"Ask him for my presence as your bodyguard." The idea of spending some time with Muninn on Midgard was thrilling.

"No offense, Drake, but Odin would not be fooled by this request. I'm Odin's daughter. Do you really think I need a bodyguard? No, you will not accompany me," she said, crushing my hopes to crumbs. "I will accompany you."

"I don't know when we might be sent over there again," I

said, thinking she was talking about the Wolves. "We won't have a reason to return to Lagardalr for a generation or two."

"Not the Wolves," she said. "You, just you."

"Oh," I said. "Just me and you then?"

"Is that a problem?" she asked.

"It isn't," I replied, and of course, it wasn't. "But I don't see the All-Father agreeing to let me go back down just like that."

"He wouldn't," she agreed. "But you will earn that right."

"How?" I asked. She suddenly looked sorry, and I knew where she was going with this. "The brawl."

I won't lie; I did not feel confident.

ᚤ

"Foes, family, lovers, and all the rest from our first life, they quickly stop meaning anything. It's not that you don't give a shit about them or anything, you just forget. It ain't natural; it's part of the magic transforming a man into an Einheri."

Gunther Cat-Whiskers

12

Odin was pissed. This was not one of his good days. He made it obvious from the way he slouched on his throne and raised his hand absently to order the melees to form. He did not even wait for the hail of his name to cease.

I was pissed too.

Muninn had gone after we agreed on her idea the night before, leaving me alone and confused in my little house. It had not weakened my motivation, but my pride was stung. She had barely left my thoughts for the day, yet whatever frustration I held against her vanished as soon as she entered Valhöll that evening.

Frigg's absence came as no surprise, but I regretted Lif's. I had no doubt she was thriving, but she would have cast Odin's mood with a wink. Instead, I had to make do with the All-Father's dark eye on me as I attempted nothing short of a miracle.

I rolled my shoulders like an oarsman about to start a day of rowing and improved my grip on the shield I had chosen, my best, a solid round painted in white with a red, howling wolf's head. The rim was thick, the boss as well, and the whole thing was as heavy as needed. Shields were rarely used in the square, space being too much of an issue initially.

Some slung them on their backs for later, but grabbing them and tossing their owner from behind was too easy, so you rarely saw one in the upper squares. But my goal was to remain until a shield would become an asset. Brawls don't last long enough for the fatigue to settle in, so we used heavier tools than during an actual battle. Wedge was well lodged in my right hand, its blade slicing the air as I made small circles with it.

Bjorn whistled when he noticed my choice of weapon, and he was right to be impressed. My long knife was formidable, and it meant I would fight up close. And while we usually used crude weapons for the brawls, not wishing to break a good blade on such an unremarkable event, I had picked a dwarfish-made knife. I meant business, and my champion saw it.

"Something to ask Odin?" he said as we faced each other. He would be the first. Men were picking their opponent or ally and envisioned their first moves.

"Nah," I said carelessly. "Just need to prove I can still kick your ass."

"As if you ever could," he said with the smug look of a man who knows he's unparalleled.

"Begin!" Thor shouted.

I breathed out as Bjorn breached the space between us. As he often did in single combat, his grip was close to the head of his axe. He would use it to punch and cut rather than hammer it down as he did in the shield wall. The arch of his blade came in a quick jab ringing against the boss of my shield, but before he could try something else, I darted my knife toward his left eye. It would have been good if I had him there, but of course, he managed to avoid it. It woke him up, though. I hadn't just meant to beat him; I had tried to end him. Bjorn now knew I was dead serious.

"You need it that bad, huh?" he asked, his voice calm but his face crisping with anger.

"More than you know," I replied as I lifted the shield to my eyes.

"Let's give them a good show then, eh?"

And a good show we gave them.

Bjorn was furious in his attacks, putting all his strength behind each strike. But I was agile in my responses. I knew him better than he knew me, for such is the weakness of the strong that they don't study their opponents. I saw each blow before it happened and avoided most with little effort. It pissed Bjorn to see me fleeing his axe and fists, as I had hoped. He went from fighting to brawling. His grip loosened until he waved his axe as he would in battle, making his attacks wider and slower.

I vaguely noticed Eigil bringing his hammer down on some poor bastard's chest and guessed Cross-Eyes was reenacting his fight with Njal.

Bjorn was all spittle as he raised his axe high above his head, the moment I had been waiting for. I dropped my knife and stepped inside his space as he brought his weapon down. Then I twisted on my feet to offer him my back and caught his right arm. Using his momentum and his weight and pushing backward with my hips, I lifted Bjorn's massive body over my right shoulder and slammed him forward.

I heard a "fuck" before he crashed flat in front of me. The impact forced him to close his eyes, and when he opened them again. The last thing he saw was the boss of my shield. I was gratified with the crushing sound of his nose, and then his arms slumped down. I heard a loud cheer from the side of the square and another from the god's dais. We hate our nose being broken; it hurts for too long afterward. Bjorn would not be happy.

Wedge was back in my hand before I stood again, which was unfortunate for the man forced backward by Eigil's hammer. I forgot his real name, but we called him Nightingale, for he spoke with a shrill voice and was one of Magnus's little pets. He had not realized I was there, and I unceremoniously knocked him out with the pommel of my knife.

"Hey," Eigil spat. "He was mine."

I had neither the time nor the patience to teach him a lesson this time. He saw my resolve and faced the threat with a scowl. His biceps tensed, turning his flat muscles into hard-knotted oak. Decades of Wolfing around had given him a solid instinct, and he came at me with his best shot, which came from the side. It was a difficult strength-sapping technique to use a hammer horizontally, but when it connected, nothing could withstand it. It crushed bones, shields, and blades. If it connected.

I jumped back, felt the wind of the hammer against my ribs, then darted forward again. Eigil tensed his grip to reverse his hammer's course, but I shot my knee up into his balls first. A cheap blow, but it did the trick. His gasp of pain reeked of mead and boar meat. I thought this might be enough to send him packing, but Eigil recovered faster than I had hoped.

He dropped his hammer and bear-hugged me with all his magnificent strength. My shield was between us, which must have hurt him more than me, though he showed nothing of it. I shouted with pain at the sensation of being compressed in this fleshy trap. Eigil shut me up with a bell-ringing headbutt. I no longer suffered from the bearhug but felt like my face had cracked open like a walnut.

I would have been proud of the big ox if I hadn't been so dazed. Instead, I felt the air leave my lungs, unable to return, and blinked some sense into my suffocating brain.

Eigil's face crisped with the effort of trying to break my bones and crush whatever my ribcage kept inside my chest. My left arm was stuck between myself and the shield, but my right still held Wedge. I could barely move it, but its sharp blade required little strength. After a few weak stabs, I felt Eigil's armor's rings give way, and the resistance of the metal turned to flesh. He flinched when the tip of the knife penetrated between his ribs, but he was not near the end of his torment. His grip on me did not weaken until I kneed the knife farther. Then he screamed and let me go.

Eigil fell on his ass, hands clutching his wound and whimpering as blood poured between his fingers.

"Are we done?" I asked, grabbing him by the collar. He nodded, and I let him crawl away from the square. The fight had lasted less than two minutes, but I was drained. I had at least one broken rib from Eigil's hug, my face hurt from his headbutt, and fighting Bjorn had taken much of my energy. I spat a gob rich in blood, then someone called my name.

"Drake! Little help here," Rune said, a hint of panic in his voice.

I had not even noticed the young Wolf fighting in the first square, so, for a second, I was afraid that I had stepped into the second one during my fight. But when I saw who he was fighting, I realized Rune was indeed in my zone.

Njal, the berserker from Hvitiseid, stood like a great bear in front of Rune, his nose caked with blood and his eyes mad with rage. Rune kept him off with two short axes, which was brave and probably unfortunate. *You need a shield*, Titus and I had told him hundreds of times.

But it wasn't his opponent who had gotten Rune to call for me; it was the other berserker in our square, Magnus Stone-Fists. Bjorn's nemesis dragged his latest victim, a solid Wend warrior with a bald, tattooed head, going by the name Jager. I had often considered Jager for the Wolves. He was tall, well-built, skilled with long swords and spears, and, more importantly, he was discreet and did not drink much. Of course, seeing him being dragged by the ankle, lifeless and broken, did not make him look glorious right now, but he was worthy.

What Rune seemed to know, and I had to guess, was that Njal and Magnus were working together, confirming my fear that Stone-Fists had already recruited Njal in his merry band. I thought this was probably how Cross-Eyes had gotten himself out of the brawl, with a combined and surprising effort of the two beasts.

Fighting by two in the brawl isn't forbidden per se, but only one man can win, so most of us choose not to get involved with someone who might betray us at the worst moment. This time, though, I thought it necessary to league with Rune rather than face the two berserkers by myself. Besides, the four of us remained only one man. He'd been a proud warrior of Bove, but as he now faced Magnus, the poor fellow probably realized by now that the first square had been a mistake. He would not buy me much time.

Wedge wouldn't help as much against those two, so I picked up Eigil's hammer. I had seen Njal fight on Midgard and had found a great weakness in his technique. He and Rune were panting when I came to stand beside my comrade. None of us had a shield, but neither did Njal and his massive axe.

"When you hear him scream, put one of those in his skull," I said.

"When I hear what—" Rune asked before being interrupted by Njal.

The berserker should have waited for his companion, but Njal was not the sharpest of tools. He aimed for me, swinging his axe downward. If I hadn't moved out of the way, it would have split my head in half, but I was prepared.

I stepped back, lifted Eigil's hammer, and brought it down with a roar. Njal leaned backward, but I hadn't been aiming at his head.

His shriek was surprisingly high-pitched, but it always was when one's foot was crushed. Njal was slow-footed; that was his flaw. He dropped his axe and meant to grab the ruin of his foot, as anyone would in that situation, and that's when Rune's axe dug itself into his skull. It was a bloodless stroke that cut the shriek and left the square in sudden silence.

Magnus finished his opponent at the same time, snapping the man's neck for the pleasure of the crowd. I heard Thor's guffaw and checked the dais. Odin was still unmoved, and his cold eye rested on me.

"Ah! I don't fight Bjorn today," Magnus said in his heavily Geat accent. He was barely sweating while I was drowning in it.

"The result will be the same," Rune spat as he yanked his axe out of Njal's head. Magnus shot a look of disdain at Rune, pursing his lips to show how little he cared about the boy's presence.

"You don't get to speak, puppy," Magnus spat. "Drake, if I win, you let me back in the Wolves, good? There is a spot, after all." Magnus had asked to rejoin the Wolves for decades. He had once won that honor in the brawl but had made such a mess of things down on Midgard that I had refused ever since. As long as I was the Drake, he would never be welcome in the pack.

"If you win, I will make you my champion," I said.

"What?" I heard Bjorn bark from outside the square. I had not seen him being dragged out but guessed Eigil had taken care of him.

"Don't worry, it won't happen. I will shame Magnus to the tenth square."

Men laughed around us, and I wondered how many laughed at me rather than with me. I was a great warrior, but some of us are beyond that, and Magnus was one of them. He was not only strong like an ox but naturally talented and far from stupid. Worse, he had no fear whatsoever, as he liked to prove by fighting barehanded. He wrapped his hands in leather thongs laced with thick plaques of iron, but that was it. As simple and disturbing a fighting style as one could be. Truly, if Magnus wasn't a drunk, rapist bastard, I would have liked him in my crew.

"*You* will shame me?" he asked, booming with a burst of short laughter. "I'd like to see that." He crouched and widened his arms like a father about to wrestle with his children.

"Any advice?" Rune asked on my left.

"Don't get caught," I said.

"Great," Rune replied with a snort. He probably thought I was joking, but my advice was honest; getting caught by Magnus was a death warrant. We were used to fighting blades, and men seldom tried to grab you in a shield wall, so when I said so, I meant it.

I had one great problem here; I still held Eigil's hammer. It was a heavy weapon that would cost me my agility. Njal had been tricked by it, but it wouldn't work on Magnus. Despite his bulk, he was fast and nimble.

Magnus understood the source of my worries and came for me. In three steps, he was in my range, but before I could react, he kicked me as a man would kick a door open. I only had time to bring the hammer pole to intercept the sole of his foot. The pole broke instantly, and I was sent rolling on my back. I was certain to be dead in the next second, expecting Magnus's fingers around my throat or something of the sort. So when I leaned on my elbows to find no one, my surprise was total, and it was nothing compared to what I witnessed.

Rune had not only stopped Magnus from pursuing his attack, he was keeping him at bay. *Fuck*, I thought, *the kid doesn't need a shield*.

Rune waved his two axes as if they were parts of his arms. They never touched each other as he swung them from every direction, and each blow was aimed at a vital spot. Magnus was doing well against this odd, beautiful form, but he was as confused as I was. I had never seen him so focused on defense, bobbing his head and twisting his body from Rune's blades with just enough time to see the next coming.

I was entranced by Rune's skill. The silence around the square was complete. Magnus took a step back. *The* Magnus Stone-Fists took a step back. It just never happened. He took another step and grunted in frustration. I felt more than I saw the berserker rise in him. Rune must have seen it, too.

"Drake!" he called, snapping me from the trance he had put me in.

I stood, picked up my shield, and removed Wedge from my belt again. Magnus had no eyes for me. In fact, I doubted he had eyes for anything but the boy who was indeed shaming him in front of the gods. Rune slowed his attacks, and Magnus punched with a shout to make the walls tremble. My shield was in the way of the punch, which I deflected more than I stopped.

"I'm here," I said when Rune stepped back, his face purple from the lack of oxygen. Magnus meant to grab my shield, but I sliced with Wedge just as his fingers caught the rim. I got nothing but a respite. His knee came up next, and this time, Rune's axe was on the way, the flat of it at least. I attacked then, jumping high enough to try stabbing Magnus in the eye. He ducked it, but Rune sliced at his face, draining blood from his cheek.

Magnus knelt, almost fell, and found a handle under his hand. Not knowing what it was, he waved it in a wide arc, but since it was a spear, I raised my shield and felt the clunk of wood against wood. Rune tried to axe Magnus's arm, but the berserker parried the blades with the iron on his fists, sending sparks flying as the two connected.

I kicked Magnus's knee when he tried to stand and welcomed his moan of pain with delight. He rolled sideways and stood in the same movement, far from his usual confident self. Not wanting to lose momentum, I pressed the attack with Rune by my side.

I can count on one hand the number of times I have witnessed a fight worthy of legend. The kind of duels that make it into songs sung at the courts of kings and gods. The kind that seemed choreographed, for everything fell naturally into place. This was one such duel, and this was the first including me.

Rune and I did not just make a great team; we were one. We alternated attack and defense naturally, read each other's movements, and moved accordingly. I felt the joy of battle like never before, and from what I heard later, my grin spanned from ear to ear as Rune and I dealt blow after blow. I forgot why I was fighting. I was doing it for the sheer fucking pleasure of it, and I did not want it to stop.

But Magnus did. That he survived this long was a testament to his abilities, but he was battered and bloodied, breathless and confused, like a deer at the end of the hunt. He was on his ass, ready to give up, and I was about to deal the killing blow; when he did one of the cheapest tricks a warrior can do, he threw a handful of dust and earth in my face.

Jumping back, I tried to rub it from my eyes, which only made it worse. The discomfort was great, but I managed to blink out the dust and saw Rune and Magnus completely still. Magnus had caught Rune's wrist when the latter tried to chop both axes at the same time. The berserker stood, his confident grin back in place, blood spilling freely from his nose and skull. Rune hadn't listened to my advice; he got caught. Or so I thought.

The boy sprang up, using Magnus's grip for support, and shot his foot in the berserker's chin. For the time of a heartbeat, Rune stood straight but upside down, feet to the sky and hands trapped in Magnus's palms. Then, he was back on his feet, free of the grip, as Magnus staggered backward. I do not know how Magnus managed to snatch one of the axes, but now both of them wielded one. And, as I dashed back into the melee, they both tried to end it there.

The attack was the same, a chopping motion aimed at the base of the neck from the right. Magnus was taller and stronger; he would prevail. I raised my shield and even put my right arm behind it to absorb the shock, which was as violent as expected and took my breath away. Magnus's blade splintered the metallic boss and the wood behind and still carried enough strength to bite into the skin of my forearm.

There was a gurgling sound. I dropped my shield to take a look behind it. Nothing had blocked Rune's axe except for Magnus's neck. It was so deeply rooted in it that Rune had to let it go. The weight on my shield increased when Magnus toppled, so I let it go.

"Who's the puppy now?" Rune asked the gaping shape of Magnus. The young man's eyes brimmed with pride and battle lust, and I wondered when he had become so magnificent. Had he always been so great, or had he just discovered his skills when he picked a second axe? The latter was unlikely, but the former meant he had been hiding something from us.

I peeled Magnus's weak fingers from the second axe, and still he grunted, as if contesting the results of the fight. He deserved little compassion, but I would make it quick.

I chopped the rest of his neck in one big, clean stroke. The head popped off in a spray of blood, and the cheers of the crowd drowned us. Magnus's carcass convulsed for the last of his heartbeats, and he became still. One of his minions would carry his head and hold it close to the stomp of his neck until it reattached itself. It would hurt for a few days, and he would not eat well for longer, but he would get over it. This wasn't his first beheading. His pride, though, would take longer to heal.

Rune opened his arms to me, his teeth white in contrast to the drying blood on his face. I opened my arms as well, still shaking from the greatness of our teamwork. And just as we were about to embrace, cheering for the pleasure of our victory, I slammed my head in his face. I had forgotten that Eigil had done the same a few minutes ago, and it hurt instantly, but not as much as it did Rune.

His eyes rolled up, and he dropped to his knees under the laughter of the spectators. I did have time for a lesson tonight, after all.

"Only one warrior wins the brawl," I told him as he fell on his ass.

It was cheap, Rune would be pissed, but I had won. I had made many people unhappy during this brawl. The crowd was pleased, though and Thor as well. The god of thunder rushed down the dais to offer me my cup of water, a rare honor. I gobbled it in one straight gulp. Muninn would be happy, too, though she did a good job of hiding it, only revealing her pleasure with a discreet nod.

"I didn't know you had this in you," Thor all but shouted in my ear, his breath heavy in mead.

"I hope you won't forget it," I replied with just enough vehemence for him to wonder if I was serious. He chose to laugh, and I must admit his laughter was infectious.

"I won't, Drake," he said, using my title for the first time in ages.

Valkyries were already passing among us, delivering cups of water and refilling the others with mead. Titus had lost his square to a shield maiden named Gunhild, the greatest of those female warriors, and I guessed it was partly due to his concern for Rune.

The lines in the ground marking the limits of the squares vanished in a green light. Immediately, the mixed feeling of relief and pain surged as bones, skin, and all the other things that made a body, mended themselves. I had received only minor damage during the fight, the worst being the headbutt from Eigil, but even that hurt like Hel when it healed.

"You fought better than ever," I told Rune, offering my hand in a silent apology. For a second, I thought he would not take it, but he begrudgingly grasped my forearm and shook it once.

"I came close."

"You did, but you let your emotions steal victory from you."

"Not my emotions," he said through his teeth.

"What then?" I knew what he would say, but I owed him some playing along.

"*You* took it from me, you old... tree-humper," he said, hesitating for so long before insulting me that it made it comical. We all laughed, even him, after some time. "Can I use those now?" he asked, showing us the two bloody axes.

Titus and I tilted our heads similarly.

"I don't like it," Titus said. "But you showed what you could do without a shield tonight."

"I agree," I said. "Maybe you'll finally be useful now."

Rune was about to blurt some kind of reply, but silence drowned Valhöll in a quick wave. Odin had stood from his throne, his hand flat in a request for our attention.

"Drake," he called. "You proved yourself worthy of your title tonight. You won, not too fairly, but bravely." The hall laughed. I knew a barb when I heard one, and Odin had meant to shame me a little. He could not dispute the result, though. "I grant you one wish. Tell me what it is."

I fought the urge to check Muninn, knowing Odin would not miss it.

"With your permission," I said loud enough for all the men around to hear, "I wish to go back to Lagardalr and need one of your nails." Few of the beings near the dais would understand the oddity of my request, but as one, they stiffened.

"A week ago, you complained about going down to Midgard too often, and now you fought like a wyvern for the right to get back there?" Odin asked, not even trying to mask his exasperation. "A woman waiting for you in Lagardalr, perhaps?" It was an easy jest, but men like those, and even mine laughed.

"Not a woman," I replied. "A man. Two, in fact. Ulf, who now awaits Ragnarök in Helheim, and Einar, whose body is being pecked by crows as we feast. They fought well, and I wish to honor them with a proper funeral. Einar will be back faster, and Ulf... Well, Ulf will have been treated as a Wolf should."

It got them quiet. It got all of them quiet. I felt ashamed for using my friends' deaths, but I was not lying either. I would use this opportunity to send them off. Muninn and I had agreed on it.

"Is that all?" Odin asked.

The only other thing I needed was for Muninn to accompany me, but that I could not ask. I needed to push Odin to send her with me. Luckily, Muninn knew how to trick her father and had taught me my next words.

"It may take some time before I am done. Probably a few days. If I don't return within a week, I would ask for Bjorn to replace me as Drake."

This was one of the worst things I could have said, and it piqued Odin's nerves even better than we intended. My words reeked of desertion. It gave just enough for Odin to guess a deeper meaning to my request. I was naming a replacement and had asked to leave by myself, all of it just after having displeased my lord. He would have been a fool not to guess some betrayal.

"I consent," he said. "And I will even send Muninn to assist you." What he meant was to send Muninn to make sure I would come back. Among the few beings who could travel the realms as they pleased, Muninn was the one he trusted the most. She had us both fooled, and at least I lived to know even the All-Father was tricked by his daughter too. She stepped forward and stood silently by her father's side. "Is this fine with you?" he asked.

I heard some chuckles at my back and prayed for Odin to notice none of it.

"It is fine," I said. "I will be as fast as I can." This was a weak promise but one I intended to keep.

"You will have your nail in the morning," Odin said. I bowed and sensed him walk away before I raised my head again. Muninn followed him, and I did not see her again that night. The feast resumed as soon as the All-Father left the hall, and I was surrounded by my men before I could breathe out. I had won the brawl and tricked Odin. Not bad for a mere evening.

"So that was your plan?" Bjorn asked smugly after he clasped my back a little too hard.

"Ulf deserves it," I said, pretending I had not understood his innuendo.

"Not that part of your plan. I'm talking about you and your little lovebird taking some vacation time on Midgard."

"I have no idea what you are talking about," I replied, faking some naughtiness in my voice. I needed my men to believe my desires to be carnal, just as I needed Odin to believe in my devotion to my dead comrades.

"Well, don't go get your beak wet for too long," Bjorn said as we crossed the hall to our table. "I don't intend to lead that sorry bunch for ages."

"Me neither," I replied. "Don't want to come back to a pack of drunks."

He punched me in the shoulder before we banged cups, any trace of the fight already gone from my champion's mind.

The rest of the evening was pleasant, and, in truth, I spent a good time with those great men. For a few hours, I drank and laughed my worries away. But no matter what, I was way over my head in this story. I had lied to Odin and hidden some information as well. Bringing Huginn home would put me back in Odin's good grace, though. Or so I hoped.

But I was not to be bothered with those thoughts for the rest of the evening. I enjoyed the company, the food, and the drinks. And it was the last time I would ever truly enjoy Valhöll.

13

Loki's cave, later. Much later.

The two Sigyn came and went with no sense of regularity I could comprehend. One minute, I was playing Loki to the warm and silly Sigyn; the next, she was back to the ice-cold crone I had started calling Frigg-Sigyn. I would not call her that to her face, at least after the first time, for her slap could knock a bull out.

Frigg-Sigyn rarely stayed as long as her other self—a day at most—but I had come to hate her. Her presence meant miserable, silent, and frightening days during which the bowl filled less. I first thought Frigg-Sigyn and I would get along because we shared a mutual hatred for her husband, but then I realized she did not truly hate him; she loved him dearly.

Years of imprisonment, the death of their son, and Loki's many affairs had twisted her love, but it was there nonetheless. She loved his rebellious spirit, his promise of an eventful fate, and his mind for beauty, but too much had happened. To protect this love, Sigyn had created this darker personality in which she stored all she hated in Loki and gave it a voice, a life, and some of her time.

I understood Sigyn and the existence of Frigg-Sigyn, but I did not like it when she was in control. Sigyn, the original giggling one, was much more entertaining. She told stories with no sense of logic, laughed at mine, and had a fertile and childish talent for fabricating amazing kennings and bynames. It even became a game between us to devise names for each of the gods.

Odin became the Three-Legged-Wanderer, Frigg, the Salt-Licker, Thor was Thunderous-Farts, and Freyja, Tits-Shower. After several weeks—or what I assumed were weeks—the list of names had grown to the point it became a game of memory more than creativity.

And then there were days when I would have preferred Sigyn to shut up. Brooding days when my thoughts went to my men, to young Lif, and to my Æsir friends. I wondered for hours if any of them still lived or if they even sensed a difference in the Drake walking by their side. For all I knew, Loki had even found allies within the Wolves.

Snekke and Karl could be bought, Eigil and Cross-Eyes fooled, and, of course, Rune was most likely an agent of the trickster to begin with. But worse were the moments when I envisioned Loki and Muninn enjoying each other and their victory over the fool that I was. My shame was nothing compared to the coming of Ragnarök, but it was more personal, and there wasn't a night I did not feel it grip my heart with jagged claws. So, on those days, I was cruel to Sigyn, and if there was one pattern I ever discovered between them, it was the presence of Frigg-Sigyn the following day.

I cried, more than a man should, but I cried, and neither

of the Sigyns handled those times well. One would follow my lead, and the other would smack me on the head. Resignation came faster than I thought it would, probably after a month.

I would remain chained to this rock until Ragnarök or the next end of the world, and there was nothing I could do about it. The snake would forever try to kill me, but Loki's body would regenerate too fast for the poison to do real damage. Sigyn would never hurt me, no matter how much I tried to trick her into doing it. And Frigg-Sigyn would never disobey her order to keep me alive.

She had faith in her husband's promise to come back, though we both knew Loki was fated to die during the last battle, so how he planned to do it, she didn't know. He told her he would come back before Ragnarök, and, for a time, I hoped it meant the end of the world had not happened yet. Then, I believed Loki had lied about this as well and had never intended to return for her.

I thought of Titus and his stoicism, understanding after the first month what it truly meant. I prayed for the snake, which I had named Skadi, after the Jötunn who had captured the reptile and charmed it with eternal life, to somehow magically slip from the rock and end my life at last. Or for Sigyn to create a third personality, one with a murderous side. Or for a bolt to shoot from the fucking sky and melt my brain in an amazing stroke of luck. Of course, I could do nothing about any of those solutions, no matter how many tricks I devised. I did not share Loki's talent for pulling gold from a barrel of shit, and neither had I Thor's strength to break those chains into hundreds of useless links.

Loki had spent twenty-seven years in this cave without a better solution than using me; how could I do better? I was

Drake, only Drake, an Einheri. Just an Einheri. And as days grew to months, I, too, lost my mind.

I first realized it as Sigyn humped me, something she did with alarming regularity. I had resisted that too, at first, wriggling like an unbroken colt. Sigyn thought it was a new game, and my attempts made matters worse. Then she broke me, and I started participating.

In my defense, Sigyn was a decent lover with no shame in her desire, and also, I was bored. For a while, I used sex as a simple time-killing activity. But one day, I surprised myself, enjoying the act fully, moaning and smiling as Sigyn rode me, and it made me shiver with fear. Needless to say, my physical reaction matched my thoughts, and Sigyn got little pleasure from that ride, which meant Frigg-Sigyn visited me the next day. This one never touched me longer than the time it took to backhand me.

Any noise from our part, whether sex, laughter, or arguments, rendered the snake furious. Skadi was a ball of anger, raging from being so close to its prey and forever denied the bite. I tried to stretch my head as far as possible, hoping it could reach me and end things. But the distance was just a little too great, and instead, it just made its venom spitting easier.

I gave up the idea of dying. When I noticed my madness, I let Skadi hit me just to feel something. Nowhere too supremely painful. A drop would fall on my forehead, drawing a shriek that turned my throat sore and my lungs empty, and for the briefest of moments, I was alive.

The cave worked similarly to Valhöll, though what Odin's hall did with space, the cave did with time. It warped it, made it stretch longer than the mind could comprehend in a never-ending loop. Nights followed each other so slowly that I wondered if I had dreamt the day in between. Each word passing my lips, each sound penetrating my ears, and each sensation coursing through my body felt as if it had been experienced a thousand times already, and I cried as much as I laughed, usually at the same time.

I missed the simplest things, like the songs of birds, the taste of ale, the smell of fresh paint on a shield. Even Karl's grumbling would be music to my ears. Odin had given his eye for knowledge; I would give both of mine for a night on Jötunheimr, my tongue for a bath in the icy waters of Lake Vanern, and my vanishing sanity for Skadi to grow another foot longer.

For a time, I thought I might actually have been in Helheim all this time, but the idea washed away, replaced by the certainty that I was nowhere in space, no *when* in time. I was stuck with an angry snake and a two-faced crazy goddess, and I laughed as she rode me.

But sometimes, when the snake and the Æsir slept while I did not, my mind retreated on itself and remembered my last day of freedom. I had been in love, ready to become a hero to Muninn and a savior to Odin's sanity. I was a fool.

ᛦ

Asgard, one day before Loki's cave

"Odin has mixed feelings about this," Muninn told me on the brawl's morning as we walked to the Bifröst.

"Something between pissed and furious?" It was a feeble joke. I had not slept well.

"On the contrary. A part of him is proud of you."

"And the other part?"

"The other part didn't like starting the day by pulling one of his nails out."

"Can't blame him for that. But getting his precious raven-son back will improve his mood." I had thought of cheering Muninn, but she seemed lost to it. In fact, if I had not been so enamored with her, I might have noticed her thoughts wriggling with doubts. Of course, if I had not been feeling for her as much, I would not have been in this mess in the first place.

"We will start with your men," she said, echoing the decision we had made two nights ago.

None of us knew what would happen in that cave. She claimed she would sense her brother once we got close enough, but maybe he could too, in which case, he might try to avoid us. It would become a game of hide-and-seek, which could go on for ages. Gods were famous for their stubbornness. Starting with my two brothers was just common sense.

"I will be fast," I told her. I didn't think she cared much about Ulf and Einar.

"Your men deserve a funeral," she said absently. "And if we see this Bove—"

"—I kill him," I said. I had not told Odin about it, but I made it clear with Muninn what would happen if the big bastard was alive and in our path. "Then I'm all yours."

"I thought that was already the case," she said playfully. We giggled like the two lovers we were not, and I don't know why I said what I said next. There was no reason, but reason had nothing to do with my relationship with Muninn.

"You know I am," I said.

She did not speak, but her eyes said plenty. They were sorry, those two black moons I loved with all my heart. I took it for pity, as if she meant that she knew of my feelings but could not respond to them.

She told me I would not need to use the Bifröst on the way back. We would use it to travel down, to preserve her *seidr,* then she would fly me up once done on Midgard, hopefully accompanied by Huginn. I would still need to swallow Odin's nail; otherwise, the border between the realms would turn me into a pile of ash, but I would not need to die this time. I was strangely excited at the prospect of flying, not only with her, but just of flying. It had been many years since my last experience of the sort, and I had loved it then.

Despite our last encounter, Heimdallr was all smiles when I arrived at the cliff's edge. The kind of smiles men throw at their friends before calling them a goat or something of the sort. He knew of my desire for Odin's raven, and I detected a hint of pride in his golden eyes as we approached. *Well done*, I could hear him think.

"Aren't you traveling a bit light?" he asked, a point I agreed on. I had no helmet, typical chain mail, a light shield, and Wedge.

"I'm not going into battle," I said. I had insisted on the shield, for no warrior traveled without, and I felt naked if it did not cover my back. The rest, Muninn had insisted, wasn't necessary and would only make the journey back more difficult for her. Huginn, she said, would tear through anything I wore if he so wanted. She claimed that only my dwarfish long knife could harm him, but she made me promise to use it only if she told me to.

"Less to remove," Heimdallr said with a wink. "If it gets too wet," he then said apologetically when Muninn caught his jest, though his last words only made it worse. She punched him in the chest, and I was stupefied to see him wince. *Was she that strong?*

"Same place as last time?" he asked, massaging his chest.

"Same as last time," I replied.

With that, he blew in his horn and called for the rainbow bridge to open. I had not been expecting much, but seeing none of my men to send me off itched my pride. I guessed to them I was just taking a trip down with the woman I longed for, nothing to worry about and certainly nothing to wake up for.

"Don't be too long," Heimdallr told me as the horn found his belt again.

"We won't," I promised.

She jumped first, diving like a prey bird and barely making a splash as she crossed the watery bridge. I nodded to my god friend and followed her.

ᛉ

Traces of the two fires we had built by the river were still present, but the scenery had changed already. White covered the land in a thin layer of black ice and snow, though it wasn't particularly cold at this moment. Muninn stood by one of the circles of ashes, already gathering pieces of wood for a fire. She wasn't skilled in this particular art. Gods didn't feel cold as we did and didn't require a fire until everything froze around them. And when they did need a fire, someone built it for them. This fire was for me.

"Thank you," I said as I knelt by her side to help pile up the branches more efficiently. It took an incommensurable effort to stop looking at the wet dress clinging to her like a second skin, marrying the shape of her perfect hips, perfect ass, perfect breasts, perfect—

"Is everything all right?" she asked when I failed to take my eyes off her.

"I just think it's cold."

"It is. That's why we're trying to build a fire. Well, *I* am, at least." The heat on my face increased another few degrees. I decided to play a bit of her own game.

"Since you too feel cold, you should know we usually get naked to warm up."

"I've been watching you for many years, Drake lie-weaver; I know you don't."

"Can't fault a man for trying," I said.

"Yes, I absolutely can," she replied, bringing a strand of wet hair behind her ear. "But as I said, I watched you for many years; I know what kind of man you are. I don't fault you for trying."

The meaning of her words took a long time to sink in. She knew of my feelings but did not shy away from them. If I ever had a chance with Muninn, it was now. But something prevented me from grabbing her by the neck and kissing her with the passion burning inside, something that would have made my men laugh. If she responded to my desire as a sign of gratitude, then we ended up discovering nothing here; she might resent me. I'd have Muninn because she wanted me and for no other reason.

When Huginn is back, I told myself.

What a fool.

Less than an hour later, we left for Lagardalr, almost dry and ready for what would come next. It was not the first time I went on a mission without the Wolves or with a limited version of my pack, but never had I been in more pleasant company. Sadly, it made the path stream faster.

We came upon the village around noon, and I wasn't ready for the spectacle offered to us. Some people had gathered the bodies of the slain in front of Lagardalr, but, for some reason, had not finished the job. It stank from two hundred paces away, and clouds of flies swarmed in the air. Einar's head rotted at the bottom of the tumulus, and I had yet to see his body. I was tempted to look for it now but needed to check the great hall, where my ashes and Ulf's remains rested.

Muninn brought her hand to her nose. If they did not mind the cold, the gods were as bothered by the stench of death as we were.

As we passed the walls that had protected our retreat, I let an astonished whistle pass my lips. My plan had worked much better than expected. Hakon's great hall was a pile of fuming dark wood and charcoal. Most of the village stood no better. A couple of houses had miraculously escaped the fire, as did the barn, but that was it. A group of four men emerged from the latter building, each armed with spears and shields.

"What do you want?" one of them asked. The silver rings on his arms marked him as their leader. I did not remember him, but this was no surprise, I had a terrible memory for faces.

"We heard there was going to be a battle," I said, keeping a safe distance from those men. "I guess we're too late."

"Aye, that you are," the man replied. "And you should thank the gods you are. This was a massacre, not a battle."

"Is your wife a healer?" another asked, eyeing Muninn from head to toe.

"I can heal a little," she replied. I liked that she took no offense for being taken as my wife.

"Good, we have a man in need of you." They invited us into the barn, and I learned everything I needed to learn there, including Bove's fate.

He had been a force of nature and had fought like a Jötunn, but Bove was done. He lay on the very patch of hay I had slept on not so long ago, eyes and mouth agape, staring blankly at the ceiling like one of those old men who do not accept death even when its fingers are around their throat.

Already he smelled of shit and blood and many other things that took me in waves of disgust and made me gag. I didn't even know one could survive with so much skull peeled from one's brain. Without the wincing of his breathing and the beating of the veins on the side of his head, I would have assumed him dead already.

"The roof fell on his head," the leader said. "The four of us were still outside when it happened. We dragged him out, but he was the only one."

Four men. We had left four men. I would have been proud of myself if my pity for Jarl Bove had not surpassed my hatred.

Bove's eyes slowly slid to me, and I saw them rounding up and heard the poor excuse of a voice screaming in his broken throat as he recognized me. Dying people had power, and Bove was close enough to Helheim that Muninn's spell had not taken him. His agitation was pathetic. Two of his men held him down as he spewed a mix of saliva, pus, and blood from the corners of his lips.

"I cannot help him," Muninn said, Bove's hand in hers. "He's too far gone."

"Why didn't you kill him?" I asked, trying not to sound harsh.

"We hesitated," one of them said. "But we don't know if he will go to Valhöll if he dies like this. Technically, he survived the battle."

I understood his issue. Folks didn't know what the gods considered worthy of Asgard, and frankly, neither did I. It was all more a guess born from centuries of experience than facts, but from what I knew, Bove was doomed. Had he died in the fire, he may have had a chance. No Valkyrie watched him now, as I told them.

"Put a blade in his hand, slit his throat, and pray to Odin, that's the best you can do." An idea popped into my mind as those four men sighed in unison. "Burn all the dead men with him and gather the ashes of those from the hall; it may attract Odin's eye."

It wouldn't, but at least my men would receive their funeral, and I could pray for Ulf in peace despite these men's presence. I sounded confident enough that none of them thought to contradict me.

With the help of the few villagers who had survived and returned, the six of us gathered the corpses. It took the better part of the afternoon to prepare the pyre and get the slain ready. I recognized some of the men I now called brothers during the process.

Njal was pale and bloated, his open wounds festering with maggots. I took great care to dispose of Einar's body at the center of the pile, his head on top of his neck. Those who had died in the hall—more than half of the dead—were mostly ashes, though here and there remained the blackened remains of a warrior. Rib cages opened to the sky, skulls with hanging lower jaws, and curling fingers forever denied the handle of a sword or the warmth of their wives' skin. Them too, we gathered. Ulf was somewhere among them, and so were my ashes.

"He's long gone," Muninn said. Her hand fell on my shoulder as I gathered some ash in a small linen pouch. I knew Ulf had been in Helheim for two days already, and yet I felt his presence in this place. His ghost had been waiting for me, and I had come.

"I know," I said, touching her fingers with the tips of mine. "Give me a second, please." She left, drifting from the burned hall like a spirit, and I let my sadness overcome me one last time.

"Your granddaughter," I told him as I shoved more ash into the pouch, "is a child of fate. And if you thought she was a wonder, you were still far from it. She has so much greatness in her that even Frigg has taken a liking for her."

A cold wind brushed the scent of death across the empty hall. It would be dark soon. We needed to light the pyre before it happened.

"Hakon should be by your side," I continued, "so I cannot help him. But Lif, I will watch over her as well as you would have. And someday, maybe, some god will marry her, and the blood of Ulf, my friend, will become that of a new line of Æsir. Who knows, your great-great-grandson might become the god of archers or sour losers if he takes after you."

The pyre was huge and burned well.

Bove died before any of his men had to cut his throat, and his body rested among his dead warriors and enemies as we sent him to the Corpse Shore or to another part of Helheim if he was lucky.

The night was thick when we abandoned the fire, sure that the wind would keep it alive and rain would remain away. Einar was now back with his son.

"What will you do?" the leader of the four survivors asked. I had learned his name and laughed inside. Thorstein the Lucky. As far as I could tell, he was a decent man and had earned his byname.

"There are other wars to fight in," I said. "Many jarls in need of warriors."

We sat in a crude circle around a smaller fire, chewing

on pieces of fat pork and juicy onions. At this point, a dozen villagers had reclaimed the village, but they had understandably made their own circle. Muninn sat by my side, playing the good wife, her arm crooked in mine. Not an unpleasant moment.

"How about you?" she asked.

Thorstein tilted his head left and right, pursing his lips as he pondered on it.

"We have enough silver to last a lifetime," he said in a great show of honesty. The four of them had looted enough silver rings and beads and whatever else they could to fill a hoard, but being only four men, they could do little about it. Possessing so much silver presented more danger than opportunity.

"I think Lagardalr will need leadership," I said, not loud enough for the villagers to hear. It stilled Thorstein in his chewing, and his three men looked at me, then at him, as if I had just solved all their problems.

"Nothing left here," he replied.

"Still a mountain full of iron, I have heard."

He shook his head as if to say he wasn't interested, but I could see his brain working on it already. His silver would find a hole in the ground somewhere nearby to be dug out when trade and war needed it. His three men would become rich and important in the region, and together, they would fill the void left by the disappearance of Bove and Hakon. And if the world still existed by then, the Wolves would be back in three or four generations. I had planted a seed in a man's head and would reap warriors for my lord. Such was the task of Odin's Drake.

"That was smart," Muninn whispered in my ear as those four men smiled dreamily, thinking of their future.

"Surprised?" I asked.

"Not at all," she replied before taking a long sip of ale.

Her eyes never left mine as she drank; the light of the fire bounced mischievously around her pupils, and all I saw of the world were those two dark, brilliant jewels. My blood thumped in my ears, no air passed through my nose, and I lost myself in my lust for her.

I decided then that I had had enough.

I stood, leaving my wooden cup on the floor, and held my hand to her.

"Come," I said.

She frowned with surprise and took a couple of seconds before accepting my hand. I did not let it go as we walked to the forest, and though I managed to keep my confidence, it threatened to leave through my mouth. The drum in my chest shot fire in my veins and would let nothing pass the knot in my throat. Muninn's hand in mine was cold and strong, the grip from her thin fingers willing.

"What is it?" she asked when the warmth of the fire was but a distant memory. I did not reply. Truth was, I had not planned what would come next. I just wanted her for myself and had acted on an impulse I would dearly regret if not pursued. "Drake," she called, using her Æsir's strength to stop me in my tracks just as we neared the first trees. She still did not let go of my hand.

I wanted to wait until we found your brother, I told her in my heart. The playful moon chose this moment to reveal itself from the cover of a cloud and cast its light on her skin. *But I can't wait longer than now. I want to be with you, and I have for many, many years.* I pulled a strand of her hair behind her ear with my callous hand, using this chance to caress the top of her ear. *It might sound ridiculous for a man like me to claim love for a woman like you, but I cannot hide it anymore. I will not greet another sun on Midgard or Asgard without you being mine.*

I don't know how long passed while Muninn and I looked at each other in perfect stillness. Then, as if they had a will of their own, my fingers went from her ear, down her hair, and ended behind her neck. I pulled Muninn to me and, with no resistance, found her lips. Her hands timidly reached for my hips, and I pulled her even closer. My left arm coiled around her waist while the other would not let go of her head, worried that if I gave her some room, she would part away. Our lips broke away after a time that could have lasted a second or an hour, but my eyes refused to open while my brain carved this moment in my memory.

"You took your time," she said.

Forehead to forehead, we giggled, our brains not having registered yet that our bodies were already moving as one.

"I am slow. Will you forgive me?"

"Only if you stop talking," she said as she pulled me to the forest floor with her. Muninn and I made love that night for the first and last time. It was not only the greatest moment of passion I had ever experienced with a woman in my very long life; it was the greatest moment of all.

She and I became one; our bodies responded to the need of the other with burning desire, and our moans of pleasure echoed in the dark as we switched from leading the dance to being led. Muninn's body bathed in the light of Mani, the moon god, and I knew in my heart of hearts that nothing had ever been as beautiful as she.

Surrounded by the stars and the spirits of the forest, we communed, turned into one body by the flesh and by our lust. Muninn was, in turn, fire and ice. She knew me and I her as if we had been hewn from the same tree. She could be strong when she rode me and enjoyed it greatly when I did as much.

On the opposite side of war, which makes a moment feel a thousand, our love ended in the blink of an eye, though our struggle for air and all the images forever carved in my mind suggested that we had been playing for longer than Bragi would need to recite a poem.

She straddled me, offering her breasts to the sky and smiling with delight when I gave up and released the growing tension in me. She was spent, too, and let herself fall like a leaf on my chest. Our breath matched again as we tried to recover it, her heart beating even faster against mine. I kissed the top of her head as she pressed herself ever closer to me, her sweat already turning cold. I pulled my cloak over her back, thinking to keep her warm and on me.

Then, when enough time had passed without either of us moving, I said, "I'm glad I won that brawl." This was probably the stupidest thing I ever said, but it broke the silence with her laughter.

Her hand moved up the cloak and reached my beard. She gently pulled on it and kissed me again, with less energy than before but no less passion.

"I'm glad you did," she said. "I just have one question."

"What is it?" I asked as her hand went back under the cover of the cloak, then a little farther below.

"Is one time enough for humans?"

ᚤ

"If I had known that women too could become Einherjar, I would have filled my ships with the plumpest women from Birka to Aarhus. Not enough shield-maidens in Valhöll as it is. And Valkyries, pwah, all bark and no meat. No, friend, give me a farmer girl from Götaland, a wench from Uppsala, even a feisty Finn, and I'll be a happy man. I'd have won more battles, too."

Jarl Ivar Nine-Fingers

14

My comrades had been sent off properly, Bove was dead, and the previous night had made me a happy man, and a happy man I woke. But Muninn wasn't in my arms when I did, though she had been when I closed my eyes late in the night, back in the barn. I wondered if she had slept or if she slept at all, but I missed her presence already. I found her by the lake, eyes lost on the horizon as it welcomed the sun's first rays.

Muninn usually clung to the shadows and dark corners of rooms, so seeing her in the glory of dawn pinched my heart with satisfaction. She looked a little older in the morning light, but even more beautiful in my eyes.

I was tempted to embrace her from behind, but I knew women sometimes felt different the morning after sex, and so I chose a more discreet approach. Yet I could not stop myself from kissing her shoulder. There was resistance when I did, and I congratulated myself for not having acted more boldly than this.

"Is everything all right?" I asked.

She did not reply for a time, but I knew everything

wasn't all right. I relived the night's events in my mind, trying to change my point of view to notice any mistake I could have made and missed. From what I saw, Muninn had been satisfied. There had been no grudge in her as we walked back to the village. I even guessed she felt more than some carnal satisfaction when her fingers found mine as we lay in the hay for sleep. Something had changed in between, as I slept.

"What do you think of fate?" she asked, eyes lost on the water of the lake as it reflected the young sun like so many mirrors. As often with the Æsir, I chose to answer honestly.

"I think fate cannot be understood until it happens, and then it's too late. I think it bites you in the ass just when you believe you've managed to avoid it."

"So you think it's pointless to fight destiny," she said more than she asked. "We should just let Ragnarök happen as prophesied?"

"I did not say that," I replied. Muninn's fate was Odin's fate, as she had told me, and Odin's fate was to be killed by the mighty wolf Fenrir, son of Loki. Until now, I thought she had made her peace with this idea, but maybe I had given her a reason to long for life. "Heimdallr told me that Ragnarök was maybe the best we can hope for. He said that if we tempered with the prophecy, things might get worse."

"And what do you think, Drake of the Einherjar?" she asked.

"I think that if there is a way to keep you from death, I will find it, no matter the consequences."

A single tear rolled down her cheek and dropped by her foot. I did not know what was going through her mind, but she was struggling with something, and I had just made it worse.

"Einherjar have all died once," I went on. "So, whether

we make it through Ragnarök is irrelevant. It doesn't mean I wish to face a more permanent death, and I would prefer some of my comrades to survive. But for you, Lif, and for Odin, I'm ready to challenge fate."

Muninn whipped the trace of her tear from her face and made herself strong. She had come to a decision because of my words. "Let's go to that cave then," she said.

Folks, Valkyries, Æsir, and Vanir all feared Ragnarök. Even Jötnar were said to view it with mixed feelings. I thought Muninn had just rediscovered her own mortality in a new light, as we all did from time to time. I guessed the gods had a harder time with the concept because it did not concern them as often as it did us, but when they considered it, you never knew what kind of reaction it could bring. Heimdallr scoffed it off, Thor drank it off, and Muninn, though I did not see it, had decided to set Ragnarök off by herself.

ᛦ

The walk toward the cave offered a much more agreeable sight than my last visit. The sun lay on the right side of the hill, and the eerie silence had been replaced by little birds chirping as they toiled ahead of a harsh winter. Muninn's company, however, did nothing to cleanse the nefarious aura circling the hill in a thick *seidr*. We breached the invisible border of the magic veil, after which Muninn called a stop.

"Is your brother here?" I asked, guessing that if he was, this was where she would sense him. She shook her head, but even I felt the tension emanating from every pore of her skin. "It's not far from here." The cave's mouth cut through the rock ahead. I swallowed Odin's nail then.

"Don't you need one?" I asked Muninn, suddenly realizing my lack of foresight.

"I'm a part of Odin," she replied as if it explained everything.

"Should we call your brother?" I asked. If he were here, I would rather him be in the open than be trapped with him in the cave.

"I've been trying for a few minutes already," she said anxiously. "I don't think he's here, at least not right now. But he's been recently; I can feel it in my bones."

I had a small firebrand with me this time, taken from Thorstein's group before we left them to their fate. Its weak flame accompanied us as we struggled in the narrow passage leading to the room with all the feathers and turned our shadows into malicious ghosts. Muninn walked behind me, and I held Wedge in my right hand by my waist.

The pressure gripped my heart and brought the taste of copper to my mouth, its origin being the *seidr* flooding the place and maybe Muninn's, who I thought might have been using some charms on us before we reached the end of the cave. Huginn wasn't there. I breathed out and tucked Wedge back in my belt.

No one had entered the place since my last visit. At least that's what it looked like. The feathers, more than I had guessed from the candle's feeble light, had been swept by the wind to the bottom of the walls, leaving the center of the room bare. The pile of furs was just as I had left it, and I could guess the shape of the torc under the first layer.

"I don't think he's been back here," I said as I checked the table for clues. There wasn't any trace of food or drink, but even Æsir needed them, usually in greater quantity than us. Muninn did not reply. Her attention was absorbed by the wall at the very end of the room, the one I had failed to check last time. She caressed the flat rock, leaving the white imprint of her fingers through the dust. The rock even shined.

"Is it Asgard's marble?" I asked as I came by Muninn's side.

My question reverberated between the walls of the room before leaving me none the wiser. Yet, I could not be wrong. The color was the same as the gigantic wall slabs protecting the citadel, and the same, slightly darker veins ran through the marble, giving it an almost living appearance.

I brushed more dust away, uncovering the same stone on the entire height of the wall. This could not be good. It did not exist on Midgard. Some Æsir or Vanir had placed this stone here. *But why here?* I meant to ask Muninn this exact question, but she spoke first.

"Forgive me, Drake."

I looked at her and knew nothing would ever be the same. Wedge was in her small hands, tip pointed at my belly. I had not even felt her taking it from my belt.

A flash of clarity hit me. One of those moments that stretched and stretched but left you in control over nothing. I knew I had been played. I thought of Rune, more sure than ever that he had brought me here on purpose the first time. Then I thought of the previous night, realizing its meaning with pain. With her body, she had banished whatever instinct of self-preservation I could have used. The only thing I could do was talk her out of whatever was happening.

"What—"

"Forgive me, Drake," she said again

The dwarfish blade made quick work of my mail, my garments, and my skin. She stabbed quickly and efficiently, all the way to the hilt. Pain came in a wave of heat, pinching my entrails as the knife shook under Muninn's trembling hand, and I screamed as I'd rarely screamed.

My hands went to the handle of my knife, not daring to touch it and unwilling to leave it there either. Already, my sight darkened and blurred, but Muninn's face still appeared clearly at its center. I thought tears were running down her face, but they were mine. I had never felt so much pain, from so many parts of me.

Slick with blood, my left hand searched for support. I would fall soon, and this would aggravate the wound. Had I been myself, I would have tried to off myself, and send me back to Asgard before Muninn's plan could take place. Odin's nail was in me, after all. But I wasn't myself. I was suffering, I was sick with sorrow, and I was losing consciousness. I used the white wall for support, and just as I did, I felt the stone drinking my blood, just as it did back on Asgard before it opened to the dead heroes. And this is exactly what happened.

The wall lowered itself, swallowed into the ground, and if Muninn had not passed her arm around me, I would have fallen for good.

My breath rasped from inside my body, and a blinding gray light enveloped us. My feet dragged lifelessly behind me as Muninn carried me to the other side of the white door. Then, echoing in my skull as if I were wearing a helmet, I heard a voice I had not heard in ages, and I cursed myself.

"Drake, so glad you could join us."

That voice, smooth and sharp, it was impossible to forget it.

Loki.

15

Loki's cave
Now.

"Oh, poor Drake," Sigyn said through her threatening sobs. She looked away while still holding the bowl between my tormentor and me, but I knew her so well by now that I guessed the first tears would soon overcome her feeble resistance. And sure enough, they broke through when her eyes fell back on me. She looked slightly cross, too. "When this plan succeeds, and he passes through that door, promise me to be kind to him, husband."

I sighed and slumped as much as my chains allowed. I had failed once again, not that I had believed I could make her see the truth of my identity. No, this fool's hope I had abandoned a long time ago. Sigyn believed I, Loki, was talking about my plan for Drake rather than the path that had led me under the cursed snake.

"I will be nice to him," I replied in defeat.

"I truly wish there was another way to punish this mean, mean Odin," she went on. "Drake is a good man; you said so yourself. Using love against him... You will be kind? Promise me."

"I promise," I told her as genuinely as the situation allowed. My reward was a smile to fill a sail with a gush of wind on a flat day. It was a half-toothless smile, rancid and yellow-stained, but there was love in it and gentleness. The snake slept at this very moment, though his slumber never lasted more than five minutes at a time, so it was just Sigyn and I. And I adored that deranged, pure smile.

Though it was for Loki's benefit, it was mine, and it kept me sane, just as her arms kept me safe from the venom. We had grown closer than most husbands and wives by then. It was not love, at least not on my side, but her dedication was touching. And I told myself I was lucky she was here. And it hit me.

A revelation.

There was no way in the nine realms Loki felt nothing for Sigyn.

In fact, I would have bet with Titus that Loki loved his wife dearly. It may not have been the case at first. Even when they were banished to this cave, I assumed Loki cared little for the wife forced on him. But no man, god or otherwise, could resist love when wrapped in such devotion.

For twenty-seven years, Sigyn had sat by her husband's side, protecting him from the snake and offering him some distraction. I felt the pang of love myself, and I had spent far less time here than Loki had, or at least I hoped. So, yes, Loki loved Sigyn. And this revelation filled me with a sense of hope I hadn't felt in a long time.

Love meant Loki would return before Ragnarök, as he had promised, so Ragnarök had not happened yet. And if the world had not ended, then I could do something about it. Heimdallr had warned me not to play with the prophecy, but he could go hump a goat; I would play my part as I wished. I was Drake, and I could do something Loki could never have done. Love had been my weakness, and he had used it against me. I would return the courtesy.

ᛉ

As a freshly promoted Drake, Odin had invited me to his hall. He asked a question when I arrived, though it was more of a riddle. "How does one hit a sparrow with a spear?" he had asked. This was way back when Odin ruled, supreme and hopeful. He liked to test people, but I had no answer.

"How does one hit a sparrow with a spear?" I had repeated, knowing the All-Father wanted to speak as much as he wanted to be heard.

"You can't," he replied, "pick a bow." Then he laughed and left me none the wiser.

I now understood his point. An impossible task requires us to change the rules more than it requires stubbornness. You can't hit a sparrow with a spear, or an axe, or probably even a sword. But an arrow, maybe.

I had believed that I could not outfox Loki, and if Loki had found no better idea than one involving years of preparations, then I would do just as well to wait. Loki was smarter than I ever was. But Loki had one weakness, he loved his wife and would never have hurt her even if it meant saving himself. I, on the other hand, did not have this moral issue.

I had no plan worthy of the name, but I would change the rules by removing one of the players from the game, and we would see what happened next. And what would happen next depended on a question I had never found the answer to during my time as Loki. *Why hadn't Sigyn killed the snake?*

She could not break the chains. That I knew because I had seen her try. She could not escape either, for the door was locked and the mountain impossible to climb down. But why hadn't she killed Skadi the serpent? She claimed the snake could not be killed. Skadi, the Jötunn, had infused some of her power into the reptile to make it so.

But Skadi wasn't immortal either. Jötnar could die and be killed, so if she had indeed given it her power, it only meant the snake was, at best, as strong as Skadi. Granted, Skadi was one of the strongest of her kind, probably stronger than Sigyn. Still, it in no way meant the snake was invulnerable. This animal, like everything else in the nine realms, could be killed; of that, I was fairly certain, and it was time to test this theory.

I'd like to say I did what I did next for the greater good. That I thought of Lif, of Odin, or even my men. But I did not. I did what I did for myself, for a chance at revenge. Even preventing Ragnarök came second on my list of priorities. And Sigyn was my sacrifice.

Sweet, pure Sigyn whose only fault had been to marry the man she was told to and to fall in love with him. On the day of my true death, I will end up on the Corpse Shore for what I did to her, and if she is there, I will let her torture me to her heart's content.

She was sleeping. Her chest rested on my belly while she kept the bowl over my face with a weak grip. She twitched as she often did in her sleep, and I waited for her to fall deeper into her slumber. My face was on the side, looking at her, the bowl on my cheek receiving a drop of venom every couple of minutes. I felt one land at its center and counted up to sixty. Skadi needed to have its next fang full and ready when I acted.

Then I shrieked a terrible scream of pain that woke the snake, who then hissed with pure anger. Sigyn sprang in terror and lifted the bowl by reflex, apologizing without knowing why.

"What is it?" she asked. It was the gentle Sigyn, not her horrible twin. I could act. I had to act.

"It got me!" I whimpered, eyes shut with faked pain.

"Where?" she asked, half panicking herself, her free hand brushing my face for a trace of the venom.

"Back of the neck," I said, giving a great show of gritting my teeth, "It's still there! It burns!"

She got closer. So close that I could smell her rancid breath and the air coming from her nose on my forehead. Her hand went to the back of my head, brushing the hair in search of the venom's burn while she checked my neck with her eyes. She had to stay low to avoid the snake's maw, but I saw the beast readying itself for the next drop, opening its mouth to an impossible angle and unfolding its two fangs.

"I can't see it," Sigyn said as she raised her head. Her eyes met mine for a second, and I almost gave up my plan. She was pure, my Sigyn, so pure that she smiled, and I will die believing she saw something of my resolve and chose to smile as if accepting her fate.

I rocked my head into hers with all the violence I could gather and heard her nose snap on my forehead. There was no smile then, only a short gasp as her head shot backward while she stood by reflex. The gasp ended in her throat when Skadi found its mark. The snake's fangs penetrated Sigyn's throat from the side and coiled around it at the same time. This was a vicious beast that could choke and poison its prey, and now was doing both.

I never heard anything as painful as Sigyn's scream.

The snake did not let go, but neither did Sigyn. Her hands clasped the snake's body in front of her throat and she pulled for air, but the beast was pure muscle and strengthened its constriction. Its leathery skin creaked as it slithered around Sigyn.

The beast pulled her up toward the ceiling, and her feet left the ground. Her right foot found the chain tying me to the rock. She used it for strength and pulled downward passionately on the snake. Skadi shook. It finally had caught something and would never let go.

The cave shook. Debris fell from the ceiling. The chains rattled, and Sigyn went from screaming to grunting. She lowered herself as she pulled on the snake, and this, more than anything, made the place tremble. Her face went from pale to purple and now to red.

Sigyn bellowed with rage when she got enough space between the snake and her throat to breathe, but she did not stop pulling on the beast. Skadi removed its fangs and screamed. I had never heard a snake screaming before, and it was not a pleasant sound. It did not recoil from Sigyn's throat, but it was losing the battle. And, in the space of two heartbeats, maybe three, I heard its body tearing itself apart. It was a horrible sound, like the sail of a boat being shredded, but only if this sail was made of meat, nerves, and blood.

Sigyn toppled like a bag of wheat when the snake broke in half, leaving a wriggling, bloody stump dangling from the ceiling while the other half dropped dead on me. The upper part showered me with blood, blinding me until I blinked the drops from my eyes. I was breathless.

I watched Sigyn's hand searching for support from the table and rising. She had knocked the bowl in her fall, and fumes from the spilled liquid flooded the cave in a pungent, yellow smoke that hurt my eyes. Sigyn stood in this fuming poison like a *gyoja* in a trance, her eyes shooting bolts of fury. I was about to receive the full ire of Frigg-Sigyn.

She broke a piece of the bowl on the rock and kept the sharp part stuck between her fingers. I thought of begging but gave up the idea instantly. I deserved her wrath; I would finally die, and the fumes hurt my throat too much to speak, anyway.

"I think I will disobey my husband after all," she said in a hoarse, broken voice. "If he's dead already, tell him—"

I never heard what she wanted me to tell Loki. Instead of finishing her sentence, foam accumulated at the corners of her mouth. Blood poured from her eyes and her ears, and she clasped her wounded throat once more. Sigyn fell on her knees, shaking like a bleeding goat and looking at me with what I presumed was a call for help.

I could not see her drop to the ground but heard her body hit it heavily. And suddenly, all that could be heard in the cave was the sound of my breathing, loud and frantic, and the drops of blood from the severed body of the snake landing on my chest. My ears rang with the absence of noise, and I waited a long time before agreeing with myself that both my captors were dead.

I howled with relief and laughed like the madman I had become. The place reeked from the mixture of poison, blood, and death. Half of Skadi lay on my belly and a dead Æsir died by my side, but I had changed something. I had picked a bow and shot that fucking swallow. My chains remained, but at this instant, it did not feel like an unsolvable problem.

And just as my joy soared, a pain, sharp and growing rapidly, shot from my belly. I wondered if I had been wounded in the struggle or if the snake itself was poisonous and exacted its revenge on me with its carcass.

Then, I realized with horror that the origin of my pain was no wound or venom. I was hungry from months of fasting, and it hurt like daggers stabbing me in the guts.

With the snake's death, time had regained its hold on the cave, and suddenly, my problems had become more urgent.

16

Gods did not hear prayers, not even Heimdallr and his unmatched hearing. Some folks hated the gods for not answering their prayers and ignoring their sacrifices. Now, sacrifices *could* be felt by the gods, the ones involving blood at least, but besides attracting their attention, it did little.

Once in a while, an Æsir would travel to Midgard to listen and even, in some rare cases, intervene. Adoration required some effort, after all. But I would be generous if I said that one in ten thousand prayers ever got a god's ear. This knowledge, however, did not prevent me from muttering my own.

"All-Father," I said, "for all I have given you, deliver me from this wretched place. Heimdallr, my friend, hear my voice and send my men to me. Thor," I said after a mere second of hesitation, "give me your strength so that I may break these chains."

None of them came to my rescue, and I grew tired and thirsty.

Hunger drew a hole in my belly, and that, more than anything else, worried me over my fate. I had Loki's body, a god, though from a Jötunn branch, and I wondered how long such a vessel could hold hunger back. From what I had seen in my years on Asgard, not much longer than us humans. And Loki had the reputation of having the greatest appetite among all the gods. Surely, such an appetite required an equal need for food.

Skadi's blood had stopped leaking from the ceiling, and for the first time since I had entered the cave, I did not need to worry about what was on top of me. Its fallen half lay dead on my lower belly, heavier than I thought it would be. The beast's head dangled pitifully on the side, maw opened toward Sigyn's corpse.

Food was my priority, and I had a good supply of it waiting on my belly if only I could get a hold of it. I tucked my stomach, which let the snake's corpse roll toward my chest a little. When it reached my navel, I inhaled and sent the air to my guts, thus pushing Skadi closer but also making it slide to the side. I froze, not daring to move until I was sure the snake would not fall.

A pearl of sweat rolled down my temple as I watched my meal about to join Sigyn's cadaver. Hurting myself against the chains, I lifted my right elbow as much as they allowed me, probably less than half an inch, which prevented Skadi from slipping farther.

The next part proved more difficult. The beast rested just under my nipples, and I could not get it moving any farther by breathing. So I gave small, tiny spasms as if trying to make it bounce on my chest, and it took me the greatest part of an hour before the snake finally rolled on itself. Its black and ocher skin was so close to my face that I smelled its putrid stench.

Once reaching the base of my neck, the snake rolled faster. Too fast indeed, and I had to roll it back with my chin.

Then, with the added pleasure of revenge, I plunged my teeth into Skadi and started the greatest, most vicious, and most disgusting meal of my life.

The meat was lean, juicy, and raw, but it beat the taste of the best beef on Midgard. Blood dripped on my chin as if it were ale, sometimes spurting as if I had bitten into a wild plum. The first bites made me sick, and I vomited whatever I had eaten, but I kept digging into Skadi as if my life depended on it, which it did.

Who knew snakes tasted so much like chicken?

My stomach, shrunken by a long-lasting fast, wanted me to pause in my feast, but I continued for another couple of bites. The pain from having a full belly was only a little better than that of an empty one, but at least I would not die of hunger. Not before a few days, that is.

I must have been a sight, face drenched in blood, a thick reptile resting on my throat like a king's torc, and an Æsir dead at my feet. The skalds, if they ever knew of my misery, would have a hard time writing this poem.

ᛉ

Skadi kept its place on my chest for another couple of days, during which I gnawed at its meat like a rodent. Then, I was taken by a violent cough that shook me so strongly that the snake fell. I despaired from this loss, though in truth, the body was decaying, and maggots swarmed in an increasing number where I had torn the flesh. They sometimes also fell from the half of the snake dangling from the ceiling, and I presumed they did as well around Sigyn. Life had invaded the cave and the terrible smell of rotting flesh with it.

Raw meat contains a lot of water, and I did not have to worry about my thirst. My situation had not improved by much though. I had regained some strength and slept for hours at a time, but everything else was changing for the worse.

All those little things I had lived with since my arrival in the cave, like resting immobile on a rock or the bite of the chains on my skin, became more painful. I suffered discomfort like never before and realized it was the cost of hope.

Everything is a question of sacrifice, as Odin would say. Folks on Midgard give sweat to make their fields grow. We give up peace for ambition, silver for a good blade, a few cows for a good wife, and ambition for comfort. I had sacrificed Sigyn for a chance to free myself, something Loki could not have done. Everything was a question of sacrifice, of exchange, and right now, my hope was costing me a sore ass.

My bed of rock had never bothered me as much, and, of course, the more I fought the edges of the rock, the more they bit into me. The pain from the tiny cuts was nothing compared to the many deaths I had suffered as an Einheri, yet they made sleep a nightmare, and if not for extreme fatigue, I would never have achieved more than a brief nap.

When I woke from those forced slumbers, all I felt was hunger, and now I had nothing to sink my teeth into.

ᛏ

If my time under Skadi's wrathful eyes had been a slow, nerve-racking torture, the next couple of days were painful to another degree. Hunger came back with a vengeance. The hollow in my stomach was so demanding that I thought of cutting my tongue to fill it. But all it would do was prolong my suffering and add some more to it. I'd rather die of hunger now than three days later with a festering mouth.

My energy slowly abandoned me. I did not sleep that night. My mind refused to rest because this would be my last night alive, and I wanted to go through all of it. This was my last battle, and like all those before, I would not give up until I had used everything in me.

So I waited for the first sign of day half-consciously. Hunger, or thirst more likely, blurred my sight and made it undulate. I smelled roasted pork and honeyed mead. Men laughed around me. Someone was pinching the strings of a lyre while a flute whistled a tune from my childhood. A hand slapped me on the back, and I felt the wood of a bench under my ass, smooth from decades of men sitting on it. I was back in Valhöll, my Wolves by my side, laughing as they always did, jesting like a pack of brothers.

Bjorn was there, and Karl, Titus, and Rune. Snekke, Sven, Einar, and Eigil were facing us. I could not understand their words, but someone said something funny, and we all laughed.

I looked at the next table where Arn sat with my two old Drakes, as well as Magnus Stone-Fists and Thrasir, the young man I had killed and who had fought as bravely as any champion. No one fought on that evening in the hall of heroes, and the Valkyries passed between us with pitchers of mead and platters of meat.

Lif, older than I remembered, sat by Frigg's side. The queen watched her husband with love and Odin replied with a charming grin full of teeth. Thor, Tyr, and Heimdallr banged cups while Freyja, Freyr, Bragi, and Idunn exchanged pleasantries. Baldur was back from the dead and laughed at a joke from Loki, and the trickster kissed his wife on the forehead when she huddled against him. Dozens of Æsir and Vanir shared in the feast, all of them beaming with joy.

Valhöll had never been so, and I wondered if there was another Valhöll. One we could reach upon our real death, where there was no need to fight, no need to compete and kill each other over and over again until the end of time. There wouldn't be an end of time either. Maybe this was the true prize, and maybe I was really dead this time.

"Wouldn't it be amazing?" a familiar voice called behind me, the first words I could distinguish since I entered this dream.

I turned, and Ulf stood, his stupid, charming grin splitting his graying beard as it so often did. I left my bench and spread my arms around him, dragging my old friend into a hug like the one we had shared moments before he died. Was it possible to cry in a dream? I wondered as tears poured freely down my cheeks.

"It would," I finally replied after we broke the embrace. "This would be a Valhöll worthy of our sacrifices."

"Some of us see it like that, you know," Ulf replied.

"I didn't. And how could I?" I asked. "Especially without you in it."

"I left someone in my stead," Ulf replied.

"Lif?" I asked.

"Lif," he replied with a nod. "Did you take care of her as you promised?"

"I tried," I said, not daring to look at him in the eyes. "I tried, but Loki—"

"Loki is on Asgard, and you're not. So why don't you do something about it, Drake?"

The hall slowly vanished in front of my eyes, its shape and the people in it evaporating in a thin smoke carried away by the wind.

"Drake?" Ulf called again. His voice lost its echo and felt more real.

"Drake?" he asked again, and this time, I opened my eyes, a feeble light drowning my awakening senses. "Are you sure it's him?" Ulf asked, not to me. His hands were on my shoulders, which he squeezed gently.

"It's him, I'm certain," another voice answered, one I did not recognize.

"Ulf?" I called. My voice sounded weak and hoarse.

"Drake, it's me," my friend said, sounding relieved. "I'm here; it's going to be all right now."

I blinked water from my eyes as my friend put a bundle of something soft behind my head. It must have been fur, and it was bliss.

So I was in Hel after all. At least I was with Ulf.

"Hel?" Ulf asked. I had probably spoken my thoughts unwillingly. "No, it's not Hel. We are... Where are we?" he asked the other man.

"I don't know what it's called," the man said, "let's just call it Loki's cave."

Consciousness came back faster as if I had been hit by the cold flat of a sword. I felt the chains and noticed the familiar shape of the surrounding walls. I was still in the cave. Ulf stood over me, offering me the same grin I had seen on his face in my dream.

He looked slightly different from my memory. His hair had turned grayer, and new wrinkles had appeared at the corners of his eyes. But it was Ulf, and if he was in the cave, it meant he was alive. I wanted to ask him how it could be, but the sight of the man by his side stopped me.

I first thought it was Odin. The resemblance was striking. But this man was thinner, skin stretched over a more angular face and gray hair gathered in thin locks. His eyes were darker than Odin's, and he had two.

He, too, had aged since the last time I had seen him,

which was why I had a hard time recalling him. He had lost weight, his discreet smile as well, and he had gained the wild aura of his father.

"Huginn?" I asked.

"It's me, Drake," Huginn said, eyes filled with wisdom and sadness. "Now tell me, what did my sister do to you?"

ᛉ

"I knew Drake when he was just a scrawny farm boy, though we called him something else back then. Hum... I forget his real name. Anyway, I was on the same ship during his first raid. Even then, all squirming and pale with fear, he had something more than the other boys. Hard to say what. It's like his feet were more solid on the ground. He still shares mead with me once in a while, when he has time. He just doesn't have much of it. Always with the gods or with his Wolves. And, of course, he can't see me because he's always searching for that dark she-Æsir. Everyone knows he yearns for her, no matter how discreet he thinks he is. At least we have a good laugh at his expense."

Brenda Dustinsdottir

17

Ulf was alive. Or, more accurately, Ulf had not died.

"The beam squashed your head like a barrel of ale, and the roof followed soon after," Ulf explained as Huginn inspected the chains, turning and inspecting each link with care. "I, too, received my fair share of burning wood. But unlike any other man or woman in the hall when it collapsed, I did not die. Odin must have been watching me because all I suffered was a headache on the level of a morning after Yule."

"It wasn't Odin," Huginn said without interrupting his task. "It was fate."

"So you've said," Ulf replied. The two of them clearly had this argument before. "In any case, I got knocked out for a minute and woke to a burning hall, the smell of bacon, and the sight of this old bird stooping over me as if I were a worm."

"I am not that old," Huginn said.

"You do look older," I commented as he walked from my right to my left.

"We age when away from Asgard for too long," Huginn said, *we* being the Æsir and their creatures.

"So, you've spent twenty years on Midgard?" I asked.

"More than that," he said. Huginn, when I last saw him, looked in his late thirties. Now, he was an old man, though he still moved with the grace of his kind.

"Odin has been worried sick since you left, you know," I said. He finally lifted his gaze from the chains to look at me in the eyes. Under his thin brows, Huginn harbored a look balancing shock and anger.

"He didn't tell you I was down here?" he asked.

"He didn't have a clue where you were," I replied. He and Ulf exchanged a glance that spoke of their many conversations on the topic. "What is it?" I asked.

"Let me finish my story first," Ulf said. I was content to listen, for my throat hurt, and my brain hurt, and I wasn't entirely certain I wasn't dreaming all of this. So Ulf told his story.

Huginn had rescued him from the raging fire consuming Hakon's hall and had taken him as far as his old wings could carry them, which wasn't far. As it turned out, Huginn was indeed living in a cave near Lagardalr, just not the one that led to this place. There, he had treated Ulf's wounds, which were more than just a simple headache. And once my archer had recovered, they worked on Huginn's mission on Midgard.

"Your mission?" I asked.

"Ordered by Odin," he said accusingly. Huginn wasn't happy with his father.

"He knew what you were up to?"

"When I left, he did. He sent me here."

Huginn stood up, his knees cracking as any old man's would. "And Grimnir does not forget," he went on, using one of the many names given to Odin throughout the ages. Grimnir, *the hooded one*, a remnant from his frequent journeys among men. "Unless—"

"Unless his Memory betrayed him," I finished for him. Ulf nodded. They had come to the same conclusion.

"It was just a speculation that she was involved," Ulf said. "Until we found her cave and all those feathers."

Not that it mattered anymore, but I knew now how far Muninn had been ready to go in her scheme. She had torn her own feathers, hundreds of them, to make the place look like her brother inhabited it. She had killed Jarl Olaf, too, for the sole purpose of attracting the Wolves to Lagardalr.

There, she teamed up with Rune, worked Loki's plan, and planted this idea in my mind that her brother could be rescued. I had worked most of it out during my time chained to the rock, but I could not understand why she had not simply acted when Rune brought me there the first time. The two of them could easily have overcome me, and while I might not have been willing, the results would have been the same.

I understood why Loki would prefer my body as a vessel rather than Rune's, but the boy could have done more than simply guide me to the first cave. Unless Rune had nothing to do with Loki, and he had been played by the trickster and his traitorous raven, too.

Hope returned with my friend, and I thought I would deal with the question of Rune once back on Asgard. Making Loki and Muninn pay took priority. And my vengeance wasn't solely self-centered. Hundreds of people had been hurt because of them, like the good folks of Lagardalr, including Lif and Hakon. The boy-jarl had died just so Loki could escape and, in a way, just so Muninn could get me to her true lord.

"I'm sorry for Hakon," I told Ulf when he paused in his tale to give me some water. No ale in the nine realms had ever felt softer than this first gulp of water except the next one.

"He didn't get to Valhöll?" he asked, then sighed when I shook my head. "My granddaughter?"

"She thrives, at least when I left. Even melted Frigg's forever-frozen heart. No offense," I told Huginn, wondering if he ever thought of Frigg as his mother.

"None taken," he replied with a surprised look, telling me he had not.

"She may have been when you left," Ulf said, "but it could have changed since. A lot has."

I did not understand. Loki's presence on Asgard meant bad things were bound to happen, but the two of them wouldn't know of it. They had remained on Midgard, and from what I gathered, Huginn could no longer fly between realms as he used to. So when Ulf said that a lot of things had changed, he meant on Midgard, and things never changed on Midgard, not that fast.

"How long have I been here?" I asked. Ulf and Huginn exchanged another glance, none of them wanting to answer.

"You came back two days after the battle, right?" Ulf asked. I nodded. "That was three years ago."

"Three years?" I asked, my voice hurting my throat.

"More or less," Ulf said. "It's hard to say."

"What do you mean?"

"The last couple of years have been nothing but snow and death," Ulf answered. "And even the last summer was a mere, shallow month. People are dying around their fire, and brothers are killing brothers for a piece of bread."

"Fimbulvetr," I said.

"Fimbulvetr," Ulf agreed.

The great winter preceding Ragnarök was upon Midgard, and the end of the world would follow. Huginn's tongue clicked in his mouth. I thought he was reacting to what we had mentioned, but he only cared about the chains.

"Wait, it took you three years to come here? Even with the help of an Æsir?"

"And some help it was," Ulf said scornfully. "A moon-crazed old raven with orders sounding like riddles."

"Moon-crazed?" I asked, looking from Ulf, who waved his finger around his ear, to Huginn, who simply shrugged.

"I have some bad days," he said.

"That's a thing with Æsir, isn't it? Odin has those bad days too, as did Sigyn," I said as if it could help.

"That's Sigyn?" Ulf asked as he tapped Sigyn's body with the tip of his boot.

"She didn't die well," I said.

"I can see that."

"What riddled orders?" I asked.

Then Huginn told his story.

Twenty and some years ago, Odin had required Huginn's presence after a day spent in Mimir's well. It was a few years after Baldur's death and Loki's imprisonment and only a few months after Odin had learned Ragnarök's prophecy. It was a time of doubt and fear among the gods, and Odin had been less than approachable in those days. Odin, Huginn said, was exhausted beyond words when he met him, but he gave strict orders to his little raven, if only vague ones.

"Go to Bandak Lake," Huginn said in a poor imitation of his father. "A hall will burn. You will find a Wolf in the fire. Trust the Wolf. Together, you will open the snake's cave. But instead of two snakes, you will find a Dragon disguised as a snake. Trust the Dragon. He will get you back to Asgard, and all will be as it should be."

"It all makes sense now," Huginn said, "but you can imagine how I felt then?"

Damn, Odin and his riddles. What was Huginn supposed to get from all of this? The burning hall was Hakon's, and the Wolf to trust was Ulf, who was not only one of Odin's Wolves but also bore a name that meant "wolf." The snake cave was the one we currently occupied, and the two snakes would have been Skadi and Loki. While I was Drake, the Dragon. Huginn must have scratched his head over this riddle since his descent on Midgard.

Odin had sent him on his way urgently, but as he left his creator, Huginn met his sister, who had also been called by the All-Father. Muninn must have acted then, somehow erasing Odin's memory and making him forget what he had ordered Huginn.

"Still," I said, "three years."

"To be fair," Ulf said, "we found the cave quickly enough. Within half a year. The problem was the dwarfish blade."

"Ah," I said dismissively. Dwarfish weapons were scarce, that was a fact, and one was needed to enter the cave. Whichever god had placed that door—Odin most likely—had reinforced it with some powerful charm and made it so that the heroes' blood would not suffice; a second key was required. The blood had to be drawn by a dwarfish blade to open it, hence Muninn's insistence on me taking Wedge. Sigyn had known about this mechanism, too, so this was no news to me.

"How did you find one?"

"Do you remember my gift from Odin when I became a Wolf?" Ulf asked. The memory came fast enough; Odin did not give much, after all. He had offered Ulf a common arrow mounted with an arrowhead made in a Dwarven forge. We had debated then if it was an insult, for Odin famously disliked archers and had not been overjoyed with Ulf joining my pack.

"That's the one," Ulf said. "I lost it in a battle near Uppsala a hundred and some years ago."

"You went to Uppsala?" I asked.

"Not just," Huginn replied.

"Some warrior found it on the battlefield, then sold it to a trader," Ulf explained.

"A trader known to sail the Baltic Sea. As did his son after him, and his grandson, and his great-grandson," Huginn said.

"We tracked the route he had taken in his days and visited the Finns, the Wends, the Geats, and finally the Jutes before learning that a jarl acquired a beautiful arrow made by the gods only two generations before. The said jarl had taken it with him as a token of the gods' favor into a war against his Swede enemies, but as you can guess, it did him little good, for he and all his warriors died in a battle by the wall of all places—"

"—Uppsala," I said, guessing where the story was going.

"Uppsala," Ulf confirmed, snapping his fingers. "We crossed the Eastern world from West to East and North to South in search of something that was a day's walk from our starting point."

"All of this during Fimbulvetr," Huginn finished.

I shouldn't have, but I laughed. I laughed as only a crazy man can, and I exorcised much of my frustration with those waves of mad laughter. It was a terrible joke from fate that I had suffered more than two years in this cave because my friend had asked the wrong jarl if he hadn't seen an old arrow nearby. If I hadn't laughed, I would have cried.

"We came back here as soon as we stole that thing," Ulf said, retrieving the arrow from his belt when I got myself under control. Poor Ulf, stuck between two men dangerously close to folly.

"That's it!" Huginn said. He snatched the arrow from Ulf's fingers with astonishing speed for an old man and, in the next moment, slashed the arrow with great dexterity near my left arm. It made no sound, and I wondered why he had waved the shaft like this, but then the chain broke. One second, it tied me as strongly as ever to the stone; the next, it buckled under its own weight. The whole thing slid off me, simple as that.

I did not move for a few heartbeats, my mind refusing to believe what had just happened. I lifted my hands. Everything hurt, my bones, the blood rushing through my fingers, the way they shook like leaves at the end of autumn. But here they were, palms facing me. I clasped them and delighted in the feeling of rubbing my two hands together.

Leaning on my elbows, I meant to sit up, but the movement was too sudden, and I felt dizzy. Ulf caught me, his left hand behind my back and his right on my chest.

"Take it easy," he said.

I looked into his eyes and thought he was about to cry, then realized the tears were in my eyes, not his. I clasped my friend, dragged him into a hug, and finally let go. I shamed myself, and Ulf did not stop me from hugging him; this way, no one saw me crying like a bairn.

I was free.

EPILOGUE

I could sit within an hour, stand in the next two, and walk at some point during the night. But it all made me so tired that I sat back against the cave wall, spent and happy like never before.

Ulf and Huginn tossed Sigyn and Skadi's bodies from the side of the mountain. They had some dried beef, a lump of hard cheese, half a loaf of molded bread, and a few sips of old water. A feast. They must have been hungry, too, but refused to take anything from me.

"What now?" I asked.

"No idea," Huginn said. "Odin told me to trust him," he went on with a nod toward Ulf, "then to trust you."

Typical Odin.

"How would you get out of here?" Ulf asked.

I sat up a little. Despite my exhaustion, I would rather break my back than lie down. I had done that enough for a lifetime.

"Can we use parts of you as we used Odin's nails?" I asked Huginn.

"If I had just been out of Asgard, maybe. But I have been

gone for so long that I am more human than Æsir now." Gods never left Asgard or their other sanctuaries for long. They quickly lost power when away from their home. Not completely, no, but enough.

"Besides," he went on, "I don't think we should cross the Bifröst."

"Why not?" Ulf asked.

"Three years," Huginn replied without looking at us. "That's a lot of time for Loki to execute his plan. No doubt he will have changed things around."

"Starting with the Bifröst's guardian," I guessed. Heimdallr and Loki hated each other, always had. It was not only possible but logical that Loki would have tricked Heimdallr away from his role as guardian of the rainbow bridge.

"Even if he hasn't, he will have the bridge watched. Plus, can you imagine landing at the feet of the Bifröst looking like this? Heimdallr would snap you in half before you could open your mouth. No, we need another way in," Huginn said.

And I knew none.

I had used other gates to Asgard in the past. Contrary to the Bifröst, those gates connected one particular part of the nine realms to one particular part of Asgard. Few existed, and they were impossible to find without knowing where to look.

The door to the cave was one-sided, so the only way out of this place was its exit. But said exit opened to a smooth, steep mountainside. We could not climb down, especially not feeble old me.

"You can't fly anymore?" I asked Huginn.

"I have lost this ability, along with most of my feathers," he answered.

"But you still have wings?"

"Of course I still have wings," he replied, vexed.

"Can they slow your fall down the mountain?" I asked. Ulf, who was remaking the bandage where he had cut himself to open the door, gazed from me to Huginn as we waited for his answer.

"Probably," the raven replied.

"Even if you are being weighed by two Einherjar?" Ulf asked, following my thoughts.

"Less probable," Huginn replied.

"But not impossible," I said. Huginn tilted his head as if to say that one way or another, we would find out.

Within the next few minutes, the three of us peered over the edge of the small path out of the cave's entrance, none of us looking approvingly at our only way out. This mountain reminded me of the one at the center of Asgard, except that it was gray, sharp, and surrounded by a strong, random wind. We could see no farther than the thick cloud hanging around the mountain a hundred feet below us.

"It's a long way down," Ulf said apprehensively. "I guess."

"Only one way to know," I said.

"I'm not confident about this," Huginn said.

"Odin told you to trust me." I tried to sound reassuring and failed miserably, judging by the way he shook his head.

Then Huginn opened his wings, and I was the one who lost confidence. If he looked like an old man, his wings belonged to a decaying raven. My faith withered. But I would not stay one more day in this cave. The only way was down. I had a revenge to claim, the end of the world to prevent, and a title to regain.

"And a body to recuperate," Ulf said with a pout suggesting what he thought of my current vessel.

"That too," I said. In fact, I had forgotten about it, but now that he had mentioned it, I was ready to jump to certain death. So we did. The three of us jumped, Ulf and I tightly gripping Huginn's waist and he grabbing us by our collars.

I had flown before. It had been one of the greatest sensations of my existence. But *this* was not flying; this was falling like a rock. The wind gained strength as we dove through the cloud, all three screaming with fear. When we burst through, I realized there was still a great distance before the end of our fall.

"Huginn!" I screamed.

"Trying!" he said. A painful look up told me he was indeed trying his best to beat his wings, and whatever feathers he still possessed were abandoning him one by one.

"Fuck!" Ulf said.

He was sliding away from Huginn's hips and from his own tunic. I grabbed his wrist and winced with pain. It completely unbalanced Huginn, who started spinning like a whirlybird leaf. I closed my eyes to fight pain and fear and focused on not letting my friend's wrist go. I then looked down, wondering how long this could continue, but the ground was nowhere to be seen. It was all white under our spinning feet.

"Fuck!" Ulf said again, looking in the same direction as me.

"Huginn!" I called again, understanding that we were actually close to the ground. It was just there, coming at us fast and covered in snow. "Ground!" I yelled from the top of my lungs.

Huginn groaned. His two wings bellied like a ship's sails taking the wind, and he pushed hard to break our fall. He didn't manage, but he still slowed us down enough to prevent a catastrophe. The change of speed was so sudden that I tasted the contents of my stomach in the back of my throat. But before I could throw up, we landed abruptly on a thick, powdery mat of snow, so thick that I thought it would swallow me. I found the hard ground, stood, and realized the snow only went up to my knees.

"You did it," Ulf said with great relief as he emerged from the powder.

"I did," Huginn said, teeth clenched against the pain. His bare back was covered in dark bruises where his wings blended and disappeared again. He covered himself with the old woolen jersey he had been wearing before, and even that simple gesture pained him. "But where are we now?"

Everything was white—pure, unmarred white disturbed by heavy snowflakes dancing in a slow yet sharp wind. Squinting, I guessed some shapes on the horizon—trees. As we struggled through the powder and the growing cold, I took them for pine trees, but their needles were black and red.

I knew where we were, for I had only seen one place with this kind of tree. And all hope abandoned me.

"Jötunheimr," I said.

We were in the land of our enemies. The realm where those who fought the Æsir gathered.

And Asgard had never been farther.

To be continued in

BEASTS OF JÖTUNHEIMR

AFTERWORD

Readers who know me from previous books might be surprised to learn that writing Viking/Norse stories predates my Asian novels. I "decided" to become a writer upon reading Cornwell, Kristian, and Low, and while watching *Vikings*. It was only natural for me to depart on this journey with great sagas, riding the waves of my ancestor's culture or what we think we know of them.

My first historical novel is titled Sword Maidens. It follows a crew of Norse warriors, rebels against their king, led by a fearsome she-jarl, guided by a dark seeress, and whose fate falls upon the shoulders of a slave-turned spearwoman named Mist. I shopped this story to several agents back when I believed my wyrd was to be traditionally published, and I actually found one. Sword Maidens did well in some literary competitions, but things were slow and barely moving, so to keep myself patient and busy, I wrote a whole trilogy, the first part of which you just read.

The Army of One trilogy was born in the midst of COVID and took me a solid year to complete. It started innocently, with a quick thought for those nameless Einherjar and how they were so much more badass than the gods and their immense powers. I love to give a voice to the little guy(s) in my stories, but I also love reshaping tales we know and adore. The Army of One allowed me to do both.

Among the main inspirations I drew from, I have to name Neil Gaiman. Norse Mythology, of course, but not just. One could even say American Gods played a more influential role in this trilogy.

The Gospel of Loki was also good fuel for imagination, as was the Rise of Sigurd and the Oathsworn series.

All those titles and writers impacted the creation of Blood of Midgard. But things got more personal for the next two books, especially with Beasts of Jötunheimr, where Drake's personality shifts dangerously close to the dark side.

I don't have much to say in my defense when it comes to historical/cultural accuracy here or in the next two books. I just took some of my favorite stories and characters from Norse mythology and mixed them into a melting pot of my creation. I actually met two big names of everything Norse-related in France during a medieval fair and discussed my stories with them to get their professional opinion. To my relief, both claimed that little was certain with Norse mythology because most of what we know came from secondary sources and was written down after the end of the Viking age. "However," one of them said, "don't mess with the names, because that's a point we have no doubt about."

Oops...

Afterword

I messed with the names. I messed with them big time. And I'm not too sorry about it. The great part of this story is that it includes warriors coming from different cultures and times, and, as such, mixing Icelandic names with Norse ones, unorthodox spelling with more popular ones, and even including a Roman officer in this mess was fine with me. This story, and those characters, are a love letter to one of my greatest passions, and I hope you felt it through those pages.

I also hope you are ready for the next chapter in this saga, and, should enough of you be enthusiastic about this story, there is potential for many more books in this world.

Skål

ACKNOWLEDGMENTS

My first thanks go to my father, who so often took care of my son as I wrote the first draft of this novel.

My second thanks go to my son, who so often took care of my father as I wrote the first draft of this novel.

You made a great team. Cheers.

I'd like to send all my gratitude to my beta readers, whether they helped with this novel or some others. One of the most positive signs regarding my writing career is how much easier it is to find you. For Blood of Midgard, I need to specifically thank Marie Sinadjan, writer of fantastic Norse stories herself, and James, who has shared his time and thoughts with me for the past year. Eternal gratitude to you two.

A thousand thanks to Lara, who jumped on the editing of this novel at the last minute and crushed it. Looking forward to working with you on the next books.

And, as usual, my undying love and gratitude to my wife, without whom none of this would matter. And, before you ask, no, she hasn't read this one either, but I'm not expecting a miracle. It's really not her type...

ALSO BY BAPTISTE PINSON WU

The Three Kingdoms Chronicles

1. Yellow Sky Revolt
2. Heroes of Chaos
3. Dynasty Killers
4. Forest of Swords

Undead Samurai

www.ingramcontent.com/pod-product-compliance
Ingram Content Group UK Ltd.
Pitfield, Milton Keynes, MK11 3LW, UK
UKHW011353230625
6537UKWH00013B/72

9 798333 533340